California Twist

A Harry Rhimes Novel

****

John A. Connor

California Twist

A Murderous-Ink paperback
First published by
Murderous-Ink Press
Crowland
LINCOLNSHIRE
England
2nd Edition
2 3 4 5 6 7 8 9 10
Copyright © John A. Connor 2013
Artwork © Dana Thompson (DTKinetic) 2020

Paperback ISBN: 9781909498174
Electronic ISBN: 9781909498181

Acknowledgements

Thanks are due to the following people for their help and support:

Barry Martin, Jan Stinson, Elizabeth Leather, Rodney Leighton, Lawrence Stribling, and the Vancouver-based Jonathon Osborne Editorial Services, for their help in keeping me both on-track and making me play within the rules of literacy. Not forgetting the last of my beta readers: Belle Wood, Dave K and Bill.

To Lieutenant Damon Minor of the Redding Police,

Rick Riggins, the now-retired Sheriff-Coroner of Siskiyou County, and

Dean Wilson, Sheriff of Del Norte County

for their valuable time and patience with my letters, e-mails and generally answering questions of the dreaded "Okay, fine, but what if…?" nature.

And to my partner, Den, as always.

Please Note:- All bands, groups and singers, along with all song lyrics quoted, are purely fictional, and merely indicative of my "disgustingly lowbrow taste in music."

Prologue

Midnight. The drizzling rain falls gently, sparkling and glittering like crystal dust in the glow from the vandalised street lights. Blue and red neon bleeds across the wet parking lot from the tired and shabby strip mall, while the muffled thump of a bar room jukebox occasionally matches time with the sign's flashing. Whenever the door swings open, the sound jumps out like an angry junkyard dog, before the door closes again, and the music returns to its muted hammering. It's Friday night in the Piederbeck district.

Across from the parking lot the sidewalk edges onto the overgrown front yards of a series of neglected houses, and at the back of Number 43 – *old Mrs Mallory's place* – the loud opera music starts; then stops again several minutes later. Outside, at the junction, a bus turns left then heads rapidly down the street, engine loud in the ensuing silence, disappearing to leave hollow echoes of noise in the distance.

From somewhere nearby, a night bird starts calling, while from inside 43's back kitchen something makes low, animalistic, mewling sounds.

Splinters of broken glass sparkle on the kitchen doormat where visitors with good manners wipe their feet, before settling down at the kitchen table. Cup of coffee and a slice of pie. Half listening to old man Carmody gossiping and setting the world to rights, while Evangeline Mallory carries on baking as if she were preparing to singlehandedly feed the five thousand.

Tonight, though, things are a little different.

For a start, there wouldn't've been any need to break the little pane of glass by the door handle if she didn't keep leaving the fucking key in the lock.

Over in the corner, by the worktop, the stove is cooling. The kitchen table has been pushed hard up against the sink under the back window, with three of the old beechwood dining chairs tucked neatly underneath it. The fourth had been placed in the centre of the cleared space.

With its arms and legs bound tightly to the heavy wooden frame by lengths of strong plastic washing line, the naked body had, two hours previous, been a young man. Back then the questions had been punctuated with a little slapping, though careful so he wouldn't bite his tongue. Otherwise how would he be able to tell where the treasure was?

But he just kept on repeating the same old, "I don't know anything," story, which soon got to be irritating. I mean, like really irritating, because he knew, and he just kept on lying. Which was a bad, bad thing to do. In the end there had been little choice but to go to the car and get the iPod docking station, the tool roll, and some wide gaffer tape.

Walk back into the kitchen, and without even touching him he'd started to blub – still making with the lying – until his voice had become as irritating as a nest of tiny red ants, biting and chewing on the nerves. It had been a relief to stuff one of his socks into his mouth, tape it shut, then just listen to the silence before slipping the iPod into the dock and picking out a track. Nothing sets the mood better than a piece of Italian opera for this kind of work....

The small tire iron didn't take long to heat up on the gas stove. It's always satisfying to watch the flame lick the metal, see the tip of it change colour. Turn up the music, nice and loud, the best way to appreciate Rossini's Barber of Seville, *then over to stand behind him.*

La la la la-la!

Arm around his throat, elbow under his chin, then pull the head up and back.

La-la-la la!

Then bring the tip down onto his chest.

Figaro! Figaro! Fiiiiii-garrrrr-ooooooh!

Boy, could he struggle! Never thought he had it in him, took him to be more a sissy boy. Then the smell of burning, and the curious way his skin and nipple blistered up. Why do men have nipples anyway?

Wait for him to calm down, then pause the iPod. Ask the same questions, over and over again, then push the sock back in, tape him up, then go back to the stove.

Rasori e pettini

lancette e forbici,

al mio comando

tutto qui sta.

Of course, after two hours – doesn't time fly when you're having fun? – he'd first pissed himself, then emptied his bowels – which had been a really serious buzz kill.

Yet even after the branding, the broken fingers, the boiling water on his feet, he'd just kept on lying and lying. Until, hell, it had started to sound like the truth, and he really didn't know where the treasure had been hidden.

But The Man *had said that this asshole knew, and it was important to get the treasure back. Find the treasure, get it back to* The Man. *Because if* The Man *is happy then everyone is happy. And that is a Good Thing.*

Of course, if this asshole didn't know where the treasure was, who did? His girlfriend? His boyfriend? His buddies? Nothing he's said makes any sense!

Be quiet and let me think!

Even the old bitch, Mrs. Mallory, was supposed to have been away on vacation with her beloved grandson. Otherwise there would've been no point in choosing her house in the first place.

Finding her in bed had been a real surprise. With her in her eighties, it had been easy to keep pushing on the pillow until she stopped thrashing about. She had some nice meds on her bedside table, though, which sort of makes up for the inconvenience.

Time to finish up and disappear. Cut a side off a cornflake box, fold it, then tape it over the broken pane in the kitchen door. In this neighbourhood it won't look out of place

Collect up the iPod dock, the gaffer tape and tool roll, take them out to the car and drop them in the trunk. Come back to the kitchen with good old Mr. Longshanks, *and a large bottle of* Pine Fresh *bleach. Stand behind him, legs spread a little for support, hand under his chin, bring his head up and hold it firm. Nudge* Mr. Longshanks *into the auditory canal, then push-twist-retract –* "It's the rubber grip that makes it non-slip! Mr. Longshanks, the **only** long shafted screwdriver you'll ever need!"

Wash and wipe down the scene with Pine Fresh – it always pays to be methodical, that way we don't get caught. Before leaving, put all the stove burners on low – get the kitchen nice and warm. With the sunny weather to help as well, it won't be long before he – and old grandma Mallory upstairs in her bed – would be wriggling fit to bust.

*****

At 3:00 a.m. the bar across the road closed and locked its doors. Patrons and staff wandered off down side streets, or got into cars, vacating the parking lot as they made their way home. One more nondescript car, moving into the flow, rapidly became as invisible as the rest.

1

Late October, and the Sunday evening was cool, clear and dark.

I was in the ground floor living room, the lights turned low, sitting in an old leather club style easy chair. The light from the hearth had died down, and out beyond the patio windows, above the canyon rim and the dark forest line, I could see masses of distant stars. Like most Boy Scouts, I could pick out the better known constellations, but that was as far as my astronomical skills went.

The logs settled noisily in the hearth, and the rekindled firelight made new-born shadows dance around the open plan room. Three fingers of something amber and smooth in a whiskey tumbler rested comfortably in my hand. As Lonnie Tewkes' slow trumpet flowed like warm, rich chocolate from the stereo, I told myself that it was time to move on.

Plenty more fish in the sea…

Plenty more pebbles on the beach…

Plenty more frogs in the pond…

Ah, who was I kidding?

Being dumped sucked.

Big time.

*****

Monday morning, and although I'd been back in the US for some time, I'd never grown out of the British habit of driving with a stick shift. Oncoming traffic had cured me of driving on the left side of the road, and although I will always miss roundabouts, I really appreciated the advantages of turning right at a red light.

Still, the drive into the city from Concrete that Monday seemed longer than usual. Not that I time myself, you understand, but there were unconscious markers between the CD in the stereo – this time it was Vicky LaPerso, the 1956 Ventura sessions – and how far I'd been able to travel down the just-getting-choked-up traffic queues heading into the city itself.

> *"Gonna buy me some deadly poison, baby!*
> *Gonna mix it up,*
> *With some strong gin!*
> *Gonna buy meeeeep– !"*

Taking my finger off the eject button, I pulled the CD from the slot and tossed it onto the back seat. The last thing I needed right then was a self-pitying, "Oh, woe is me," attitude. I blindly rummaged in the scatter on the passenger side, and moments later another CD was sucked into the player's waiting maw. Cranking down the windows and cranking up the volume, I let the Jinxtones take wing and scare a couple of teenagers in their open top Jeep, stuck in the next lane to mine.

> *"How you call all your lover-boys? White TRASH!"*

Yeah, tell it like it is, Danny. Tell it like it is.

Out of boredom, I watched as several drivers started talking to themselves. Around here that usually meant they were either off their medication, or on hands-free and their cell phones had locked onto a stable signal. Given the scant coverage, and with no intention of installing masts, most of us Concretes don't bother with cell phones much. It's always been one of the town's saner attractions.

With a population approaching two and a half thousand, the small town of Concrete, Northern California, lies strung out, in, and around a long canyon. Access was by a bunch of back roads which, in turn, eventually connected to Highway 299. From there it was only a hop, skip and a fender bender away from the Interstate – the good old I-5.

The first settlement had originally been named after the bird, the Corncrake, way back in the 1850s. In those crazy gold rush days, when all around were striking it rich, the best the town could come up with was pyrites and dust. So it diversified into whiskey and brothels. Times were good and the money kept rolling in.

However, when the gold ceased, so did the town. Dead and dormant – a fitting tribute to the equally dying Wild West – it became just another Northern Californian ghost town. That was until 1910, when Dr. Theodophilous P. Jacksonhammer founded his *Resort of Health & Inner Beauty*. The good Doctor, formally a philandering snake-oil specialist from Alabama, discovered that by the judicious use of assorted herbs and compounds – which, years later, topped various Narcotic & Controlled Substance lists – he could easily part his patrons from their parents' money. This he used for the advancement of his own research into luxury living.

Like the whores and hoteliers of the previous age, when the scam finally came to an end, he took the money and hightailed it back over the state line – leaving the old ghost town with a new ghost spa. In those days the ghosts never had it so good.

The Depression, the Second World War, the Edsel and the Hoola Hoop, all dropped in and out of fashion during the next lull in the town's time line. It wasn't until the Summer of Love regenerated old smoker myths of a forgotten Nirvana, that a slow but regular trickle of hippies and other free thinkers start migrating from the east – giving a whole new meaning to the term, Way Out West. Especially when it was discovered that several generations of Narc-less and Fed-less interference had let the good doctor's gardens of *Cannabis sativa* and *Erythroxylum coca novogranatense truxillense* grow wild. Once the rumours had been confirmed, people were eager to repopulate the area.

After the Summer of Love, there came the Winter of Discontent. Biker gangs had found easy pickings from the land and the nearby towns, until their activities attracted the attention of the County Sheriff, as well as the city police. In true Wild West tradition, they arrested any and everything that moved, in as short a time as possible, leaving the ghost town to itself once more – albeit now with a mescaline-aided Make Love, Not War makeover.

Today, Civilisation is slowly rediscovering the legal joys of living out in Concrete. Businesses have started to come out here, and the mail service delivers to the community on a daily basis, so somebody must know we're here to stay – even though most of us have to go to the city in order to earn a living.

After a slow hour of stop-go-stop-go car shuffling, I turned onto Chancery, then into the cool of the underground car park beneath the Kincade Building. It's a classy address, I'll give you that, and my old Ford PoS always looked out of place among the BMWs, Jags and Toyotas. But it's where I work. Well, to be more exact, it's where I come when I don't have work.

I parked in my regular Visitors Only bay, eased my six foot one frame out of the car, and stretched a little to un-kink some of the muscles in my shoulders. Safe in the knowledge that no one, in their right mind, had enough sympathy for me to steal the damn vehicle, I took a steady walk over to the building's elevators.

These days, taking the stairs is considered the healthier option, but I just can't get excited over it. True, not everyone has their own home gym, but after fifteen years of active military service, such things as regular exercise are ingrained into my subconscious. Anyway, after the first eight floors, stairwells become passé – and at my age I've seen more than enough stairwells to last me a lifetime.

Then again, the ride up to the 10th floor had never failed to impress me. The scenery shifts from underground car park to grass and trees as the elevator climbs above ground to street level, then it travels up the outside of the Kincade Building. Some people always faced the wall, in order to avoid vertigo from the height and the view, but I still got a schoolboy kick of excitement every time. The whole block was an innovative award winning design, for its time, constructed completely out of recycled materials. From the reconstituted cement and steel in the walls, to the recycled plastic and glass for the windows. True, when it's kicking over 98° outside, you're thankful for the air conditioning, but at least some of the construction was ecologically sound.

On the way up, the floors and businesses were announced by a calm and emotionless feminine voice, and I wasn't sure if it was designed to tell you where you were or, by omission, who had ceased trading. However, with both the 9th and 10th floors occupied by *Orion & Nadler Investigations & Security*, I was sure they were going to be around for some time to come. Mind you, I have a vested interest – they throw work my way from time to time.

When the elevator reached the 10th, I stepped out into the open plan reception area and nodded a cheerful "Good Morning!" to Michelle and Darlene, the regular daytime receptionist staff. Michelle smiled and gave a little wave back while still talking into her headset. Darlene silently mouthed something impressively gross before continuing her conversation. "I can really empathise with your grief, Mrs. Gorretski. Believe me, I truly can."

I took a quick time out and looked over the maze of cubes and walkways. It's a sight which reminded me why I never wanted a proper 9-to-5 job.

Muted, bland cubical walls. Neutral cord carpet the right shade of nondescript. Constant overhead lighting, despite all the natural light from the building's three glass sides. Heads bobbed, telephones chirped or berrrrrring'd, keyboards clattered, and photocopiers made those noises only photocopiers do when in captivity. The only thing missing was the rattle of chains and the sound of a drum slowly beating time while an overseer called out, "Stroke!" Still, as I headed towards my office, the call centre operators seemed to be smiling and happy – going about their daily tasks of righting wrongs, ensuring people were protected, and referring callers to others who might be able to help with their questions.

Architecturally, the floor plan closely followed the shape of the Kincade Building itself, which had been designed by several ergonomics experts. The layout was based on a right angle and although I'm not a child of Sesame Street, it always gave me the impression of a big, fat, capital L. From the reception area, you entered around the middle of the down stroke, with two vending machines and coffee break areas at the top. Travelling down the L you came to a water cooler and an office waiting area, off to your right, before the corridor bent 90 degrees to the left.

At the far end of the base, there was a fourth, smaller alcove, on the left, with a single water cooler and just enough space for two adults to hide in, at a push, at, say, an office Christmas party…. Let's just leave it at that.

Walking along the base, I loitered in the alcove by the water cooler, pulled a cup from the dispenser and let water slowly trickle into it. Across the way I could see the old-fashioned dark varnished door, with a frosted glass top panel – incongruous in the modern office environment. The matt gold lettering was tastefully arched, and in classic old style lettering, it read: Mr. Harry Rhimes.

That's me. A little old fashioned, a little retro. It helped keep the kids on their toes, not knowing if I was just a touch eccentric, or completely loony tunes.

Underneath my name was: Private Investigator.

I've always felt it had a classier ring to it, when put like that. More upmarket and respectable than Private Eye. And there's no way I'd ever have Private Dick beneath my name, no matter how fancy the lettering. A touch eccentric, maybe, but certainly not a certifiable screwball. And anyhow, my name's not Richard.

I was contemplating bittersweet memories of mistletoe and gin-tainted minty breath, when a female voice beside me asked, "Is he in yet?"

She was young, late 20s to early 30s, and I guessed around five nine in flat shoes. Her mousy brown hair was cut in a short, tomboy style, which gave her face an elfin look, reinforced by intelligent brown eyes and small nose. She was neatly dressed in a white blouse and a modern no-nonsense two piece, in dark navy wool. Power dressing, but without the coldness to pull it off successfully. Her shoes and shoulder bag matched, but gave the appearance of being an afterthought, rather than by calculated design. She'd carefully applied a minimum of make-up, which highlighted rather than hid her natural complexion, and made for a refreshing change. Attractive, in a girl next door sort of way, if that's what you found attractive.

She appeared impatient and in a hurry, dividing her attention between the closed door, her watch, and glancing down the corridor. Annoyed, she pursed her lips, then bit lightly on the bottom one.

Between sips of water, I asked, "Have you knocked?" I tried, but failed to make eye contact.

A mixture of anger and frustration flashed across her face. "I …!" Then she half turned and took a hesitant step, as if she was about to leave.

I coughed politely. "Perhaps I can help?" I took her by the arm and walked up to the door. Without stopping, I turned the handle and strode in, trailing the young woman behind me.

My office was small and oblong, like a shoebox in comparison to the surrounding floor space. In keeping with the trend, it had been done out in the same bland, oatmeal-tasting colour scheme as the rest of Orion & Nadler. At the far end sat an old oak desk and in front of it was an executive leather chair. Behind it, with its back to the large picture window, was its partner. Thankfully the office faced north, which kept things cool in the summer and, in the winter, helps to steal light off the south facing skyscraper opposite. I got to see the world reflected off its frontage, the windows reminiscent of a large bank of TVs. Sometimes I would spend an hour or two, sitting in contemplation, just looking at the sights reflected back at me.

Half a dozen drab grey filing cabinets along one wall provided a resting place for the coffee maker which, in true office fashion, was always nine-tenths empty and in need of refilling. Humming away to itself, in the corner by the window was a small refrigerator, the sort you find in the not so cheap but still sleazy motel rooms. It usually contained a can of not-so-fresh ground coffee, a plastic tub of sugar and some powdered creamer in a jar for people who felt they needed it. Alongside that I kept a dozen bottles of water, plus several brands of lite beer, for when I needed it.

I picked up the empty coffee carafe and pointed to the chair in front of the desk. "Make yourself at home."

I took some water from the refrigerator, reloaded the machine with the makings, and set it off to do its drip-drip-drip magic as she watched in silence.

Hospitality thusly taken care of, I sat behind my desk, pulled a yellow legal pad towards me and selected a pencil from the desk caddy. I eased back in the chair and said, "Now that civilization has been restored, what can I do for you, Ms.?"

She looked at me incredulously, and sounding slightly bewildered, she asked, "You're Mr. Rhimes?"

"Often imitated, but never bettered." I gave her a reassuring smile. Maybe she didn't appreciate the trapdoor spider approach to client gathering?

Another show of indecisive lip biting, then, "My name is Lindsey Fairfax." She stared down at the edge of the desk. "I want to hire your services. I need you to find someone for me."

In a large script I wrote *Missing Person* at the top of the legal pad.

"Does he have a name?"

She looked surprised. "How did you…?"

"Most people want me to find something, or someone. You didn't qualify it with brother or sister, father or mother, and you're not wearing a wedding ring so I just assumed it was a friend or fiancé." I gave her a friendly shrug.

She sighed a little. "Well, he's my fiancé – or was going to be, before he disappeared."

"And does he have a name?"

She looked flustered, then shook her head as if to clear it. "I'm sorry, I seem to be going at this all wrong – I probably even sound like a crazy person, but I'm not. I know he wouldn't just leave without…."

I let her trail off and gather her thoughts.

Getting up I asked, "Coffee? How do you take it?"

"Thank you, yes. I prefer it strong and black."

I busied myself filling two mugs, taking my time, and allowing her to compose herself once more. Getting comfortable again, I smiled in an attempt to get her to relax. "Tell me about him."

"His name is Preston Llyle, that's Llyle with three L's. His father is Roger Llyle, the business entrepreneur, though his mother – Margaret – is Roger's second wife. Preston still gets an allowance from his mother, even though he's twenty-five." Conscious of how that sounded, she quickly added, "But he's involved in some businesses himself, so he's not living solely on family handouts."

"Do you have a recent picture of him?"

She looked at her hands as she started to worry at the shoulder bag in her lap – her fingers twisted at the catch. "He's very self-conscious about people taking his picture. I tried to get him on my phone once, but he was so upset I immediately deleted it. The only thing I have is this." Opening her bag, she withdrew a small four by six photograph and placed it on top of the legal pad.

The picture showed half a dozen young men out on a football field somewhere, all dressed in dirty, sweat-stained uniforms. From their frozen positions it was clear they were breaking away from a professionally posed shot, and only half realised someone else had been taking a picture. It was very much a post-game snapshot and, from the scattered background crowd, I assumed it had been taken not long after the final quarter. In the foreground, the players' faces were flushed, their bodies still pumped full of adrenaline. Most had their helmets off, their hair mussed up, damp and clinging from sweat or from having water bottles emptied over them. One of the jocks had two of his fingers taped together; another had been caught in the process of spitting out his mouth guard. All were either smiling, or laughing, eyes bright with success. The downside was it had all the blurriness of a candid shot, taken with an unsteady cheap camera, making it difficult to distinguish any real details.

She pointed to the one with the protruding mouth guard. "That's Preston. He said it was taken about three or four years ago."

"Can I keep this?"

"No, it's…" Self-conscious again, her teeth white against her upper lip as she bit at the bottom one, two or three times, then, "I'd rather you made a copy."

"No problem." I picked up the phone and pressed a button. Darlene answered, using her professional voice, "Orion and Nadler, how can I help you?"

"Darlene, could you come by my office; I need something copying."

Without changing her tone she said, "Get screwed," then hung up on me.

Looked like I was going to have to tangle with the photocopier myself.

I eased my shoulders and rubbed the back of my neck a couple of times. Something felt out of sync somewhere, but I wasn't sure what. She was a pretty, organised, and clearly intelligent woman. Yet here she was, emotionally confused over this guy's actions – at odds with her initial image.

"Why do you want to find him, Ms. Fairfax? You're not–?"

"Pregnant?" Anger and resentment flashed across her face. Cheeks flushed, she looked out the window. "Why does everyone think the worst of our relationship? His parents. My parents. You…?" Again her voice trailed off, and I thought she might finally crack and show more of her real self. Holding back her anger was doing her no favours.

Sitting back, I held up my hands defensively. "Hey, I've got to ask awkward questions, no matter how intrusive they seem. It's the way I get to find out things." I took a long breath before continuing. "So I take it you're not pregnant?"

"No." She glared at me like a truculent child.

I let it pass, and moved on with the questions. "And you were engaged?"

She fidgeted, now mildly embarrassed. "Preston said he was going to talk to his family, assure them it wasn't just an impulsive decision on our part, and that we were genuinely committed to it. In a way I can understand the family's concerns. Preston stands to inherit a large part of the Llyle fortune, especially after the death of his half-sister, Jacqueline."

In the back of my mind, something nudged me about the name, Jacqueline Llyle, but I didn't want to break the rapport building between us.

Lindsey continued, "She killed herself just over twelve years ago."

"Much to the delight of the local newspapers who dredge it up on a regular basis." The media always loved an anniversary.

She nodded. "He's the only child from his father's second marriage."

I brought us back on track. "Did Preston actually propose to you? Give you a ring?"

"Not officially, no, but he showed me his grandmother's diamond wedding ring, and said he would get it resized for me once his parents agreed to the engagement." She looked at her hands worrying the snap clip of her bag again.

And there it was. The shell, partially peeled away, revealed the confused child beneath, thrown head-first into the grinder of life. Wearing big girl shoes meant you got big girl problems, whether you liked it or not, and I wondered if she was going to release some of the pressure and start crying. She opened her bag, pulled a fresh tissue from it, delicately blew her nose, and tucked the tissue into the bag. Then the shell was snapped back in place. Maybe later, somewhere more private, I'd get to see the real her again, but for now it was back to business.

"How much does it cost to hire you, Mr. Rhimes?"

I jotted a figure on the legal pad, and turned it around so she could read it.

"That's per day, plus expenses."

She sounded slightly taken aback. "I've got some savings I can transfer…." Another bite of her lower lip. "I can pay you for two days, provided the expenses aren't excessive." She looked back at the pad as if it were a complex math problem.

Giving her more time to think, I reached across the desk, picked up my forgotten mug of coffee, blew on it for effect, then took a large mouthful. It was lukewarm and bitter, just like most of my own failed relationships, and I wasn't prepared to start walking down that road again. It would only take me back to the land of depression, and me, myself and I had made a unanimous decision to move on.

Swallowing hard, physically and mentally, I coughed lightly to regain her attention. "Okay, look, here's what I'll do. I'll find out what I can over the next couple of days. I'll report back to you at the end of each day, and you can cover the expenses once your money's transferred."

In my head I heard my late father's sonorous banker voice calling me a fool. So maybe the next client would be the one destined to bring in the millions. I just wanted to give her a break, is all.

She looked at me to see if I'd meant what I'd said. Then the shell cracked a little again, and the innocent peeked out and smiled – happy in the knowledge that Bad had been vanquished from her life once more. Well, for the next 48 hours, at least.

She dipped into her bag, pulled out a chequebook and a slim silver ballpoint, then wrote out a two day retainer. She tore the cheque free and started to thank me, but I got up, walked around the desk, and handed her a business card from the holder by the phone.

With her chequebook back in her bag, she jotted down a phone number on the legal pad, then wrote 'Lindsey Fairfax' beneath it and ensnared both name and number with a circle.

"That's my home number. I work for Claite Electronics, up

on Palmetta, but they don't like employees taking private calls. I've a new Smartphone, only it keeps breaking down and I haven't had time to exchange it yet." Then, with genuine emotion she added, "I really am grateful for this."

I picked up the photograph from the desk. "I'll drop this back to you with the first report, sometime tomorrow evening."

She nodded her thanks and, as I opened the door for her, she paused to look at the photographs and prints on the wall. On one side, a surreal still life and a couple of abstracts rubbed shoulders with a framed copy of my licence. On the other, a framed clipping from the London Evening Standard, which displayed a picture of one Major H. Rhimes, of the Reds & Royals. Next to that were several photographs of my late Uncle Nathan, on my father's side. One of them showed him beside Jack Orion, shaking hands over the business agreement which had founded *Orion & Nadler* back in 1958.

The newspaper clipping was from July 1st 1997, with the caption "The Handing Back of Hong Kong." It's one of the few things I'd kept which still tied me to my former life.

She pointed at the clipping. "Is that you?"

I stood to attention, and saluted smartly. "At your service, ma'am!"

She giggled a little, which I appreciated, then I escorted her back to the main reception area, making sure she was on her way before going to the Reception desk.

Thankfully Darlene was away, taking a break somewhere. Michelle smiled warmly at me as I asked if she would make several copies of the photograph. It's not that I don't like modern photocopiers – they just have a pre-programmed aversion to working for me.

Waiting for Michelle to return, I slipped through the fire doors and into the stairwell. The heat from the midday sun hit me as I looked down at the street below. With her image still fresh in my mind, it was easy to pick Lindsey Fairfax out as she stepped off the kerb and crossed the street, heading north – a dark blue blob in a sea of shifting colours.

It's been known, as far back as Jung and Freud at least, that the human mind gains pleasure and peace from patterns. We have a need to make sense out of chaos, and create order out of randomness. Which was why it was easy for me to spot the tail.

I couldn't tell if it was a man or a woman, but no matter how good they were, their lack of variation gave the impression they were somehow tethered to Lindsey. She dodged to the left, so did the tail. To the right, and the tail followed as if on a leash. What clinched it was when Lindsey stopped to get something out of her bag. Oblivious to the flow, other pedestrians were forced to dodge and swerve around her in their efforts to keep going about their business. In such confusion, a second stationary object stood out all the more.

I was surprised to see it was just a solo operator. A good double act would have crossed and re-crossed their paths without hesitation, in order to avoid detection. But with no second to take over, the job of tailing someone was infinitely more difficult. And all the more detectable.

As I saw her move off again, I didn't think she would've considered the possibility that someone was following her. Why should she? She'd struck me as intelligent, resourceful, but naïve in some respects. Had the Llyles sicced an investigator onto her? It was clear someone was carrying out a background check. And now her visit to Orion and Nadler would be logged and filed in a report. Great. Just what I needed.

There was nothing I could do about her tail, or to tip her off. Even if I'd taken one of the elevators and kept track of them on the way down, I would've still ended up losing them at ground level. So I watched as they disappeared further into the madding crowd, then I headed back through the fire doors. I crossed the reception area, and stopped at the front desk to collect the photo and the copies from Michelle. In my absence Darlene had returned. She looked at Michelle, then gave me the skunk eye as I started to walk away. Thus, with my life fulfilled, I headed back to my little office.

2

It didn't take long for me to track down the information I wanted. Surveillance companies often have the ability to deploy a diverse number of investigators. But sometimes a client might prefer to keep things simple, or be forced to use a smaller firm due to cost, or availability.

After an hour of checking business entries and phoning around, I finally got lucky. Tina Parker's smooth voice answered on the third ring. "Parker Detective Agency, how can we help?"

I tried to sound casual and bored, killing time before taking lunch. "Hi Tina, its Harry. Is Dawson there? Nothing important – if he's busy I can call back another time."

"Hi Harry!" Tina changed from professional to warm and friendly. "No, Husband Number Four isn't here right now. He was out early this morning. A client at a legal firm hired him to follow someone for a while. He's been doing it for a couple of weeks now. You want me to pass a message on?"

Still with the casual tone, I said, "No, nothing in particular. Just a social call before I head out to an interview. When you see him, tell him I'll call him next week." I didn't want to seem ill mannered, but I needed to free up the phone. "Oh, I've got another call. You never know, it might be a new client. 'Bye Tina."

She managed a confused "Er, yeah, 'bye Harry!" just before

I cut her off.

To the left of the phone I have a Newton's Cradle, something which had fascinated me since childhood. I reached over, lifted one ball then released it. Every action has a reaction.

To the left of the cradle sat a fancy digital clock set in a glass pyramid, which had been a present from an old friend. It showed the time in large black figures on an LCD display. Running off everlasting batteries, it automatically received a time signal from a government funded radio station deep in the Nevada desert which, no doubt, doubled as a telephone exchange for our little green friends from Alpha Centauri. The display told me the time in Beijing was 01:17. Provided I remembered Beijing was 15 hours ahead of California, then it was accurate to the millisecond.

Sure, there was a way of changing the time zone – and the procedure was bound to be simplicity itself – but the manual had been de-stapled and gleefully fed to the shredder after the fourth or fifth abortive attempt.

I shook my head. Maybe, one day.

At 01:21 the phone rang.

Picking it up I said, "Hi Dawson." From the background noise, I could tell he was outside on a street, using a cell phone, and probably trying not to attract attention to himself.

"Hi Harry. Tina just called. Don't have to be a rocket scientist to join up the dots. Tell you what; you show me yours, and I'll show you mine. You first."

I set the Newton's Cradle in motion again – two chrome balls this time – as I pretended to consider his offer. Freud would've had a field day. "Okay. I've got a missing boyfriend and I'm curious as to why you're tailing my client. I saw you from on high. I was up on the tenth floor."

"You must have damn good eyesight."

"Yep. I eat a lot of carrots."

"So do rabbits, but most of them never see what hits 'em."

I smiled. Dawson Parker was a typical easy going West Coast sort of guy, and I knew the banter was helping him kill the boredom of surveillance.

"C'mon, Dawson, ante up – what you got?"

"Two weeks of aching feet. I pick her up in the morning, she goes to work, and I hang around doing coffee and Danish until the evening when she leaves to go home. I keep an eye on her, usually until around midnight, then I'm off the meter until I pick her up again in the morning. For about the first ten evenings she goes out. Does the rounds of several restaurants and bars, asks if anyone's seen some guy, then back home, thankfully before the witching hour. But last Saturday something changed and all she did was stay at home. Guess she figured on getting professional help?"

"Well, she hired me for a couple of days." I paused, waiting for Dawson to crack a funny, but he remained silent so I moved the conversation along. "Don't suppose you could keep me out of your log? Just that it might mess with a particular line of enquiry."

"Well, you know what I'm like for neat and tidy paperwork, Harry. If I start changing it now it'll mean annotating stuff in the margins, or scratching in some kind of footnote. Far easier for me to just leave the entry as 'Visited Kincade Building, floor unknown,' and leave it at that."

"Thanks, Daw. That's one I owe you."

"Ha! Get in line buddy. Talk to ya later."

Gathering the coffee mugs, I went to the restroom and

rinsed them off. As I dried my hands, I looked at myself in the mirror. Was I turning into the world's biggest cynic, or did my apprehension about Preston Llyle come from a subconscious dislike of the man?

Maybe Lindsey's emotional shell was there for another reason?

Whatever it was, she was confused and hurt – and desperate enough to hire me.

I waved the mugs dry under the air blower and wondered if the obvious answer was the right one – that she really was a gold-digger just after Preston's money.

I walked back to my office, put the mugs back on their tree, and sat at my desk. With the restrictions imposed by Lindsey's limited funds, I was left with little choice. It was going to have to be quick and dirty if I was to meet the deadline.

Picking up the receiver, I hit one of the speed dials. The phone purrrped several times before the far end picked up.

"Hello Harry." The voice in my ear was smooth, low and female. Elizabeth.

In many respects, to me she remains an enigma. She'd arrived in Concrete one evening on a Yamaha Royal Star, accompanied by David Frederic Earl. He was a white-haired Harley Davidson fanatic who had more than a passing resemblance to Hulk Hogan. In addition to his business skills, a framed certificate proclaimed him to be a fully ordained and licensed reverend of the Holy Moley Rolling Church of the Born Again Brotherhood. They were based out of Modesto, California. Where else? Whether Freddy actually believed in it, or not, was between him and his maker. It meant he could legally perform marriages – Las Vegas style if requested – which was always a profitable sideline to their hospitality business.

The pair had successfully purchased and renovated a derelict three storey hotel. Previously known as Missy Mae's Cat House, they had given it the more respectable name of The Star & Belle.

At first the community didn't know just what to make of the new couple, especially given Concrete's biker gang past. But most of us believed the refurbished hotel would be good for the tourist business in our trickle of a backwater. So Elizabeth and Freddy were readily accepted into the Concrete community.

It was also a strictly business relationship. Freddy managed the hotel, while Elizabeth took on such activities as tracking, survival and woodcraft adventure holidays. She was good at it, too. I suspected she was ex-military, but something more than just your run-of-the-mill G.I. Josephine.

She also knew how to gather information quickly, all of it quality, on a don't kiss, don't tell, cash only basis.

From the receiver, her voice asked, "I take it this isn't a social call, Harry?"

"I'm about to start working a missing persons, and I need some of your time and expertise." This time of year, with the tourist trade down to nothing, I knew any extra was appreciated. And what the IRS didn't see, the heart didn't grieve over.

"You know you only have to ask, Harry." Soft and low. It was the sort of voice which made telephone sex profitable.

I had seen her clear 100 rounds at her private firing range. Five different weapons, three fixed and one rotating target. Her score was debatable – either 99 or 100 hits – if you believe two rounds went clean through the same hole.

Handguns or rifles, she was equally at ease with either, and The Star & Belle had regularly staged the annual Shoot The 'Nads Off a Gnat at a Thousand Yards tournament for the last five years. Those type of events had little appeal to the rest of us Concretes, but they brought a much welcomed supply of dollars all the same.

"I need some background on a guy – Preston Llyle. He's the privileged offspring of Roger Llyle."

"That's a little judgemental, but I'll assume Roger is the patriarchal head Llyle International. Very upmarket, Harry. Sounds like you're widening your circle at last. How detailed do you want the report?"

"I'm on a shoestring budget and a forty-eight hour deadline. In other words, it's quick and dirty at best, as I need it ASAP."

"I'll see what I can do, but no promises."

"Does that mean I get a discount?"

"Ah, Harry. Despite the world recession, the wages of sin remain the same – as do my rates."

We agreed on a price, then she hung up. That was the easy part.

I spent the rest of the afternoon getting the number for Roger Llyle's personal assistant. He sounded pleasant with an Ivy League accent, so I added a dash of English to help level the playing field.

"Would it be possible to interview Mr. and Mrs. Llyle for a series of freelance articles I'm putting together? The working title is The Great American Good."

He said something polite, then put me on hold. There was a short burst of audio disharmony, which had possibly been music in another life, then his voice came back on the line.

"Would tomorrow morning suit? Mr. Llyle has a free slot

between 10:30 and 11:30, and both Mr. and Mrs. Llyle will be happy to see you at that time."

"One moment while I check my planner."

I put him on hold, doodled on the legal pad, then told him 10:30 would be fine by me. He asked for my licence plate so house security could recognise my car, then bid me a cheerful good afternoon.

I drank more coffee, gazed out at the office block across the way, and thought some more about the questions I wanted to ask. My plan of action was simplicity itself. Talk to the parents, find where their son was, and why he'd decided to remove himself from Lindsey Fairfax's life.

In an ideal world, I would find the missing boyfriend, discover it was all a mistake, right the wrong, be invited to the kids' wedding and we'd all live happily ever after.

In an ideal world.

By the time I'd finished staring at Window World, it was heading towards evening and I was ready to go home. The yellow legal pad was now covered in numbers, names and times – along with several doodles of daisies, an oval football, and something which could've been a house. In amongst the scribbles was Lindsey's handwriting. Her figure sevens had the distinctive European bar through the stem, so you couldn't confuse them with her ones.

I took a business card from the desk holder, flipped it over, and wrote her name and number on the back – mimicking her ones and sevens, her precise threes and sharp fives. They brought back memories of my father's notations. He had always insisted my handwriting be legible and distinct, regardless of how quickly I wrote.

Tearing off the top sheet, I jotted out a brief précis of the day's events – more an aide memoir – so I had something to hand over once her 48 hours were up. Later I'd type the pages into the office computer and do my best to make it presentable, though I doubted it would be longer than a page. Two at best. Aside from some dollars for gas, I didn't think I was going to charge her any extra for lunch money.

I spent the next half an hour contemplating Window World again, wondering who worked behind which window, while slowly sipping a Mandel Lite beer from the bottle. I hadn't eaten anything since breakfast, and the cold beer felt warm in my stomach.

Maybe tomorrow would bring the million-dollar client and, naturally, I would be out chasing runaway grooms for disillusioned brides.

The drive back home was easier once I was out of the city and into the countryside. For me, the best part was seeing the cement and glass give way to trees and open spaces.

I let my right hand diddle with the radio, found several shit-kicker and bluegrass stations, but decided life was too short and the evening too beautiful to go driving myself off of any nearby cliffs. Tuning into a local soft-rock station, I settled back and coasted on home – the commuter traffic thinning until I was on the 299 again.

Finally I parked at the top of my drive and walked down to the front door. There was a thin manila package propped against it. Elizabeth had been quicker than usual, which wasn't a good sign. I picked it up, unlocked the door, reset the alarm, and walked into the large, open plan living room.

The view through the sliding glass doors made me stop just to take it all in. The canyon, at my point, went from East-West. In the mornings it caught the sunrise, and at the end of the day the large glass panels would often frame impressive sunsets. Ever since moving in, I had been able to immerse myself in the colours and the textures of Mother Nature. Along the canyon sides, the sparse clumps of pine and shrub were home to a variety of wildlife, which helped to keep us Concretes entertained when the TV and radio reception got too bad and the phone lines were down.

Uncle Nathan had also loved nature, and designed the house to present the best views from all its levels.

Externally, the house had been constructed like a three-tiered wedding cake. Cut down the middle, half of it had been stuck onto the canyon wall 60 feet above the river. He'd thought about the position in regard to the changing shadow cast by the opposite canyon wall. That was why foot square pieces of armoured glass had been inserted into the living room roof, which doubled as the kitchen veranda. The same stolen light technique had been used on the kitchen roof, which also formed part of the third tier's open decking area.

Access to and from the house varied, depending on the dictates of the weather, as to which dirt tracks and paths you took. CalTrans ensured the roads were maintained to a high standard throughout the year, so Concrete annually helped out with the Adopt-A-Highway programme, by way of saying thank you.

The open plan living room sat at the front of the house, with two of the four bedrooms off to the sides towards the back. Up a dark wood staircase, the landing opened out to the kitchen at the front, plus two more bedrooms to the rear. Up again, and the third level was yet another large living area-cum-observation room.

The whole place had been built from natural materials

found around the canyon itself. Cemented, locked and pinned into the canyon wall, it blended in with the background.

Both the house and the office had been my inheritance from Uncle Nathan. The office is mine, rent and utility free, for as long as I made use of it. After which Jack Orion – or, more likely, one of his descendants – could then do with it as they saw fit.

For the life of me, I don't remember Uncle Nathan, so I have no idea why he left me anything in his will. He never visited the family, or myself, while we were in England, but I didn't know what contact he'd kept when Mom finally left Dad for a new life in Paris. The trouble was, with him being close family, a regular DNA test wouldn't prove anything. Which was saying I was able to find some of his DNA in the first place. I had my suspicions, but Dad had always treated me like his own son – even going out of his way to write to all the family about my success in getting a place at Sandhurst.

However, with repeated postings to Northern Ireland, the Gulf and the Balkans, our politics had diverged and further coloured our relationship over his final years.

But that was in the past – time to get back to the here and now.

The lack of food was finally getting to me, so I picked up the phone and ordered myself pizza.

Captain Chilli's Exploding Tomato Pizzeria – "Every pizza guaranteed to blow your head off!" – was run by a pair of extreme-sports fanatics, and although they appeared to be overly bohemian and laid back, they actually cared for their product. They were also the only place who would deliver for no extra charge.

Tossing Elizabeth's envelope onto the coffee table, I walked through the back and into the master bedroom. Stripping off, I hung the suit to one side for dry cleaning and tossed the laundry in the basket for a wash day, then spent ten minutes under a hot shower, trying to get the city out of my skin.

Drying myself off, I went back into the bedroom. Despite the evening's warmth the room felt cold and rejecting. The large double bed was still unmade, the cover and top sheet rucked up and pushed to one side, pillows still crumpled, two depressions still clearly visible.

I exhaled heavily, yanked open the wardrobe, and caught sight of myself in the full length mirror fitted to the back of the door. I'd always tried to keep myself in shape, cared about my appearance, and exercised both body and mind whenever I had the chance. True, the jagged lightning bolt scar on my chest wasn't what I'd call attractive, but at least it was on the right hand side, and didn't look like bypass surgery performed by some crazed Dr. Frankenstein. And the rest of the chassis was in excellent shape as well, considering the mileage it had racked up over the years. Okay, so maybe there was a visible whiff of smoky grey in with the light brown hair, but so what? All the finest meat has been aged before being put out on display, and feeling good about yourself was really all that mattered.

Impulsively I pulled on a robe, grabbed some stuff off the rail and marched myself into the adjacent guest bedroom. Ten minutes later, with fresh linen on the bed and some personal effects on the nightstand, I figured it would do until I got my head back together.

As my spirits started to lift, I put on a pair of light slacks, an old RMA Sandhurst T-shirt, and a pair of flip-flops before going back into the warmth of the living room. I switched on the hi-fi and relaxed as the rich sounds of Concrete's own jazz-orientated *Night Train* flowed softly from the speakers. I poured a small Irish whiskey and nursed it as I looked out at the night sky. Experience had taught me there was no point in drinking to forget; you just end up forgetting to stop. Then you'd waste your time trying to remember what you'd successfully forgotten.

The sound of the delivery man knocking on the door indicated the arrival of pizza, and the smell from the Mutant Margherita he handed over was sinfully seductive. As I paid the guy, I wondered how he'd made it over to the canyon. It wouldn't be the first time he'd been pulled over for speeding in a wind-powered land yacht. Not forgetting the time I had to lend a hand to pick bits of broken gyrocopter off the canyon wall.

*****

Later, with the pizza slowly dissolving my stomach lining, I lay on the long couch and went through a two minute relaxation routine. In a more receptive mood, I opened the envelope, and started to read Elizabeth's report.

I don't remember making it past the first half page.

3

I woke feeling cranky, despite the bright sunshine already starting to slide through the glass patio doors. The radio was still on: "You're tuned to Concrete's Community Radio! This is the Morning Coffee Show, and I'm Robbie Moore, the boy next door, letting you know the weather forecast for the city is hot and breezy. So don't forget to wear something thin and flimsy girls! Meanwhile, here's The Carmichael Brothers to tell you about their footwear fetish."

Glaring at the speakers, I carefully got up and started to work the stiffness out of my back and shoulders – not completely sure if the pain was from sleeping on the couch, or from the terrible pun on the song title.

"I'm a soul man…."

I shook my head. At the next Concrete Council meeting I was going to have to table a motion for getting "the boy next door" whacked and laid six feet under.

Picking Elizabeth's report off the floor, I cut through to the guest bedroom at the back, stripped off and stepped into the ensuite shower. It felt good just to let the hot water and a bar of Simple Sally soap work their magic. While still under the jets, I shaved with my eyes closed – an old Army time saving habit I've never been able to break.

I dried myself off, flossed, brushed, then dressed in khaki cotton pants, loafers and an open-necked polo shirt. I checked myself out in the wardrobe mirror. Maybe more Wal-Mart than Wall Street but, damn, I was surfing on a wave of happiness and actually feeling good about myself.

Closing the wardrobe door, I looked at the guest bed, and the grey clouds swept into my mind again. Wipe out. I wondered if it might do me good to move in here properly for a while, let my emotions calm down before venturing out into the waters once more. Plenty more… Yeah, right. Time to pick up the board and go looking for a tube to shoot.

Positive actions, positive thoughts. They say – whoever they might be – the best way to start the day is with breakfast, which was all the incentive I needed to climb the stairs to the kitchen. The morning sun was coming up over the trees and canyon rim, spreading a bright zone across the veranda decking and the hardwood kitchen floor. Can't beat a jolt of heart-warming sunshine for putting a smile on the lips of any good and honest creature. That's how you can tell the bad guys. They don't smile.

Nodding sagely to myself, I took some eggs and three links of sausage from the refrigerator. Dropping the sausages in a heavy fry pan, I left it on a medium flame while I broke the eggs into a bowl. A little salt, a little pepper… Pepper? Ah, now I knew what had been missing. Reaching over I pressed a button on the kitchen sound system. From the speakers came, not the expected sound of Art Pepper, but Miles Davies. One of his classic early albums, in the original mono mixes.

The sausage started to pop and spit, leaking a little pork fat, and I started to beat the eggs with a fork in time to Jimmy Cobb brushing the hi-hat. I was just about to take it to the bridge when the sausages began crying to be taken off the heat. Putting them on a plate, I poured the eggs in and stirred them around with the fork to keep them from sticking too much.

When they were done, I dished them up with the sausage, pulled a couple of paper towels from the wall dispenser for napkins, rolled back the patio door and went out onto the veranda. Off to one side I'd put a small, square, pinewood patio table and two simple wooden director's chairs. I slid the plate onto the table, then tucked the paper towels under its edge to stop them from getting away in the light breeze.

I walked over to the rail, found the garden twine I'd wrapped around it, and started to pull up the morning newspaper tied to the other end of the line. From behind I heard a slow, methodical, thump, thump, thump of something hard and heavy hitting against the wooden decking. Without turning around I said loudly, "Wait your turn!"

Unhurried, I freed the newspaper and tossed the weighted line back down again. Reading the front page, I went back to the table, picked up one of the sausages and flipped it across the decking. Some more thumping, then the sound of slobbering and chomping as the sausage was devoured by the Richardsons' dog.

He was a big and old golden Lab who could usually be found lying on his side on the kitchen veranda decking. He wasn't part of the original inheritance as such – he was here when I moved in, so I just assumed he was kith and kin, so to speak.

It wasn't until I'd asked some of the other canyon residents about Uncle Nathan's Labrador, that my suspicions had been confirmed.

"Oh no, that's not his dog. That's the Richardsons' dog!"

Try as I might, I could find little or nothing about the elusive Richardsons, except that through no choice of my own, I now had their dog as a permanent house guest.

His short coat had a scattering of grey and white in amongst the gold and, given his nature, it was hardly surprising as he'd certainly seen some action in his time. He was missing a couple of toes, which didn't seem to affect his ability to come and go as he pleased, and while one eye had that slate grey cloudiness of an obvious cataract, the other was as clear and clean as a mountain spring. Years of practice meant he knew how to manipulate human pity and he was adept at squeezing the very last drops of sympathy from almost anyone. He even thinks it still works on me – but that's just because I don't have the heart to disillusion him.

The thumping of his tail on the decking slowed, then stopped as he stretched himself out, shuddered a little, broke wind in the key of C#, then settled down to sleep again.

He was also the reason why the newspaper got tied to the string.

Some time back, the paperboy used to ride out on his mountain bike and throw the rolled-up paper onto the kitchen veranda. On more than a few occasions, I'd caught him trying to hit the dog. I'd shout as he was cycling off, but it didn't seem to have any effect on the kid.

A few days after his last successful hit, I came out onto the veranda with a plate of breakfast, sat down, then heard a terrified voice calling out, "Mr. Rhimes? Can you call your dog off please?"

I strolled over to the railing and looked down. At the bottom of the driveway, the paperboy was using his bike as a defensive barrier. At the top of the drive, blocking the kid's exit, was one very pissed off Richardsons' dog. The dog's hackles were up, teeth bared, and even at this distance I could hear his angry growl. Maybe pissed off was an understatement.

Offhandedly I called down to the kid, "He's not my dog, kid. He's the Richardsons' dog."

I was tempted to say 'dawg', but resisted, on the grounds I wasn't smoking a corncob pipe or chewing on a plug of tobacco.

"Please, Mr. Rhimes! I promise I won't do nothing to tease him no more!"

"Won't do nothing no more is an extra-double negative, kid. Don't they teach you nothing at school?" Ah, Harry Rhimes, leading by example.

But the kid was obviously scared, and while tossing newspapers at dogs then trying to outrun them on a bike wasn't the smartest of moves, it was time to put an end to the situation.

I went back into the kitchen, took some twine out of a drawer, tied one end around the railing and threw the rest down to him.

"From now on just tie the paper to the end of this, okay?"

"Whatever you say, Mr. Rhimes. Just call the dog off!"

I turned my head a little and looked the Richardsons' dog in the eye – either the good or the bad one, I can't remember which – and shouted "Hey, Fuckwits, get in here now!"

The dog stopped growling, let his hackles down, and snorted contemptuously. Then he casually sauntered back along a trail and onto the kitchen veranda's edge, his tail swinging from side to side as if nothing was wrong.

For the record, he responds to, "Hey," rather than anything else – as in, "Hey! Nice dog!", or, "Hey! Who are you, old fella?!" Usually, though, it's, "Hey! If you're going to do that, do it downwind!" Let's face it, if I were to stand on the veranda and shout out "Hey, Fuckwits, get in here now!" every time I called the dog, I'd have half the town's human population showing up at my door in no time.

I settled back and finished my sausage and eggs, Miles still playing in the kitchen, and flicked through the newspaper. As usual, a lot of nothing, interspersed with coupons and adverts. Not surprising considering it was late in the year, and with the tourists thin on the ground it was up to the local inhabitants to keep the journalists' insatiable appetites for sleaze and scandal sated.

Time passed, the sun continued to climb, and it was around 9 a.m. when I finally set off for my appointment with the Llyle family. I'd changed into a white shirt, plain tie, and a charcoal grey cotton two-piece suit. All the better to make a good first impression. The Ford might not have had the best air conditioning, but it always paid to dress for the occasion, regardless of how warm the weather. For all I knew, the Llyles could become regular clients one day.

Driving out from the canyon wasn't so bad once you'd gotten used to the switchbacks, the summer dust, the occasional rock slide here and there, and the fact the hill climb grinds your transmission into an early grave. A 4x4, or maybe one of the new style pickup trucks, would handle the back roads far easier. Trouble was, it was too easy to spot such a vehicle, three or four cars back, when you were trying to tail someone. Whereas my old PoS, with its dusty windshield and tired paintwork, usually remained invisible to most drivers, even when close up.

Rounding the top of the canyon wall, it was just a case of cruising along the 299 until I'd skirted the city. From there, the highway climbed back up into Shasta County, and was easy cruising before I turned off onto the back roads once more.

As I drove along a parallel track road, I caught sight of the Llyle place. It was imposing and impressive, even from a distance. The architecture looked more like an official public building rather than someone's home, regardless of whom the someone happened to be. The front entrance was protected by a white painted, semi-circular, cement wall. To the rear, the grounds were protected by a double run of wire fencing. Add in foot patrols, along with camera surveillance, and it was doubtful the Llyles could ever be taken by surprise.

Following a signpost, I turned onto a length of sun-greyed tarmac driveway and coasted up at the front gates. They were large, wrought iron and wood constructions, which wouldn't have been out of place in a remake of *Fort Apache* or *The Alamo*. Along the top of the wall ran loops of razor wire like some kind of S&M slinky. Sunlight glinted from jagged shards of broken glass fixed into the top as an extra defence. Not so much a gated estate, more a case of heavily fortified.

To the right of the driveway was a 3 foot deep storm gully. To the left was a brick-and-wood shelter, which gave a rain and wind break to those who had to use the intercom.

Killing the engine, I got out and ducked into the shelter. On the back wall sat a brushed steel intercom with a pierced grill, a well-thumbed call button, and the protected eye of a miniature camera. Hmmmm. I'll be another five minutes, Mr. DeMille.

A laminated sign had been nailed up beside the intercom. In big black lettering were the words Buzz and Wait. So I buzzed, and waited.

There was a loud click, then the speaker hummed and crackled into life as a thin, metallic, male voice said, "State your name and your business."

I pushed the button. "Mr. Harry Rhimes. I'm here for a ten-thirty appointment with Mr. and Mrs. Llyle."

"Wait."

So I waited until the speaker hissed and crackled at me again.

"Okay, Mr. Rhimes, show the camera some ID."

I reached into my jacket pocket, withdrew my wallet and flashed my driver's licence. Another bout of silence. In my mind's eye I pictured a bored security company guy. Dressed in a pseudo-military rent-a-cop uniform, I figured he was sitting in an operations centre up in the main house, finger-pecking the information into a computerised form.

From the speaker, the voice came back. "Everything seems to be in order. Mr. Steadman will be waiting for you up at the entrance to the main house. Er, you might want to back up a little though, before we open the gates. I take it your vehicle still has reverse gear?"

Ah, another loss to the entertainment industry.

I started the car and rolled several yards back down the driveway as the gates shuddered, then swung slowly outwards. Driving through left me in no doubt. This really was Fortress America.

The road leading to the main house curved out to the right before hooking back to the left in a crescent – more, I suspected, for effect than for any practical design. Seeing several other vehicles already in place, I parked to one side of a brick and flagstone carriageway which led to a short flight of stone steps and the main entrance. Fronted by ornate Doric columns and an impressive set of doors, the image and tone was of an 18th Century Governor's Residence, enhanced by an atmosphere which spoke of old money and older politics.

Another intercom greeted me at the door and a faint buzzing helped me locate the closed-circuit security camera as it rotated in my direction. Before I could do anything, the doors swung inward, revealing the hallway and, at a safe distance, the reception committee. It had consisted of a 30-something Hispanic security guard in a neat uniform, and to one side, a late middle aged man I took to be Mr. Steadman.

On one side of the guard's belt hung a matt black security wand, and the other side had an ugly, square-barrelled tazer within easy reach of a relaxed and steady hand. Steadman was impeccably turned out in a modern cut double-breasted suit, though there had been something about his stance and his body language which seemed at odds. If the reception committee was designed to impress, then it was certainly living up to expectations.

The guard stepped forward, took out the metal detector and proceeded to check for any concealed weapons. Although I'm licensed to carry, I didn't feel there was any need to this time. I mean, what sort of trouble could I get myself into just by asking about their son?

Once checked, the guard nodded an okay, then moved back to his safe spot, off to one side. Taking that as my cue, I smiled as warmly as I could before heading towards my escort, hand outstretched, ready for the initial shaking of – though as I approached he looked slightly perplexed and confused.

In a Southern fried accent he said, "Pardon my ignorance, sir, but am I right in the assumption you are a freelance journalist? Is there a camera bag? Recording equipment? Paraphernalia to be collected from your vehicle?"

Paraphernalia? Without even thinking about it I slipped into my best English. "I carry with me only the time-honoured tools of my trade, namely a notebook and pen. Now, lead on, dear boy, lead on!"

A look of pained resignation creased his face before being replaced by a mask of indifference. "If you would care to follow me, sir." He turned and pushed open another impressive set of doors which, in turn, opened out into a reception room.

Probably considered large in the real world, the room was decorated in tasteful opulence. Not so much as to say Gaudy, but enough to say Never Ever Been Strapped For Cash.

With the walls painted in sympathetic pastel colours, the room focussed on a sculpted Italian marble mantelpiece and surround, which framed a large cast iron fireplace. Above hung a massive mirror in an ornately carved and gilded frame which, on closer examination, confirmed its Pre-Independence Georgian roots. The drapes hung cinched over window shutters, which had been folded back to let in as much natural light as possible.

Halting in the middle of the room, Steadman turned to me. "If you would please wait here, sir. Mr. and Mrs. Llyle will be with you shortly."

He left, closing the doors behind him, leaving me wondering why a staff member would need an overly generous cut jacket and wear a button-sized transceiver almost totally concealed in his right ear. At least now his body language made more sense.

I took a slow walk around the room, pleasantly surprised at the way the early seventies Conran pieces blended in with more modern European designers. Several occasional tables were within easy reach, while along the far wall was a Japanese-influenced sideboard with an Art Nouveau Tantalus sitting on top.

The click of the door catch brought me back to the present. Turning around I was first greeted by Mrs. Llyle, then Steadman again, pushing Mr. Llyle in his wheelchair.

I knew Roger Llyle was in his 70s, but his frailty still surprised me. Originally from a wealthy family, he'd made his money through a string of businesses, and lost a small fortune in alimony to his first wife in the process. The wheelchair was down to an accident he'd suffered on a sub-contractor's construction site. Despite the surgeon's best efforts the damage to his spine and neck had left him paralysed from the waist down. He sued the company for every penny they had, literally, and when the company was bankrupt, stepped in and bought it, lock, stock and Chapter Eleven barrel, for the sum of one dollar. Before he finally sold it on though, the company had been placed in the Wall Street 500.

Regardless of his power and status, sitting in the wheelchair he came across as atrophied, small and doll-like, in a French blue three-piece suit, white shirt, and a powder blue bow tie. His bald scalp and face was reminiscent of an early Boris Karloff, in the RKO version of *The Mummy*, and I guessed he had more wrinkles than an elephant's scrotum. Not that I'm readily conversant with elephants' scrotums, but I've seen enough issues of *National Geographic* to recognise one, even at a distance.

His fingers were thin and bony, attached to wrists and forearms which seemed swamped by the shirt and jacket cuffs – the frailty amplified by an overly large, loose fitting Rolex – while his fingers twitched and fluttered listlessly in his lap like two small birds squabbling over a crust of bread. Yet his clear, bright grey eyes, were youthful, quick and still full of sharp intelligence.

Margaret Llyle, on the other hand, was somewhat of an enigma. Despite good plastic surgery and regular hits of Botox, I knew she was mid-50s, if she was a day. From what I'd read in the social columns, she'd married Roger Llyle right after his divorce. So quickly, in fact, some people believed she had been waiting in the wings, with her bouquet and bridesmaids at the ready, even before the *decree nisi* had landed on the family lawyer's desk. Depending on whose social commentary you followed, she had either been a cocktail waitress, a lap dancer, or a personal services type of masseuse. Perhaps even all three. But whatever her past, it had been successfully buried from prying journalists. The one thing everyone seemed to agree on, however, was that she had married way above her station.

She stood around five-seven tall and had chosen to dress very Jackie Kennedy. It was a semi-formal two-piece in light salmon, which did her no favours. Her hair, having dyed a thousand deaths, had been lacquered to within an inch of reanimation. I wondered why she hadn't thought to employ a stylist, or some other professional to advise her. From her body language it was clear she felt self-conscious and uncomfortable.

Closing the doors behind him, Steadman wheeled Llyle closer to the chairs. I expected him to leave. Instead he took up a position directly behind Llyle, feet slightly apart, hands behind his back. Relaxed, yet attentive. I waited for Mrs. Llyle to settle herself before I sat down across from her.

Smiling, she broke the ice. "Out of interest, which magazine will your series be appearing in? There are so many these days that–"

The sound of Roger Llyle sighing stopped her mid-sentence.

"I don't think Mr. Rhimes is here to interview us for any

proposed article, are you, sir?" He chuckled a little, which merged into a slight cough. "Mind you, I was taken with the title. The Great American Good. It has a ring of plausibility to it, I'll give you that." His expression told me not to push the cover, so I just held up my hands in surrender.

"You're right; I'm not a freelance journalist. I'm here to discuss a delicate and personal matter." Deliberately I looked towards Steadman standing behind Llyle's wheelchair.

Llyle nodded. "Don't worry about him. When it comes to family scandal, he's as deaf as they come. Isn't that right, Steadman?"

Steadman deigned not to answer.

Across from me, Margaret Llyle covered her embarrassment with an aggressive, cold anger. "Who the hell do you think you are, coming into this house and invading our privacy? Steadman call house security. I want this filth thrown out. How was he able to make an appointment in the first place? Roger, do something to stop him and his kind digging around all the time." Her face flushed, despite the colour of her make-up.

"No need to get upset, Margaret, Mr. Rhimes is here to talk about Preston, aren't you?" He looked over at me, a thin smile catching the corners of his mouth. "I didn't think Ms. Fairfax had it in her to hire someone, but I'm assuming she's your client? Otherwise there's no reason for her visiting you yesterday, is there?"

"Seems you're way ahead of the curve, and I apologise for any offence I might have caused." Sometimes a little humility pays back with dividends, and I could see no point in being confrontational. Nor in denying something Llyle had obviously checked up on, despite Daw's promise of anonymity.

Margaret sat back on the davenport and glowered at me.

With that avenue closed, I turned to Roger Llyle. "Ms. Fairfax hired me to find your son. Once I have that information, I'll pass it on to her. After that, it's up to her what she decides to do with it. As far as I can tell, she wants to ask him why they broke up. Beyond that, I've no other interest."

Again the thin smile danced at the edges of the old man's lips.

"That's gratifying to know, Mr. Rhimes. However, I fear you're on a wild goose chase. From what I understand, the two of them were romantically involved for a while – about a year and a half I believe?" He looked over to Margaret, but she remained silent. Turning his head to me, Llyle continued, "But, for whatever reasons, Preston felt it was not in their best interests to continue the relationship. Perhaps, in hindsight, he could have been more tactful and diplomatic about it, but it appears this young woman has taken his departure to heart. I believe Ms. Fairfax felt there was more to the relationship, yet to Preston it was more platonic than anything of a physical nature."

Margaret Llyle suddenly moved forward in her seat, the hem of her skirt riding up a little as she did so.

"She's not claiming she's pregnant by Preston, is she!? I swear to God, as soon as it's safe to do so I'll have the little bastard DNA tested!" The look of raw hatred slowly faded as she made an effort to sit back again, trying to discretely adjust her skirt at the same time.

Roger Llyle waved a hand in her direction, obviously annoyed at the interruption, then looked inquiringly at me.

I tried to smile as I reassured her. "I believe she's not

pregnant, if that will help ease some of the tension between the family and herself." I waited to see if Margaret would react, but her anger seemed deep and irreconcilable.

I shook my head a little. "I can appreciate the relationship came to an end and that it seems my client is not prepared to admit it's over, but…." I looked towards Roger again. "It might be best if Preston met with her and told her to her face."

Roger Llyle coughed out a short laugh. "They're hardly star-crossed lovers, Mr. Rhimes. I doubt very much there's anything to be gained from such a meeting. As it is, both Margaret and I have no idea where he might be. We have extensive grounds around this house alone, and that's before we start talking of holiday homes, cabin retreats, vacation sites…."

The vague movement of his jacket made me think he'd shrugged his shoulders. When I looked across at Margaret, I could have sworn she was gloating rather than smiling insincerely at me.

I smiled insincerely back. "So you've no objection to me asking around for information?"

Her grin compressed until her lips formed a thin red slash in her efforts to contain her anger. Roger sighed heavily. "If I can help with any questions you might have, then I will. But I insist this is the last time."

I nodded. "Seems fair to me. Can you tell me anything about this?"

From my jacket pocket I pulled out the copy of Lindsey's photograph. Steadman moved forward and carefully took hold of it, so Llyle could study it in detail.

"My word…. Well, I have to admit this is a few years old. About four or five I think…" He looked over to Margaret, but she pointedly refused to glance at the picture. Roger went back to studying it. "It must have been when he was involved with some sort of pro or college football business. The Greagson's eldest, Wesley, got him involved with something along those lines. Preston has always had a very strong interest in sports and athletics."

"Does he have any other girlfriends, ex-college sweethearts, cheerleaders?"

"You'd have thought so, but no, not that I can immediately recall. He's more focussed on competing and winning. He's always been very performance driven. At least, in some areas, that is. Can't say I know much about his personal relationships."

There are times when, no matter what you do with the dice, you always throw snake-eyes.

"In that case do you know if Preston is gay?"

The atmosphere in the reception room dropped from merely cold, down to frigid.

With a great amount of control Margaret Llyle half whispered, "You filth. Tell him to leave, Roger. Now. I want him gone. Now!"

Roger looked over to me. "I'm afraid Margaret is right, Mr. Rhimes. It's time for you to leave. Before you do though, to answer your question. Firstly, no. Preston has never shown any sign, or intimated such to either of us, that his orientation is anything other than heterosexual, regardless of how outwardly dysfunctional his private life may appear. Secondly, even if he were gay but not yet out to friends and family, it's still none of your business. And thirdly, Steadman will see you off the premises. Good day, sir."

I nodded my thanks to both of them, then followed the aide

through into the entrance hallway again.

Unceremoniously he said "Farewell, sir," then handed me over to the guard. "Michael, once you've escorted Mr. Rhimes to his car, make sure you put his name on the Undesirables list."

Without giving me a second glance Steadman turned and headed back into the inner sanctum of the house.

Michael looked at me, shaking his head in sympathy. "Guess you've been a bad boy," he said as he walked me up to the main door and watched as I headed back to my car.

4

Driving back through the gates, I watched as they closed behind me, then pulled up onto the verge. Getting out of the car I decided to do some reconnaissance to see what the perimeter was like. Five minutes later, and having found no easy access, or vantage point, I took my jacket off, loosened my tie a little, and rested my back against the white painted wall.

I had intended to go back to the office, write up a neat report, drop in a gas receipt, then hand it all over to Lindsey, sometime in the evening. I'd certainly not planned on rubbing the Llyles up the wrong way so spectacularly, nor getting myself thrown out by the hired help. By the same token, I hadn't expected to roll up and find Preston wandering around the house, either. But then I'd not figured on the whole sorry business running for longer than a day – or even a day and a half at best. Yep, an' it don't rain in Indianapolis in the summertime, either.

The way it looked, all I could do was bag up what I had and take it back to Lindsey Fairfax. If she wanted more, then I'd have to either talk her out of it, or stick her with a bill. Hopefully she'd listen to reason.

With my jacket over my arm, I headed back to the car.

I'd almost made it, too, when I was greeted by what looked like a pair of 30-something thugs in rent-a-cop uniforms. I'd not heard them, but from the dust in the air around their white

Chevy Tahoe I guessed they'd only just arrived. Clipboard in hand, one was in the process of checking my licence plate, while the other lounged against their vehicle.

By the brightly coloured paint job on the Chevy, and the logos on their uniforms, I knew they were from another local security firm. It was different to the company badge I'd seen on Michael's uniform, and it made sense to keep the internal separate from the external security. I suspected these guys had been hired to patrol the roads and perimeter walls – probably covering a dozen or more addresses in the immediate vicinity. They had been kitted out with an assortment of electronics, connected via Bluetooth earpieces, and good old fashioned radio for when the cell coverage ceased. At least, that's what one of the whip aerials on the Tahoe was obviously for. Still, they didn't look like hardened professional road warriors to me, and as I approached I purposefully slipped my hand into my trouser pocket and pulled out my notepad and pen. If you treat fire with fire, then the same can be said for pseudo-authority.

"Names?" I barked at them, continuing to walk to the car, pen ready to write. If nothing else, a military background gives you the ability to put an authoritative tone into your voice.

"C'mon boys," I snapped out again, "You've checked with house security. They know who I am, and they've confirmed my meeting with Mr. and Mrs. Llyle. So give me your names, or I'll put it down in my report you didn't know what was going on, and were uncooperative with it."

I glanced at both of them to make sure of their confusion, then added, "You have checked with house security, haven't you?" in that smug tone normally used by IRS inspectors when savouring an imminent kill.

They gave me their names, but as I'd already christened them Tweedledee and Tweedledum, I wrote those down in the notebook instead.

The one with the clipboard became a touch defensive. "We've already got you on our list of cleared visitors. We were just curious as to why you'd left your car parked up on the grass."

"Call of nature, nothing more exciting than that."

Tweedledee looked slightly confused. "Call of what?"

"I had to take a whiz."

Tweedledum looked over at my car. "So why the clunker?" Then, when he saw my expression, added hastily, "If you don't mind me asking."

"How would you two have reacted if I'd turned up in a car marked Security Inspector, eh? I'd bet it would be totally different to what you just did. This way, I get to see how you'd react in a real situation."

Thankfully that satisfied them. I checked my watch, and pretended to note down the time while both of them climbed back into their vehicle, slowly turned it round, and drove off back down the road again.

Once they were out of sight I breathed a heavy sigh of relief, got into my old Ford, and silently thanked Michael for not being so quick to put out an amendment to the access list.

Traffic was good on the way back into the city, and it was mid-afternoon by the time I got to my office. Winding down, I got a bottle of Italian sparkling water from the fridge, then spent time writing up my report in longhand before typing it into the computer. It might be double the effort, but every time I sit down at a blank screen, my mind goes blank to match it.

I printed off two copies; put one in the filing cabinet, the other into a large brown envelope. Satisfied, I upgraded the water to a bottle of beer, popped the top, and pulled Elizabeth's report from my jacket pocket. It didn't take long to skim through it.

Preston Llyle, now 26, had been silver spooned into a world which had provided him with everything. His early life was nondescript. Apart from a long bout of private tuition, he had no real public presence until the death of his half-sister, Jacqueline.

The County Sheriff's patrol had been called to the house in the early hours of a July Saturday twelve years before. Confronted by a distraught Margaret Llyle, she'd told them Preston had found Jacqueline, floating face down and naked, in the indoor pool.

Being heated meant the body had been kept warm, which made fixing the time of death difficult. Combined with the humidity and pool chemicals, the forensic team stood no chance, so her death had been attributed to drowning, aided by a combination of alcohol and drugs.

House security had been of little help back then. For reasons of privacy there had been no camera systems in place, and areas such as the indoor pool were considered off limits to patrolling security guards.

Preston had been physically unharmed, and had maintained an air of detached emotional coldness during his interviews. In his statement he'd said he'd briefly seen a young man with Jacqueline that evening. Though he couldn't provide a reliable description, he didn't think Jacqueline knew him from university.

Piecing things together, both Margaret and Roger Llyle had left the house, late in the afternoon, and had plans for the

Friday evening. With differing tastes, Roger had taken in a piano recital while Margaret had taken in a show. With both the parents out, 18-year-old Jacqueline had given the rest of the staff the night off, then she and her unidentified male friend had raided the liquor cabinet. According to the pathologist's report, sometime between the parents leaving and her death, she'd smoked a joint or two, drunk a fair amount of good vodka, taken some LSD, then stripped off and went for a swim. They had found no evidence of any recent sexual activity, consensual or otherwise, prior to death.

The newspapers had been given a press release by the family lawyers. It stated that Preston, coming from his room after watching late night TV, had heard music and seen the pool lights still on. His initial reaction on finding Jacqueline had been to drag her body out of the pool, and attempt CPR. When that had failed he'd sat by her side – apparently in shock – until his parents had returned. It had been Margaret Llyle, arriving home around midnight, who had dialled 911 and reported the incident.

Apart from two crystal tumblers found at the bottom of the pool, and several lipstick smeared roaches, there wasn't much evidence regarding the young man. And, despite large sums of money being offered for information over the years, the investigation had become inactive and eventually cold cased. It had remained that way, despite regular reviews.

Time to focus back on the boy.

Academically, Preston had been an average student, with little aptitude in either science or the arts. Only his sports prowess, his family's social standing, plus their charitable donations to academic causes, had ensured Preston a good placement.

After graduation he'd become involved with a variety of sports related business ventures, but unlike his father, he hadn't inherited the same Midas touch. The failures had helped generate problems with his father, who'd expected his children to follow his example. To that end, Roger Llyle had supposedly placed a massive amount of money in trust, which Preston couldn't touch until his 40th birthday. Until then, it was down to Preston's brains, and the kindness of strangers.

I flipped to the last couple of pages, which concluded with rumours about Preston supplying Mexican steroids and performance enhancement drugs to the gym and jock crowd. Personal service and quality assured, rather than some Internet credit card scam. However, the authorities had not been able to prove a positive connection, so it had remained all just suspicion and hearsay. The only things on his record were several teenage driving offences, which had been conveniently dealt with by one of the family lawyers.

The report only confirmed my own suspicions. Preston Llyle wasn't as good as Lindsey Fairfax believed, and certainly not what I'd have called a catch. I trusted Elizabeth as a reliable source, and decided to put a copy of her report in the envelope as well. Lindsey could read it all, then decide what to make of it herself.

According to the desk clock, it was 09:15 in Beijing by the time I'd finished. Lindsey would still be travelling back to her apartment, taking the early evening cross-town crush-hour special, or walking and doing a little window shopping along the way. I picked up the envelope, straightened my tie, put on my jacket and walked through the semi-deserted office area. Reduced lighting and the on-coming night shift until 6 a.m. *"Orion and Nadler – making sure you sleep safely."*

I drove downtown, took a side street, and parked near a little diner. Billy Fong's Noodle & Chop Shop. Fast food for the working masses.

You enter the restaurant first through the street door, then another at right-angles to it. That way bad spirits can't find their way in, and good spirits can't get out easily, or so Billy tells me.

Inside, the place was a shrine to a classic 1950s style diner, which was what Billy had been aiming for. There were private booths along one wall, while others looked out onto the street. Basic, one-size-fits-all, family sized affairs which sat four, or six if you were comfortable being up close with each other. Ivory and candy-apple red paintwork, strawberry vinyl upholstery, and cream Formica table tops. The overhead lighting was provided by peach tinted fluorescent tubes, which gave the place a warm and homely feel.

Opposite the booths was a counter with stools down one side, and mingled in with the smell of coffee was the aroma of Oolong, Jasmine and the earthy undertone of green tea.

I walked in as the place was starting to fill up with early evening diners. They provided a steady murmur of conversation to the background noise of the TV at the far end by the cash register. It was an old Zenith, hanging close to the ceiling, and it had an old-fashioned remote control, the size of a house brick. For convenience, Billy kept it tuned to one of the local news stations.

Sitting at the counter, I called across to Billy for a bowl of glass noodles "and an eighty-seven Carrere to go."

Billy glowered at me. "Pork chop! How many freaking times I gotta tell you?! Pork chop! No cars!" Along the counter several of the other diners smiled or laughed quietly to themselves.

Billy's a native San Franciscan, with a BA in business studies from Washington. I'd often seen him defeating local politicians at city meetings. Not only on points of law, but with the eloquence of his English as well.

Setting the bowl of transparent noodles and broth in front of me, he smiled sympathetically. "Long day?"

"And getting longer." I picked up the spoon and start eating.

When I'd finished, he came by to clear away the empty bowl.

"Sorry, Harry, looks like your order's going to be another three, four minutes, maybe." He nodded at the booths behind me. "What can I say? Business is good, or we're the cheapest place in town."

I pulled a dollar and Lindsey's number from my wallet.

"I can wait." I handed him the dollar bill. "I need to make a call anyway, can you break that for change?"

He fished around in his apron pocket and pulled out some coins. "Here, on the house."

I thanked him, headed towards the back where the rest rooms and payphone were situated and dialled Lindsey's number. She picked up on the fifth or sixth ring.

"Hello?"

"It's Harry Rhimes. I've put together a preliminary report. I talked to Preston's parents this morning and I'm pretty sure they've no idea where their son is." Before she replied, I continued, "I've had an associate of mine run a background report on Preston. You might want to read it before you think about paying more good money to find him."

There was a defensive, brittle edge to her voice. "Are you saying there's something I need to know?"

I sighed, perhaps a little too loudly. "I have no idea what you know, or don't know, about Preston. All I know is, the report doesn't put him in a good light."

"Nobody's perfect, Mr Rhimes. Not even you."

That stung, but I figured she had the excuse of ignorance, and certainly some grounds for her emotional anger.

I checked my watch. "I'm just about to eat, but I'd still like to drop this report off to you. Tonight, if possible. Say around eight-thirty?"

"Eight-thirty should be fine." The brittleness had gone, replaced by something more cheerful. "I'm at twelve-fifty-seven Carmaline; apartment four C." She was silent for a moment, then added, "I know you have your doubts about Preston, Mr Rhimes, but all I want is to find out why he left the way he did."

I went back to my waiting pork and greens, still smarting a little from the unintentional jab she'd given me. I knew she wanted closure – that much was obvious – but I still didn't like the idea of taking her money knowing it would all just end in grief.

5

I drove away from Billy's and headed south and west, catching the lull between the evening rush hour and the regular night time chaos. I pressed the auto tune button a couple of times, and let the radio climb through the stations. With little to choose from, I settled on a local college running a Brit-Glam special. The DJ was good, and with the retro music on a low volume, it wasn't long before childhood memories of that crazy period started to surface. Three-inch platform shoes, Lurex, Spandex, sequins and make-up for boys. All part of growing up in 1970s London, and made fashionable by successful glam rockers such as David Bowie, Mud, and The Stickies.

> *"Lipstick, powder and furs!*
> *I like to dress up in!*
> *Lipstick, powder and furs!*
> *So good, it's gotta be a sin!"*

Maybe there was a future in nostalgia after all?

It didn't take me long to locate Lindsey's address. It was in one of the latest up-and-coming redevelopment areas. Well-lit deserted streets and an air of Upwardly Mobile Isolationism. Nobody knew their neighbours, because everyone worked every hour of the day or night just to make the rent. It all added to the sterile, plastic-wrapped feel, and made me wonder just where the old sense of community had disappeared to.

I drove past the apartment block and found a space a little further down the street. Collecting the envelope off the passenger seat, I locked up and slowly headed back to the entrance – hard to miss with the bright security lights. In amongst regimented rows of metal buttons I located Lindsey's apartment number, thumbed the stud a couple of times, then waited for her to answer. Through the thick glass doors I could see the lobby and the area the developers had put aside for potential buyers.

Originally the building had been one of the city's old malt-house breweries. Beaconsfield Beer – *"Beer so good, you just won't wanna pee!"* Developers had stepped in when the brewery closed, and had wasted little time in gutting the place down to just the four external walls. Then they had divided the space up into fashionably small apartments. Looking through the glass at the publicity shots, they seemed like studio boxes with the bed set up on a mezzanine shelf, accessible by an artistically constructed ladder-cum-stairway. The photography was done with a touch of wide angle which gave a deceptive appearance of space, and going by the lack of availability notices I guessed the units had already been snapped up.

I was about to press again when a tinny voice called out, "Who is it?"

I put my mouth near the speaker grill. "It's Harry Rhimes."

"Come on up." The door buzzed like an angry swarm of bees and I walked through into the small reception area. It was neat, clean and utilitarian, done in mock marble walls and plastic wood flooring. Security cameras in two of the corners blinked their little red eyes every few seconds, and a large sign told bikers and delivery personnel to remove their headgear before proceeding into the building proper.

At the far end was the elevator, while off to one side were the stairs. I admit the stairs looked tempting, but by the time I'd come to a decision I'd already pressed the up-button, and the elevator doors pinged seductively open. With no canned music to deter me, I stepped inside and pressed the button for the fourth floor.

When the doors shamelessly pinged open again, it was a short walk along the corridor before I stood outside a plain door with 4C in shiny chrome lettering on it. Off to one side was an ornate doorbell. I pressed, and waited: something which was becoming a habit.

From within I heard Lindsey check the peep hole, then the door opened. Where her office suit had given her an air of authority, her faded blue jeans and baggy pullover added, rather than subtracted, from her tomboyish appearance.

Her smile was warm and genuine. "Come on in."

The apartment felt small and compact, even a little claustrophobic – but then I'm luckier than most. Still, if the apartment met with Lindsey's approval, at a price per month she could afford, then who was I to deride it?

The décor was light, but colourful, and Lindsey had obviously gone out of her way to make it homely. One corner was the compact kitchenette, with just enough room for a microwave and a two burner hotplate. Crockery and china had been stacked neatly on the shelves by the sink, while a small refrigerator completed things. Open backed bookcases broke up the floor space and helped define other areas of activity, while several vases of flowers added to the fresh, clean smell of the place.

The remains of her evening meal still sat on the table – dirty plate and cutlery neatly to one side with the condiments, chair pushed back under. In the small area bounded by a two piece suite sat an oblong coffee table. On it, an open bottle of red wine – the cork pushed part way back into its neck – and a half-full glass sat next to several neatly stacked magazines. The sight of so much precise tidiness made me wonder if there wasn't more than just a touch of OCD at work.

I walked over and sat down on the sofa, which gave her the protective safety of the easy chair. Sometimes it helped to let others feel they were the ones in control.

I wondered about mentioning the fact I'd spotted Dawson tailing her when she'd left Orion and Nadler, but thought better of it. Although he hadn't said he'd stopped, I hadn't seen anyone hanging around the apartment block as I'd walked up to the front door. No one had tried to slip in with me when I'd entered the building either, so I was guessing the surveillance had been called off. What with everything else happening in her life, I thought it best just to forget about it.

Without ceremony I held out the large manila envelope, then settled back while Lindsey read both my initial report, along with several sections I'd deliberately highlighted in Elizabeth's thumbnail profile. They were mostly the rumours and some hearsay which, knowing the quality of Elizabeth's work, would have solid foundation rather than being wild or malicious gossip.

After a while she looked up from the paperwork.

"This doesn't change anything, Mr. Rhimes." She tidied the pages, stiffly tapping them on the coffee table before slipping them back into the envelope. "I just want to find him and have him tell me what's really going on. If nothing else I deserve that, regardless of what the rest of the family think. I know about the lack of money. I was the one who suggested a palimony agreement to help ease his parents' fears."

"You've met his parents?"

"Not exactly…." She let the comment trail a little before adding "I wanted to talk to them, let them get to know me. But Preston said they always questioned his relationships, especially in view of what happened to Jacqueline, and his mother could be quite hostile to strangers."

"Did he say why?"

She looked thoughtful. "No, I don't remember him giving me any reasons. It all seemed very guarded and cold. I mentioned it several times, but Preston said he didn't want them reacting to my past until they got to know me better."

I closed my eyes as a sinking feeling settled heavily in the pit of my stomach. It never occurred to me she might have a past which would cause problems.

"Okay. What might have upset the Llyles?"

Her face flushed in embarrassment, and she stared at the envelope still in her hands. "I admitted myself for rehab. Six years ago I was hooked on prescription painkillers. Vicodin at first, then OxyContin."

She slowly put the envelope down on the coffee table, then sat back in the easy chair. Her fingers fussed with her hair before she carried on.

"It had started off innocently enough, after I'd fallen down two flights of stairs and damaged my back and hip. Soon after that I twisted my knee, so the doctor kept me on the same prescription from one injury to the other. It wasn't long before I was tending to take them on a daily basis, even though the pain had disappeared. I kept telling the doctor I needed the pills and the old guy kept on prescribing them. When he finally stopped, I just went on the Internet."

In the past I'd known veterans who'd endured serious pain, both real and, in some cases, psychosomatic phantom pains caused by amputated limbs or paralysis. A small number of doctors used to find it easier to keep on prescribing, without regular case reviews, getting the patient hooked on the junk. Demerol, Percodan, OxyContin – the Hillbilly Heroin. All opiate-based prescriptions. When used and controlled correctly they did the job they were created to do. But, over the years, people had become addicted to them just as others had to tranquillizers and amphetamines in the 60s and 70s. Mother's Little Helpers. At least Lindsey'd had the sense to seek help.

"I wasn't hooked as such, it was still in the psychological dependency stage. The third time I ordered some from the Internet, it made me realise I needed help. The tablets didn't arrive, then my credit card account was hijacked. I always thought it would never happen to me. When it did it came as such a shock. I spoke to several close friends, and they all suggested I get help. It took a while and some interesting therapy, but I've been off them ever since."

With the information now public knowledge there seemed little point in damage limitation.

As calmly as I could I asked, "Do you know how the Llyles found out? It's not the sort of thing rehab clinics or therapists like to release, even to investigators or the police."

"I told Preston all about it. It was our third or fourth date." Again she smiled, showing just a hint of teeth before looking down at her hands folded in her lap. "He took me to Albizzi's, the Italian restaurant off of Saratoga Boulevard. It sort of became our place." Biting her bottom lip again, she added "I haven't been back since Preston left."

Having been slightly blind-sided by the rehab incident, I decided to ask a little more about their relationship.

"So talk to me about your relationship with Preston. How did the two of you meet?"

"I'm not really sure how we met, but we had been aware of each other since college. We were at different ends of the school spectrum; I was into the debating societies, discussion groups and student politics. Preston was…" She tried to find the precise words to describe someone she obviously felt emotional about. "Preston was more than just a sports-fixated kind of guy." Her nose moved a little as her mouth scrunched up, unhappy with her choice of words. "That doesn't really do him justice."

The more she continued the more I realised what she felt for him. The emotional attachment seemed genuine on her part. It wasn't the blind infatuation of teenagers or young adults, nor the obsessive desperation of a lonely woman grasping at failed relationship straws. Whether it was reciprocated was another matter.

"Preston is fun to be with. He makes me feel good about myself." Her eyes were alive with emotion and she smiled as she spoke. "We might not have had the same interests, but then diversity is the spice of life. Or so we're forever being told by the experts."

"And Preston felt the same way?"

Without hesitation she replied, "Yes. Otherwise why would he have kept asking me out on dates, or showed me his grandmother's ring?"

Inside me the Bad Fairy of Recent Experience flexed its dark wings. "So why has he gone into hiding? There must be a reason, and if the two of you were as close as you say, then you must know what's behind it all?"

Her smile crumpled like a side-swiped fender as her anger and confusion returned. I could empathise with the way she felt. Let down and betrayed by the seemingly callous way he'd deliberately walked off without any explanation. It wasn't the coldness of the action which hurt, nor the anger at being deceived – used even – but the pain which came from discovering all the lies. The sharp sense of betrayal. It was the realisation that I had no idea – or no conscious idea at any rate – as to exactly why they had walked out on me.

Her. As to why Preston had walked out on *her*. I had originally thought I was there to just deliver the report and go, not go delving into my own psyche while things were still raw inside. Mentally I put the lid back on the Bad Fairy's jar and screwed it down tight again.

Lindsey looked to be on the point of tears. In a small, quiet voice she said, "I don't know why he's stopped seeing me. That's why I came to you."

I made a mental note to ask Santa for a pound and a half of Stiff Resolve, to be taken as required.

"Look, excluding expenses, you've hired me for forty-eight hours. So far you've had about half. Let's call it twenty-four hours for argument's sake. I'll keep to our agreement and carry on looking. But, once the time is up, and if you still want me to carry on, then I'm going to have to ask for some more up front. Deal?"

She considered it, then nodded in agreement. It was the least I could do, I thought, though the closeness of her at that moment made me feel uncomfortable. I needed to get out and re-focus myself, sort out my own head before too long. But above all, I needed to finish my commitment to Lindsey, then move on to something more profitable.

I got up and headed for the door. "I'll drop by tomorrow evening and give you an updated report – though I doubt there'll be much that's new. By that time you should have worked out if you want me to take it further."

Lindsey got up out of the chair, crossed the room, and opened the door for me. "Call first, just in case." She left it at that. She closed the door firmly behind me as I stood in the hallway, the noise of the deadbolt being thrown sounded loud in the silence.

I took the elevator to the ground floor and walked back to my car, all the while cursing myself for not being hard-nosed enough to give her the brush-off. It was clear to me things were going nowhere. For some reason, Preston had gotten cold feet. Or else they had been cooled for him. No doubt he was off somewhere, waiting for Lindsey to lose interest, or just give up and get on with her life, probably oblivious to the way she felt about him.

I started the car and headed back towards the 299. Maybe I could contact the Llyles again, see if I could get them to talk some more? I doubted I'd get much from Margaret Llyle. She'd been like an angry diamondback rattler poked with a stick – quite venomous in her attitude towards me. Maybe there was more to her relationship with Preston than met the eye? Roger Llyle, on the other hand, didn't strike me as having ever lost control. In fact I doubted he would have been as successful in his businesses ventures if he had.

The late evening traffic going out of the city was light, making the journey home thankfully uneventful. Just as well; I was feeling physically tense and emotionally tired. It had been one hell of a long day.

Parking the car at the bottom of the drive, I killed the lights, got out, and walked slowly to the front door. The sound of my shoes on the loose surface added a loud crunching to the evening's background noise.

Up in the kitchen I put the day's mail on top of the breakfast bar, then started a pot of tea. If the British Army had taught me one thing, it was how to make a proper cup of tea. With boiling water poured over loose leaves in a teapot. The fact I drink it black – no milk, no lemon – is again down to Army logistics and personal survival. That had taught me when out in the field, any milk was to be considered suspect no matter how fresh it looked.

Leaving the pot to mash and brew, I checked the refrigerator. Some salami and a block of Monterey jack. There was no way I was going to risk doing cheese at that time of night, so I sorted out a couple of slices of white bread and toasted them while reading the mail.

That's another good property about tea. It's an anti-depressant. Especially after opening several bills which were guaranteed to knock a hole right through the middle of my cash flow.

I buttered the toast, and looked around for something spreadable in a jar. With nothing to hand, I decided life was too short and all I really wanted was a couple of aspirins and some time to relax.

Throwing the bills to one side I topped up my mug, took it down into the living room, selected a copy of Minchfield's *Observational Techniques for Forensic Investigators*, then headed for the guest bedroom again.

Someday soon I was going to have to face up to going back

into the master bedroom, if only to change the linen and pick up the laundry basket. But I didn't feel like it. At least, not after Lindsey and her blind optimism.

I had the feeling, in some respects, that she had never grown up. That somewhere in her childhood had been created a strange duality I failed to understand or appreciate. Outwardly she was the level-headed young career woman, who took her responsibilities seriously. Inwardly, though, she still believed in the teenage dream of schoolyard sweethearts, white weddings and two-point-four children.

Maybe she didn't realise Life was the consummate joker. Because even when you think you're safe and you've moved on, it sometimes taps you on the shoulder, turns you around, and kicks you four-square in the nuts. Just for a laugh. That was where Lindsey was lucky. Women didn't have any physical balls to be kneed in.

I turned over a page and tried to pick up the threads of Minchfield's underlying argument. She put forward a hypothesis that all observers are prone to subconscious assumptions, which they had no control over, thus tainting their supposed impartiality. But I kept drifting back to Mom and Dad's failed marriage. They were never, officially, divorced. To do so would have been an admission of failure, and both of them had always been far too proud for that.

Maybe there was some truth in the saying after all, that fruit never did fall far from the tree. Maybe I should have asked, rather than just assumed. Or been more assertive instead of passively compliant, despite my hidden reluctance. Perhaps if one of us had been more sensitive to the others' needs, then we would still be together, without the festering threads of displaced anger.

Come midnight I finally put Minchfield to one side and turned out the sidelight. Half an hour later, with the Bad Fairy once more in its jar, I put it back in the cupboard alongside my other monsters, shut the door, and finally went to sleep.

6

The following morning I felt restless. I didn't want to go to the office first thing, but I didn't want the isolation and solitude of the house. So I did what I usually do when I wanted to sit, relax, and contemplate how things were going: I went and sat in the city's Bicentennial Park. It's a large, tranquil, green expanse in a sea of high-rise cement, tarmac and cars. Perfect for regaining your perspective on life.

Originally, it had been laid out long before the Bicentenary itself. However, to celebrate 1976, the city governors decided it should be remodelled and refurbished, in the hope it would become a place devoted to inner peace, harmony, and culture. Landscapers, ecological professionals and wildlife specialists had been involved with the project from the start. The aim was for it to become one of the city's major attractions, showcasing physical skills in material construction alongside the more aesthetic and artistic.

Thankfully, unlike similar projects, it had retained most of those qualities over the intervening decades. The lawns were kept trim and neat, the paths meandered and wandered naturally, and wildlife was evident throughout the whole of the year. Reproduction sculptures, changed and rotated on a regular basis, were dotted here and there, while benches had been positioned to allow people to sit and contemplate their surroundings. And, of course, there was the famous

Bicentennial Park bridge.

The construction spanned from one side of the park to the other and was easily one of the most impressive sights the city had to offer. As you walked along it, the arc gradually lifted you high above the ground, so you could take in the entire park from an aerial viewpoint. There were protective windbreaks, and railings helped to deter any but the most determined of jumpers. However, with the impressive surrounding architecture, and the fact the walkway wasn't all that high off the ground, there had been very few accidents or successful suicides. You're more in danger of being hit by flying candy from the kids flicking M&Ms through the railings at the people below.

The morning was still overcast with darkening clouds, which kept the morning sun at bay, and a light breeze kept the heat down. As I walked over from the Kincade Building, I picked up a couple of fresh bagels and some coffee from a corner deli. Then it was just a matter of walking into the park, finding a bench, and slowly eating breakfast in quiet contemplation of some cultural artefact.

This time round, it was of a sixteenth-century Italian sculpture. To me, it seemed to depict one of the Roman Emperors in combat with someone who, I originally thought, was supposed to be a representation of Mars, the God of War. On closer inspection of the information plaque, it turned out it was a representation of Christianity's war against Roman paganism and other false deities.

Over a battlefield-style body-strewn plinth, two large, perfectly muscled, semi-naked men were locked in a close-quarters wrestling match. It was clear from their faces and positions – also from the fact it had originally been a Papal commissioned piece of work – that the old-style Roman polytheist traditions were being conquered by the newly emerging world of Christianity.

It was a quality reproduction of the original piece, made from weather- and pollution-resistant acrylic resin designed to look like marble. It certainly seemed good enough to fool the local bird population – at least going by the guano deposited on the sculpted heads and other perchable body regions.

When I half closed my eyes, it wasn't difficult for me to imagine the struggle. The intensity of traditional ideals and philosophies, losing ground to newly emerging theological beliefs. The impact of Christianity on a culture which had produced not only some of the greatest military leaders, but had encouraged some of the greatest innovative thinkers of all time.

As they wrestled in my mind, the sound of rock warriors locked in mortal combat had intensified, until it had finally become the sound of Marty Beddows' mutated New York accent, grumbling and muttering as he sat down beside me on the park bench.

There's no denying it, Marty has always been one very ugly creature. People often said he bore more than just a passing resemblance to Lurch, from the 1960s TV show, *The Adams Family*. Kissing 6ft 3, but with broader than average shoulders, his macabre appearance wasn't helped by his taste in midnight black double-breasted suits. Coupled with his high forehead, morticians' morose countenance, and general downbeat aura, and the result had been something which only his late mother could ever have admitted to loving. And then probably only while under duress.

If you listened to station house gossip then you'd know he

either slept hanging upside down from the rafters of the nearest derelict church, or else in a bed on top of graveyard earth, taken from his motherland.

Never able to settle in one place for long, Marty had travelled the East Coast, moving from one police force to another, until finally moving west to Northern California. He was one of New York's finest mongrels of no fixed ethnic origin, who had successfully worked his way up the food-chain by hard graft and honesty.

We sat on the park bench in silence for a few minutes, while I continued my appreciation of the sculpture and its artistic merits. I tilted my head a little to one side, then the other. Then I stood up, slowly walked around the sculpture, and sat back down alongside Marty again.

He took a long, sideways look at me, then looked back at the sculpture. With a pained expression on his face, he said, "K-rist."

"Nope. It's more a physical interpretation of Homo Superior."

"Looks more like homo pornography to me."

I looked off into the distance, slowly shaking my head. "Your family tree wasn't involved with the sacking of Rome, by any chance?"

Beddows looked at me from beneath his dark eyebrows. "I don't know about sacking, but we'd've sure as hell bagged something less queer for a souvenir, that's for sure."

We sat there in silent contemplation for a few seconds more, before I reached into the paper bag beside me. I pulled out the last warm bagel, broke it in two and offered him a piece.

He accepted it, stuck a bite of it in his mouth and chewed a little before saying: "I understand you've been upsetting important people."

"Sorry?"

"So you should be. Talking to the Llyles like that was bound to set the dogs loose, and you know it. We've had a complaint from a pet pit-bull at Sphincter Hard-on and Sphincter."

"You mean Spencer Hartman and Spencer, shysters to the well-heeled?"

"You see? With that kind of talk, is it any wonder you've been rubbing people up the wrong way? What's your interest in the Llyle kid?"

"I'm working a missing persons on him."

"Who for? According to the father, his kid's not missing. They just don't know where he's disappeared to. Anyway, he isn't a juvenile, he's a grown man."

"His almost-fiancée, a young woman by the name of Lindsey Fairfax, hired me to see if I could find him."

"Almost-fiancée? Is that like as in he almost –"

I cut him off sharply. "Proposed, yeah. C'mon Marty, she's a nice kid. She's in love with the guy, for Christ's sake."

He held up his hand, thumb and forefinger barely apart. "Well, according to the pit-bull, they're this close to banging her with a restraining order, on the grounds of harassment."

I was surprised. "Why the heavy stuff?"

"They say it's because of her chasing that the Llyle kid's gone into hiding."

I thought back to our previous meetings. Lindsey didn't strike me as being the stalker type. But then, was there a particular type which could be labelled stalker, even if they hadn't started stalking yet?

"So, are you warning me off?"

"No, nothing like that. Your name blipped up on my radar,

is all, and I thought I would come and get the real deal from the horse's mouth, rather than the horse's ass."

"And how is Karrel these days?"

"Hey, you know he just lives for you to keep biting on him."

Karrel Johansen was a born and bred country boy who had been fast-tracked up the promotional ladder. To his credit, he had brains and intelligence, and used them to good advantage, borne out by an impressive record of successes. He'd recently been promoted to Captain, heading up the Investigations Division of the Major Crimes Unit. He'd installed Marty as his right-hand man from day one. If there was an ounce of fairness left in this world, then their roles should've been reversed, as Marty would make an excellent Captain given his background and experience. But that was never going to happen, mainly because I knew Marty would never have gone along with the level and depth of office and city politics which went along with wearing that particular hat.

Actually, it had been Karrel who had saved my ass when it came to securing my PI licence.

Completing the required time I needed to put in had proven difficult. Especially when my original mentor had put himself in hospital the fortnight before. I'd already done the bulk of the 6,000 hours required to obtain the California State licence. It was now just a case of getting down and doing some old-fashioned grunt work. Over coffee and donuts with Marty, I'd vented my frustrations.

"With the dispensation they've given me for my Army time and legal experience, plus time already served, I'm down to my last seventy hours."

"Are you sure you really want to do this?"

"C'mon Marty, I was in the military police. What else can I

do?"

"As the old proverb goes, be careful what you wish for. As long as you're sure?"

"Yeah, I'm sure."

"Okay, I'll see what I can do for ya."

Marty had left, all sweetness and light, which should have tipped me off. But no, like a spring lamb to the slaughter I had no idea what was going to happen next.

Several days later, and he'd called by the office again. This time he said he'd found a way for me to qualify. I could top up my hours, double quick, if I were to help the department out with some community service work.

As long as the time went towards my hours, then fine.

It transpired that Karrel had volunteered Marty, along with some rookies, for one of the Crime Prevention roadshows. The sort of thing which regularly toured the elementary schools, trying to teach the kids right from wrong.

How difficult could that be? Just a bunch of Second and Third Grade kids in a controlled environment, a little theatrical style re-enactment, usually done in slow time to help emphasise the point to the kids. Then home before the sound of the bell.

In my defence, when the suggestion was mooted it was towards the end of a dull and boring day, so I was in no fit mental state to question such a purveyor of idyllic gifts.

Two days later the cat suit arrived.

For three days per week, over the next four weeks, I was Charlie Kat. Yes, with a K. I was the only one around when the boys and girls, played by a bunch of rookies, did bad things to each other, to themselves or, more usually, to me. Well, to Charlie Kat.

They would pull on my tail, yank at my whiskers, twist my ears, and I would take it until they ran off. At which point I would put my head in my paws and pretend to cry.

Marty would then step up and talk to the kids about what they'd just seen. Those not too terrified by his gargoyle-like appearance would answer his questions as best they could. Those who kept silent were probably mortally afraid he would eat them if they got the answers wrong. In real life, Marty's tastes run the full gamut from Texas truck-stop chilli and crackers, all the way through to modern New World-Thai fusion cuisine.

Well, the first week went quickly, and I was starting to get into the role, when the rookies realised I wasn't a fellow law-enforcement officer. By the end of the second, things had started to get a little bit rough-house, and by the end of the third week's performances word was out I was working for my P.I. ticket.

Now I don't know why it is, but in my experience, public-sector law-enforcement personnel have never taken kindly to the private sector. And, rookies being rookies I suppose, they thought it might be fun to beat up on Charlie a little more realistically than they had been doing. Some of the punches and kicks were not pulled as they had been before, and even though the cat suit offered a degree of padding and protection, I was still coming away with bruised ribs, a bruised back, and several lumps on my head which I was sure I never had three weeks before.

On the final day of the four week tour I decided I'd had enough.

It was halfway through the show when one of the main troublemakers, a big rookie from the Redhill precinct, called

Marconetti, was scripted to pick a fight with me. He was over six feet tall, with air between his ears, and he had been cast in the part of a school bully. Smart money said he'd been successful when he'd auditioned for the role way back in kindergarten.

The storyline had him follow me around, then pick on me after school. Only, when it came to the confrontation scene, instead of just saying, "Oh no! Please don't hit me!" I dropped my voice down in volume and added, "you dumb-ass sasquatch."

He froze, unsure about the deviation from the script. Then his anger started to crank up, and I took a step away from him as he half-shouted, "What did you say?"

Reaching behind me, I picked up my tail so as not to trip over it, and held it firmly in one hand. As cutely as I could, I looked over his shoulder and into the audience.

"I said, Oh no! Please don't hit me, you peckerhead."

Then I flipped the top of the tail up and brought the end of it down squarely against his ear.

Marconetti's head jerked sideways and he dropped to his knees, which was the desired effect, considering the night before I had removed some of the kapok stuffing and replaced it with six ounces of finest quality birdseed. With that sewn into the end, it had turned the tail into the perfect fur-covered blackjack.

After that, I have to refer to editions of the local school and city newspapers, mainly as their photographic evidence purportedly doesn't lie. But, to this day, I refute the statement that, after cold-cocking him again with the end of my tail, I commented, "Choke on this pussy, you," at which point most sources differ as to the expressive expletive used.

As the photographs go on to show, I was quickly wrestled to the ground by four of the remaining rookies using batons, handcuffs, and in one slightly blurry shot a folding chair of some description. Somewhere in the confusion I have a memory of Marty looking faintly bemused, though later he stated it was just gas at the thought of the paperwork to come.

When all the brouhaha had finally died down, it fell to Karrel to decide what actions needed to be taken. For the good of all concerned, he'd thought it best to just forget about the whole incident, so no charges, or counter-charges, were ever brought.

A month later I was a fully paid up member of the Californian Association of Licensed Investigators.

Sadly, despite repeated requests from both the teachers and the kids, I was never invited to tour with the roadshow again.

The distant sound of shouting and laughing from children, high up on the bridge, brought me out of my reverie and back into the real world. I smiled at their innocence and the fact they had no fear of what the future held in store for them. I had no idea what it held for me, either. Like one of Dawson Parker's rabbits, I was just an optimist on the midnight freeway of Life, trying to stare down the headlights of the on-coming eighteen wheeler of Destiny.

I looked up at the sky. The clouds were getting darker, and tension seemed to be on the wind. Something Roger Llyle had said came back to me, and I looked over at Marty.

"Can I ask a favour?"

He leaned back and stuck his hands in his pockets. "Ah, what the hell. Ask away."

"Does the name Wesley Greagson mean anything to you?"

"Greagson?" His foot tapped out a heartbeat rhythm, one-two one-two, while his database mind correlated information. "They're a well-to-do family but the son has a record of drug abuse and failed rehab promises. Convicted of possession but never of dealing. I'm pretty sure both his parents publicly disowned him a couple of years ago."

"Was he involved in any business ventures, pro football, anything like that?"

Hands still in his pockets, Beddows shrugged his shoulders. "Couldn't tell you. I only get to know the bad boys, and then only when they've been caught. Or gotten off on a technicality."

I nodded and looked across at the park again, thinking about the team picture still in my jacket pocket. The photo was old, or so both Lindsey Fairfax and Roger Llyle had implied. Yet Roger had spotted Greagson right off in the photo.

I turned my head back to Marty. "I don't suppose?"

"Ha! Not a hope in hell. Can you imagine what Karrel would do if he knew I was running errands for the likes of you?"

I smiled. "It could induce a heart attack."

Marty looked at me. "He's a good guy, Harry. He's getting things done for this city."

I nodded in agreement. Despite my disparaging comments, I knew Karrel cared just as much as Marty did when it came to keeping trouble off the streets. But relations had never been good between us. If you were to put us in a room together, then we'd end up beating each other's brains out within an hour. Opposing forces. Yin and Yang. Though, theoretically, we're both supposed to be The Good Guys.

Marty got up, brushed imaginary bagel crumbs from his trousers, then stretched his calf muscles a little. "Tell you what I'll do. If I hear of anything about Greagson, that might be relevant to your missing Llyle, then I'll give you a call."

"Fair enough," I said to Marty's retreating back.

I watched him walk away, his slightly uneven gait due to an old bullet wound, and I kept watching until he'd disappeared from view, beyond the park gates. Looking up over the bridge, I could see that the clouds had turned a darker, smoky grey, edging themselves with hints of brooding malevolence.

I bit into the remaining piece of bagel and washed it down with a mouthful of coffee. There was nothing for it. I would have to start working on a new angle in the hope of discovering some new information.

Crumpling the empty paper bag into a tight ball, I put it in the coffee cup, then dumped them into the bin beside the park bench. For a moment I thought about buying a packet of M&Ms and joining the kids up on the bridge. It would sure feel good, but wouldn't solve a damn thing.

With a heartfelt sigh I stood up and started heading back to my office.

7

The ride up the side of the Kincade Building felt like a scene from Wagner's *Ring Cycle*, and the horizon was getting crowded with ugly looking thunderheads. Even from this distance I could see them moving slowly closer, letting everyone know a mother of a storm was on its way. Call me Southern Fried, but it still made me feel uncomfortable all the same.

As I walked past the reception desk Michelle said "Hi!" and Darlene flipped me the finger. It was a good sign. It meant we'd moved on from public stony silences to expressive hand gestures, and even those were becoming less dramatic, yet still managing to convey their anatomically impossible messages. It was progress, of a sort. Baby steps, little baby steps.

Entering my office I turned on the lights then checked the coffee maker, pushing the On button to reheat what was still in the glass jug. The sky in Window World looked ugly as well – snitty, as my mother used to call it. Despite the glazing I knew the outside temperature was dropping and the wind was picking up. With a touch of luck it would pass by, or just touch the city with squally showers. But I doubted it. Like the Llyle business, I just wanted it to be over and done with as quickly as possible, but I had a feeling it wasn't going to be that easy. As my thankfully late Uncle Morty used to say, "You get a feelin' in your water, son, it's usually a sure sign of prostate trouble. Or stones. I passed a stone once, did I tell you? Big as a pea. Took a chunk of porcelain clean off the rim."

Armed with a fresh mug of re-brewed coffee, I sat behind my desk and flipped through my address book. Once I'd located the details of a sports writer I knew, I tapped out his office number and waited for a response.

Tony "Bam-Bam" Sinclair had been a childhood friend from around the time my family moved to England. We had sort of kept in touch, mostly through our parents, though over the years it had become an if-and-when thing. He had been a very competitive kid, even from an early age, hence the nickname, Bam-Bam. It had followed him all the way through college, and into his professional life.

Early on he'd had a promising career as a South Carolina rookie pitcher, coming through the tough Royals in the 1980 to 1984 seasons. Training alongside the likes of David Cone and Kevin Seitzer, he seemed to be on course for the big time.

But a fast car and a slow bend put paid to both his right shoulder and his career. When he came out of hospital, he'd started looking around for something he could do, and in no time he'd figured out the solution. As he was no longer able to play, why not follow the next best thing, writing about it instead? Which was why he'd taken a time out for some college courses before making a start as a cub reporter. He was a passionate but fair commentator, with his writing style firmly down at the fan roots. With the contacts he'd gained as a player, he was able to climb up the ladder to the dizzy heights of successful freelance. Had regular columns. Syndicated, no less.

The sharp click from the receiver brought me back to the present. Without waiting I said, "Hey, Tony! I understand you're still doing the college stuff."

"No way, buddy, I checked her driver's licence! Hey, who is this?"

I put on my best Southern Belle accent. "Why, Mistah Sinclair, how soon you forget!"

"Fuck off, Harry, I'm busy!"

I grinned into the phone. "Hey, your mom says to play nice. I'm trying to track down a guy who played college football. All I've got to go on is a name – Wesley Greagson – and an old picture of him. He's holding a gold and red helmet, with something that looks like a space rocket in blue, on a white background."

"You sure about the space rocket? It's not skyscraper, or a radio mast?"

"It's about the only thing I am sure of, going by the quality of the picture."

"Lemme see." The conversation died, while over the receiver came the sporadic machine-gun fire of his keyboard being tapped into an early grave.

A burst of silence indicated a break in hostilities, then, "The guy you want is Mack Martinez. He's a small to medium time shoestring promoter, happy to work the outfields. About five, maybe six years ago he put together a collection of young football jocks, all twelve- to eighteen-month contracts, that sort of thing. Went out touring as a showpiece and exhibition package. I think he was seeding the ground in the hope some talent scout would headhunt, and he could then sell the contracts on. The circus would turn up with an Outer Space, Area 51 theme, hence the rocket logo. Hell, I'm sure he even based himself out of Nevada to add to the kitsch, along with luminous paint, Day-Glo and tin foil. The guy really knew how to go the whole nine yards of cheesy."

I sketched another doodle on the legal pad while I mulled things over. "How successful was the show?"

Tony snorted a little down the phone. "Mostly he recruited from around the sidelines, so the talent wasn't that hot. You stick enough cheerleaders with big jugs into tight tops and quite a few frat-boy fans will walk out of the stadium happy, regardless of how the game went. Martinez usually made his money on other things, like concessions and merchandising, but after a couple of good years he surprised everyone when he upped and dropped the whole thing, half way through the year. Must have been three seasons ago now."

"What's this guy like?"

"Martinez? Well, you wouldn't miss him in a crowd, that's for sure! He's still dreaming of the big time while more than happy working the county fairs. Sometimes it's all you need to pay the bills."

"You got a number?" My pencil was poised over the yellow legal pad. A couple of football-shaped alien eye doodles looked back up at me. I added a pair of nostrils then jotted down Martinez's cell phone number as Tony reeled it off – all the while feeling good about how things were progressing.

I put on my best Southern Colonel accent. "You, Suh, are a scholar and a Gentleman."

"And you, Rhimes, ain't no fucking lady!"

Out of politeness and good manners I let him slam the phone down on me.

I looked down at the notepad again, added a half-smiling mouth and wondered if it was worth trying to get my doodles analysed by a professional. I wrote Mack Martinez's name beside the cell number, mentally crossed my fingers and called it, hoping he was within signal range.

The connection made, and a distant voice said "Yellow?"

"Mr. Martinez? I'm Harry Rhimes. I got this number from Tony Sinclair, the sports columnist. He suggested I talk to you about a guy named Wesley Greagson."

"Wesley Greagson? Why do you want to know about Wesley? Nothing personal you understand, only I don't know you from Adam, so I'm going to need more from you, before I'm prepared to tell you more about him."

Nice to see he still cared, even though Greagson was no longer under his contract. I eased myself back in my chair and started in on what was rapidly becoming a familiar line. "I'm working on a missing persons case. My client is trying to find Preston Llyle–"

"Ah, Mighty Mouse! That figures. Sorry. Please, do go on."

"My client has a photograph of him, as part of a group shot, and Llyle's father identified Wesley Greagson as being one of the others in the photograph."

"I see. And?"

"And after talking to Bam-Bam Sinclair, he pinned down the decals and the logos as being one of your previous promotions. I just want to know where I might find Wesley. By the way, what was all that Mighty Mouse stuff?"

"Okay, Harry, I'll tell you what. Let's meet up for lunch. That way we can get to know each other and the conversation will flow easier."

"Fine by me. Where?"

"I'm staying at the St. Waterford resort, near Mount Shasta, north on I-5. I'm thinking of getting into the pro snowboarding line. Maybe run some franchises, that sort of thing."

I checked the clock – 02:50 Beijing time. "It'll take me about forty-five minutes, say an hour. Make it one o'clock this afternoon?"

"It's a deal. See you at one."

*****

The drive turned out to be less of a problem than I first thought, the lunchtime traffic light, and the resort was easy to find along the I-5, near Dunsmuir.

One of the joys of travelling that stretch of the Interstate was the lakes, long with the scenery. Some say Trinity is the more diverse, but for me they're just as beautiful as each other, especially during the fall.

With year-round snow on the Heights, the area had no problem in maintaining a steady flow of tourists. Skiing, snowboarding, cross country and extreme – all augmented with seasonal hunting, fishing and woodcraft trails during the summer.

Not quite in the same league as Freddy and Elizabeth, who were more left field in their range of outdoor pursuits. The *All You Can Eat Survivalist Weekend* was one of the more outré, which sprang to mind.

Fifty miles later I pulled into the forecourt of the St. Waterford. Parking towards the back, I felt almost lost in a sea of SUVs, 4x4's and RVs. In the summer the place was an island of luxury for those who didn't want to spend their nights under canvas, getting their veins sucked dry, or their asses bitten off, by insects they couldn't identify, and were usually too citified to squash. After years of taking logs from woodpiles, experience had taught me to whack it first, then ask questions about its genus.

From across the parking lot I got a clear view of the resort.

A massive, two-story affair, built in the mid-1980s, with a woodsy, countrified look created by its natural pinewood log-and-stone construction. Although not major league, it was close enough to offer the snow fans easy access, at a more affordable price tag, with all the amenities and none of the hassles which over-popularity brought.

Inside, the front desk was being driven by a tidy-looking middle-aged man in a nondescript department store suit. Laying his pen aside, he looked up expectantly as I walked across the lobby.

"Good afternoon, sir, and welcome to the Waterford. How can I help?"

"Mr Rhimes. I'm here to see Mr Martinez. If you could tell him I've arrived?"

The receptionist rang the room, spoke to Martinez, then put the phone down. "He'll be with you shortly. He suggests waiting in the restaurant, behind and to your left. We're serving lunch until three."

I nodded my thanks and headed through a pair of double doors into the dining area. Martinez had already made a reservation and the head waiter led me through the room to a small table towards the back. Seating myself so I faced the door, I waited for Martinez to make his entrance. Five minutes later he appeared, and I had to admit Tony Sinclair had been right, Martinez was easy to spot. I stood up as the waiter collected him and brought him over.

He was an unusual man for a sports promoter. I guessed he was around five-five, and it looked like he weighed in at 250-plus pounds. Given his heavy physique, he moved effortlessly between the tables, rather than pinball from one chair back to another.

His striking red hair, having successfully won the battle against the combined forces of comb and hair products, proudly proclaimed its victory by wisps poking out at odd angles. A thick moustache nestled over his upper lip, like a hibernating ginger rodent, and from his mouth protruded an overly large cigar. It was obvious it had never been lit, but he handled and worked at it as if it was, clamping it between bejewelled fore and middle fingers, then regally waving both cigar and hand at me to indicate he knew where I was.

Both hands were crowded with ostentatious gold rings – coins, gemstones, or just plain gold with his initials diamond-cut crisply into the surface. Again, any loss of dexterity went unnoticed even though the metal bands looked restrictive and constricting on his sausage-like fingers. His three-piece suit had been hand-made, and despite the fact it was being subjected to treatment which would have sent most tailors screaming from the room, it still retained a newly-cleaned and pressed look.

Seating himself, he seemed oblivious to the stares of the other diners. As I sat back down he treated me to a very broad and genuine smile, which was eighty percent teeth and twenty percent gold.

"Mr. Rhimes!" His voice was rounded, fruity, full of energy and an inward happiness as he offered his hand across the table for me to shake. The metalwork felt strange, but his grip was firm and unhesitating. Without looking at the menu he said, "Have you ordered?"

I shook my head

"Then I can wholeheartedly recommend the surf and turf, with a side of greens and another side of pasta salad as well. It's the healthy option, and we've got to keep our eye on the cholesterol and the calories, haven't we?"

Red meat and two salads?

Suddenly he burst out laughing, again seemingly oblivious to the captive audience around him in the dining room. In a slightly loud voice he said, "Harry! Sorry, may I call you Harry?"

I nodded.

"Harry!" He spread his arms wide and wiggled his shoulders a little, "This is all paid for and is the end result of pure pleasure! If I die tomorrow, then I go to my grave a happy and unrepentant fat man."

I smiled with him, rather than at him. His happiness was infectious and it felt good to laugh a little.

"Okay," I waved my hand a little flamboyantly, "Waiter, two Surf and Turfs, two green salads and one pasta salad for Mr. Martinez." I looked back at Martinez apologetically. "Sorry, I've been missing training so can't give you a run for your money."

Martinez added a bottle of house Shiraz to the order.

"Care to join me?"

I shook my head. "No, thanks. I've got a drive back, and with the weather the way it is…."

"Just the one bottle it is then."

Inside, a little part of me felt admiration and a tinge of jealousy at this man's attitude to life. Maybe, one day.

Martinez leaned forward slightly, putting his cigar down onto a side plate.

"Okay, tell me again what it is you're after?"

I took a deep breath and let it out again.

"I'm working for a client who is trying to find Preston Llyle. Part of the investigation turned up a photograph which helped identify Wesley Greagson. Now I'm trying to track him down, to see if he knows the whereabouts of Preston Llyle." Before he had a chance to reply, I added, "You said something on the phone about Mighty Mouse?"

"All in good time, Harry. Things come to he who waits. You only want him to supply you with a possible address for Preston Llyle? Nothing more?"

"No, nothing more. But having piqued my curiosity, should there be more?"

Martinez put the cigar back in his mouth, puffed on it theatrically a couple of times for the benefit of the disapproving around us, then put it back down.

"Around six years ago I put together a football show. I supplied just about everything – advertising, programs, T-shirts, catering, and a production guaranteed to entice even the most hardened sports fans off their couches and into the stadiums. The team was put together from all over, and most were on a tight little contract, with the option to buy into the show should they want to. It was a way of generating seed money, pure and simple."

He stopped when the wine waiter reappeared at our table, and paused until the wine had been poured before he continued.

"After a while it became obvious the three of them were becoming trouble, especially when the other players dubbed them The Three Musketeers."

I jumped in as he paused for breath.

"Three?"

"Yep. It was something of an unholy trinity. Wesley Greagson, Preston Llyle and Harrison Tylor. All regular Beta Kappa Keylime Pi sort of guys. Of the three it's hard to say who was the worst. Greagson with his incessant obsessive gambling, Tylor who seemed to be able to procure anything provided the price was right, or Llyle with his unpredictable personality swings, probably down to steroids. Hence the nickname of Mighty Mouse. He'd been taking so much junk and enhancers his balls had shrunk to the size of peanuts and his dick was like this." He wiggled the little pinkie of his right hand a few times. "One minute he would be all pally-pally. The next," Martinez threw his hands up wide, "he would be going ballistic over some imagined slight or off the cuff comment."

I frowned a little at this new revelation.

"Don't believe me? Ask the guy's mother. She was the one who had to bail him out of a serious aggravated assault charge. He'd beaten another player, Andy Newhart, half to death, using a can of deodorant knotted in a bath towel. Believe me, Harry, others in the locker room said Preston just lost control completely. Totally zoned out on his anger. It was lucky Newhart curled into a ball and let the rest of the team take Llyle down. Know what it was over? Who should walk out onto the field first. I ask you. Mom Llyle said she would make sure he went back into therapy again, her words, not mine, and paid Andy Newhart off with a new car. She made good on her promise to me, and bought Preston out of his contract. For twice the severance fee."

Filing the information away, I tried to bring him back on track. "You said you had an address for Greagson?"

"I have *an* address. Whether or not it's *the* address is another matter."

He handed over a piece of paper torn from a spiral-bound pad. In an odd, childlike hand, someone had half printed and half written: If the BASTARD owes You money Then You can find HIM HERE.

The address was in one of the more skankier parts of the city, and certainly not a neighbourhood I would want to stay in for any length of time.

"How did you get this?"

"Somebody returned some of my mail from a previous address. There's still a lawsuit pending in regard to Greagson's contractual obligations. Team members were liable for a percentage of any debt still outstanding when the company finally closed the road show. I'm not worried about the loss financially, but it's the principle of the thing that's at stake here." He smiled his golden smile in a 'Some things you just got to do, regardless' kind of expression.

Our food arrived, and the conversation drifted off into other directions. Was I interested in backing his new venture? There were some "wickedly kewl" half-pipes in the area gaining good reputations. Plus, there was the hot-dogging and cross country speed skiing events, which were always good for a quick financial turnaround. A little seed money, invested early, was bound to reap dividends. Maybe as soon as six months down the line, who could say? Of course, once things took off it would be a completely different proposition as it would be more difficult to keep the buy-in share price down to the same level....

He was a great salesman, I'll give him that, but I'm the world's worst punter when it comes to those once in a lifetime offers. Unsurprisingly, by the time I left, I'd managed to keep the same shirt on my back as I'd walked in with.

8

I took a slow drive back down the I-5. It seemed the further south I went, the more oppressive and darker the atmosphere became. The storm still hadn't broken by the time I got back to my office, and it felt more like mid-evening rather than just turned 5 p.m.

I pulled the card with Lindsey's number out of my wallet, and after half a dozen rings her voicemail kicked into life. I left a message saying I was going out to find Greagson and, if all went well, I hoped to get back to her shortly with the whereabouts of her beloved Preston. Given what I'd recently learned from Martinez, Llyle was someone she could well do without.

I flipped to a clean page on the legal pad and sketched out my report of the day's progress. By the time I'd typed it up and printed it off it was a little after 6. Time to make a start.

I went over to a filing cabinet, opened the second drawer, and took out a lock box. Tapping in the combination and opening it, I took out a cloth-wrapped, snub-nose .38 revolver. For most of the time simple was always the best, which was why I preferred the Smith & Wesson Model 637 Airweight J-frame. The Chief's Special. Despite repeated assurances as to the reliability of modern automatics, I used a revolver for the simple reason they didn't jam up when you needed them most. Okay, so it was inaccurate over distance, and had a limited number of shots. But if it's going to take more than five bullets to do the job, then it's the wrong tool for the job in the first place. Another advantage was they didn't spew casings whenever you had to use the weapon in anger. Believe me, the last thing you need are round metal casings underfoot when you're involved in a shooting match.

I put the box back, lifted out a simple leather and nylon shoulder rig and slipped it on over my shirt. To me it was a work tool, not a fashion accessory. With the .38 safe in the holster, I put my jacket back on, turned off the coffee maker and the lights, closed the office door behind me and headed for the reception area.

The internal light in the elevator car turned the glass walls into black mirrors, so I rode down to ground level watching myself watch myself, rather than get too concerned about the impending storm.

The parking lot was deserted, and when I got to my Ford I opened the trunk and swapped my jacket for a zip-up windbreaker. It's part of my standard kit. Foxhole spade, jumper cables, empty fuel can, flashlight, road flares, tow rope. Everything a budding little Triple-A cadet could wish for at Christmas. You go down rough roads in a standard city car and you're just asking for trouble. Best to be prepared for the worst, regardless.

Easing the Ford into the evening traffic, I figured I could pick up Llyle's address from Greagson, deliver it to Lindsey Fairfax, then head on home. Tomorrow was going to be a brand new day, and that made me feel good. So good, I felt I might even get some stale sheets washed, and some fresh bed linen aired.

The further east I went, the more neglected and depressing

the scenery became. Taken as a whole, the city didn't appear to have much of a major gang culture, but it was there. Just ask the Shasta Anti-Gang Enforcement teams. Not only did SAGE go up against the Norteno and their forever on-going gang war against the Surenos, it tackled others such as the Bloods, Crips, White Supremacists and the outlaw motorcycle gangs – the One Percenters.

It didn't take me long to start noticing gang colours on street corners. Spray paint tags and graffiti became more prominent on walls, buildings, even the sidewalks. Anywhere which could indicate where one territory stopped, and another started. From the news and the court reports, such names as The Cheddersen Deuces, The Ballard Street Boyz, or The Cliffton Centre Crew, had become more familiar and commonplace by the day. Kids as young as 6 or 7 ran crack and called people either blood or 'ho, all wanting to aspire to be gang leader by the time they'd reached 15. Having seen the money, they believed it could all be theirs if they just got with the program.

Sad to say, the weight of the shoulder rig, and knowing the .38 was within easy reach, made me feel a lot better.

Further out toward the suburbs, I found Greagson's apartment block. The address was on the second-floor, in a particularly ugly four storey concrete complex. It looked as if it had been constructed in the mid-1960s, and despite the intervening years it had retained its cheap nastiness. Driving around it several times did nothing to change my mind, nor dispel the reek of neglect, rancid grease, stale beer and urine. Weeds growing from the paving looked starved and desperate, in keeping with the grey-white cement, stained by pollution and the tenants who lived there.

An open parking lot took up most of the ground floor, with areas for dumpsters to catch the residents' garbage. Most of the vehicles were battle scarred survivors, and the tarmac base was cracked and broken in places.

Enclosed stairs bolted to the side of the building led to an entrance door on the first floor. At one time there had been a security system, but judging by the splintered door frame I doubted it was high on the landlord's priority list.

Inside nothing changed my first impression. The smell was strong – a mixture of urine, mildew, and forgotten garbage. Cigarette butts had been repeatedly ground into the carpet, and the coals had created patches of hard acrylic where the fibres had melted and fused together, like scabs over infected insect bites. The mail boxes were gouged, blackened – some held together with thick strips of coloured tape – and overhead the fluorescent tubes flickered irregularly behind discoloured armoured glass.

Outside 204, I unzipped the windbreaker and positioned myself alongside the door hinges, my shoulder braced slightly against the wall. As a precaution, I withdrew the revolver and knocked on the door several times. From inside I could hear the muffled sound of music, blurry and indistinct. Not heavy metal, but heavy all the same – vaguely familiar, the vocals foreign. German, or Slavic – it was hard to tell.

I knocked harder, this time with the butt. The singing was in classic High German, and a choir was in full throat, knocking out Beethoven's *Ode to Joy* with all the Teutonic subtlety they could manage.

There was the sound of several security bolts being released and the door opened. Immediately the sound torpedoed out of the apartment and ricocheted down the hallway, echoing slightly off the stark flat walls in its effort to escape.

"Seid umschlungen, Millionen!

Diesen Kuss der ganzen Welt!"

Through a strong smell of cannabis and tobacco, a dishevelled man in his late twenties poked his head out, and looked down the corridor towards the broken entrance door. Immediately he froze as he heard the revolver being cocked, inches from his right ear. Slowly he moved his arms away from his body, spreading his fingers to show he wasn't carrying anything.

With the music blaring, I moved around to stand in front of him, then using universal sign language, I indicated with the gun we were going to go back into the apartment. Once inside I hooked my foot around the door and swung it shut behind me. I guided him over to the worn couch, motioned for him to sit down, located the music system, and simply yanked the power cord from the wall socket.

The single bedroom apartment had originally been done out in Abject Squalor, but it was clear that a succession of conscientious tenants had let things slide downhill over the years. Newspapers had been piled and stacked on every available free surface, smothering the small dining table and the corners of the living room. They were turned to the sports pages, with circles around names and odds scribbled in the margins. From some of the choice comments, it was obvious the action had been running against the punter.

An overflowing ashtray was on the floor by the sofa, and looked like a weird school kid science project. With the crater in the middle of the deep glass dish, it was a miniature volcano, spewing out cigarette and roach butts in equal measure. Surrounding it, the leopard spotted state of the worn carpet was testament to Greagson's inaccurate aim.

Underscoring the tobacco and weed was a distinctive rancid milk and rotting food smell, coming from the kitchenette area, which left a palpable taste in the back of my throat. Stepping away from the couch, I tapped open the bathroom door to make sure we were completely alone, letting it swing back shut again and hopefully imprisoning any monsters certain to be lurking in the bowl.

Putting the revolver back in the shoulder rig, I moved around the floor as best I could until I was standing in front of the sofa once more. Ignoring me, Greagson picked up a battered pack of cigarettes, and with stuttery fingers he managed to get one out and into his mouth. Lighting it with a cheap disposable lighter, he made a big production of taking the smoke down, then loudly exhaling it out in a steady stream.

He was dressed in stained and grubby grey sweats and cheap, Chinese no-brand running shoes. The sleeves of his loose cotton T-shirt had been raggedly ripped off in an attempt to accentuate his arms and to keep things ventilated. I thought about his football career and the photograph. His upper body now seemed less defined, the tautness and muscle tone softening in favour of the flabbiness which haunts the lapsed bodybuilder. At one time he had probably been good. All jocks, while under contract, kept themselves game fit, and sometimes that's all they would ever know. But, out of the limelight, and with no coach to impress, things had started to slide.

His face still looked very much like that in the photograph, but there was now an underlying sallowness, which made me wonder about the state of his liver. His brown hair had started to recede but still appeared stuck to his forehead, this time from grease and stale sweat. His hazel eyes were bloodshot and dilated, and although his breath had the sweet edge of opiates, he looked like he was coming down from a late afternoon pipe.

He blew another stream of smoke towards the carpet, and in a voice that sounded like he'd been gargling ground glass, said, "If Geddies thinks I've got anything left that's worth any money, then he's fucking nuts. I'm going to be getting some from a friend shortly, but I thought we'd agreed that putting me in the hospital wasn't going to get him his fucking money."

I kept my hands free, but parted the windbreaker so that the butt of the .38 was just visible, in case he started getting ideas. "I'm not from any bookies. I just want to know where Preston Llyle has hidden himself, and the last time you spoke to him."

Greagson kept his head down, still looking at the floor, but I saw his shoulders tense, the cigarette nervously switched from hand to hand. "Who the fuck wants to know?"

"I do. I'm a private investigator, and I'm trying to locate Preston Llyle. Believe me, I don't want to be here, or in this neighbourhood, any longer than I have to, so let's just make this quick and simple. If you know where Preston is then tell me and I'll be out of your life forever."

His face tilted back and he looked up at me. "It's Harrison, isn't it. You're working for Harrison. Well, tell him from me–"

The flicked cigarette came up as expected, and I let it bounce off my windbreaker without distracting me.

Greagson may have thought he was fast off the sofa's edge, but in reality he was slow and slightly cumbersome. Coupled with the effects of the junk he'd been doing since dropping out of football, and taking him down quickly was doing him a favour. There was no way I was going to underestimate him, either. I'd known other drug abusers, in the past, tap into reserves of strength which made them feel and act like super-humans. And, to be frank, I was already getting a little tired of the whole thing.

Stepping inside his wide-swinging right, I raised my arm level with his forehead then brought my fist and arm down in one smooth movement, seemingly brushing his nose in the process. The septum broke with an audible snap, and blood gushed over his mouth and off his chin. By the involuntary watering of his eyes I could tell whatever he'd previously been high on, was starting to wear off pretty quickly.

Pushing me away slightly with one hand, he staggered backwards, and put his hands up to his face, feeling around his nose and mouth. When he looked at them again, covered in his own blood, his eyes rolled up and he collapsed to the floor. I let him lay there, then nudged him carefully with my foot, even going as far as tapping his broken nose several times with the tip of my shoe just to make sure he wasn't faking it. Not even a flicker. He was out cold.

To be honest, I've known bigger and better men fold at the sight of their own blood. Anyone else's and they wouldn't bat an eyelid over, but the sight of their own put them down and out for the count. Something about having the belief in your own invincibility broken by the sight of your own mortality. Not that I'm a big fan of seeing myself bleed.

I had two choices: I could search the place for anything useful, or go into the kitchenette, find a cold wet cloth, then revive Greagson for some more questions.

The smell of the sink came back to me, so I decided in favour of a cursory search. If I felt I needed to, I could come back later when he'd recovered and would probably be much more responsive.

Searching the place was not something I relished either. From the piles of newspapers protruded old pizza boxes and lumpy half-flattened Chinese take-out, along with greasy burger wrappers. The takeaway debris had been left on top of the stacks, only to be buried when the next day's newspapers were eventually dumped on top of them.

I looked around for anything that might contain drawers, or at least something which might hide an address book of some kind. Nothing. Moving past the small dining table, I bumped against it. There was an ethereal slithering sound as about four months' worth of newspapers and trapped detritus avalanched across the tabletop and over the side, flopping heavily to the floor.

Out of sheer frustration I lashed out with my foot, kicking a load of them back into the air, and venting my pent-up anger at the whole situation. It was a futile gesture, but it made me feel better inside.

Then something on the table caught my eye.

Originally hidden to the side of the newspaper towers were a key ring with some keys, an old and well used cell phone, a couple more cheap disposable lighters and a small oblong made of plastic, slightly smaller and thinner than the disposables.

Grabbing the cell phone, I navigated through the menus. No entries under Preston, or Llyle. A little more navigation, and I started skimming through the few saved text messages. Like most junkies, all the texts older than a week or so had been deleted. Common practice to delete them as soon as they'd been sent or received, because there was nothing more incriminating than a cell phone with dealer traffic on it. Especially when it ended up being confiscated during a raid.

Throwing the phone back onto the table, I caught sight of the odd-looking oblong again. I found the cap at the end, and with a gentle tug it came away, exposing the shiny metal nose of a computer flash drive.

Though I was often considered to be a devout Luddite, even I knew flash drives needed computers in order to work. And, looking at all the crap and garbage around me, I was sure that if Greagson had once had a computer of some kind, it had long since gone through the doors of a hock shop or a fence. To make sure, I did a more intensive search of the apartment, but still turned up nothing the USB drive would fit into.

Back in the living area Greagson was starting to come around. I grabbed him by the front of his bloodstained shirt, hauled him up to his feet, then pushed him onto the sofa. He was still in no real state to be conversational, but his eyes were starting to calm down, even though there was now an angry hump in the bridge of his nose.

I stooped over him, held the USB drive up to his face, waited for him to focus on it, then saw his shoulders sag. I had no idea what was going on, but from Greagson's reaction I was prepared to gamble on a hunch.

"Is this it?"

He kept silent and just looked at me with a half smug, half dumb, expression.

I let some of my anger start to show. "I'll tell you now, you don't want me to start beating on you again. Because the next time, I won't stop when you start bleeding. That's a promise."

Still the silence. Only one thing for it, take command of the situation. In one movement I grabbed his shirt front with my left hand, took half a step back, yanked him to his feet, hit his stomach with a short right jab, and followed it through with my left to push him away from me and back onto the sofa, leaving him doubled up, dry retching and badly winded.

Carefully, I put the lid back on my anger. Control it. Channel it. Master it. Use it.

After a minute or two he finally got his breath back. Like a sulky child he said "Yeah, that's what Harrison's been looking for."

"You sure there isn't anything else? Like a computer or something, maybe?"

Greagson shook his head, then wished he hadn't done it so hard. The areas around his eyes were starting to puff up, and I had no doubt, come the morning, he'd be looking like a panda.

"It's the only copy – I wiped Bobby's laptop before I sold it. There's just a mass of old music files on there anyway."

Another piece of the jigsaw. "Who's Bobby?"

Greagson tilted his head a little to one side and looked at me curiously. "You don't know about Bobby? Preston's little cyber-geek?" His look became more smug and devious. "You don't know what's on that stick either, do you. Ha! Harrison really sent some dumb-ass old muscle!"

There was nothing to be gained by asking Greagson any more questions. It was clear he didn't know where Preston was, or what was so important about the files. Tomorrow I would talk to someone who knew about that kind of technology. If she couldn't figure out what the flash drive was holding, nobody could. For the moment, though, it was time to leave.

I tucked the flash drive away in a pocket, pulled out my wallet and thumbed out a business card. "Tell Harrison I've now got the goods."

Greagson remained silent, glaring down at the carpet while

he continued to hug himself and rock gently backwards and forwards. I reached over and put the card on the chair arm, so it was within easy reach. Then I drew the .38 and held it loose down by my side. The metallic clicking of the hammer locking back sounded loud and ominous in the room.

Greagson's head jerked up, and he suddenly looked startled and confused. "If you're not working for Harrison or Preston, who the fuck are you working for? It's not Bobby Weams, that's for sure…"

Again, Bobby. I figured the best course of action would be to let Greagson stew for a while. Then come back when I had a better idea of what the USB drive was all about.

Making eye contact, I said, "I'm going now. If you try to step outside of this apartment before ten minutes are up, I'll fix that broken nose for you once and for all."

It was a hollow threat, but it had to be said. Greagson tried to smile, but the damage to his face was getting painful whenever he moved.

I backed towards the door, opened it, stepped through, and pulled it closed behind me. Ten minutes was more than enough time for me to get back to my car and drive off, and I doubted Greagson would have the wherewithal to contemplate coming after me. He was probably trying to work out how to get back into Harrison Tylor's good books. I felt the USB drive in my pocket. I had no idea what I had, but it seemed to be important to the three of them. And if it brought me nearer to Preston then it was certainly worth investigating. At least that was my logic at the time.

There was a new player on the scene as well. Bobby Weams. From Greagson's contemptuous tone, I'd assumed he didn't rate Bobby all that highly.

As I pulled away from the protection of the parking lot, there was a long roll of thunder, followed by the start of the rain. Heavy drops bombed down out of the black sky and splattered hard against the windshield and roof, the noise almost drowning out the sound of the engine. On the horizon forks of lightning arced in jagged flashes of blue-white light, knocking out any hope for the radio. The wipers fought as best they could, but as I travelled back through the city, I was forced to pull over several times as waves of windblown rain cut vision down to almost zero.

The dashboard clock said it was 22:45, and it was already too long a day for my liking. I was no nearer to finding Preston Llyle, yet I still felt duty bound to give Lindsey a call and let her know I wasn't likely to be keeping our appointment.

Illegally parking in front of the Kincade Building I got out, threw the windbreaker over my head and ran through the automatic front doors. The security guards had been watching when I pulled up, and I recognised two of them behind the reception desk. The third, someone I didn't recognise, had kept his eyes on the revolver in the exposed shoulder rig.

George Simms, the shift supervisor, called out, "You sure picked a night for it, Mr. Rhimes. What can we do for you?"

"You guys have a phone I could use? I need to contact someone, let 'em know I won't be around this evening."

From below the counter one of the other guards lifted a phone and put it in front of me. I dug Lindsey's number out of my wallet, dialled, then waited as the receiver purred in my ear. It kept on purring until Lindsey's voicemail kicked in.

I waited for the message to finish, then said, "If you're screening calls, Ms. Fairfax, this is Mr. Rhimes." I waited to see if Lindsey would pick up. But when no one came on the line, I continued, though somewhat confused, "I'm afraid the lead I had turned into a waste of time, and I still don't have an address for Preston. I'll put it all in a written report and drop by tomorrow evening. Call me with a convenient time."

I quoted my office number, hung up, and wondered why Lindsey hadn't answered. Maybe she was out? Maybe she was next door keeping someone company until the storm had passed? I shook my head. Not my problem. No, sir. I thanked the guards one more time, dashed out to the car, then set off for home.

Back on the 299, I took it slow, pulling off the road when things got too heavy, even though the storm was shifting and moving out towards the coast.

I was almost at my turnoff when I was flashed by a patrol car. It cruised slowly past before turning round and coasting up alongside me, its red and blue strobe lights muted in the wind-blown rain.

By the time it had rolled to a stop, I had already wound down my window and had my hand sticking out with my driver's licence ready for them. Let's face it, they had slickers and other rainproof protection and I didn't particularly want to end up looking like a drowned rat should they invite me to, "Step out of the car, buddy."

We exchanged pleasantries, and I explained I was on my way home while they ran the licence plate. When the okay came back, the storm had moved on, leaving behind a soft, drizzling rain, and a clean smell to the air.

I parked alongside the house around twenty past midnight, and with the aid of the security lights, I was glad to see nothing much had been washed down from the hillside. Unlocking the door, I reset the alarm, then walked upstairs to the kitchen.

Out on the veranda, close by the potted herbs, was the indistinct sleeping shape of the Richardsons' dog. Without turning on a light I opened the refrigerator, took out a bottle of Rickards Dark, popped the top, then headed back down into the lounge again.

When the dregs of the beer had been nursed warm, I kicked off my shoes, swung my legs up, and finally called it a day.

Finding the place had not been easy, but talking to some skag and charlie dealers had finally paid off. From the outside it certainly looks like a fucking hole.

Easy, child, we both have memories of other cities, where life on the streets made this shit look like a palace.

But The Man *says the treasure is here, and once it's safe then it doesn't matter what happens to the asshole.*

Maybe we could get a little artistic this time?

Martial arts flick on the late-nite slot yesterday. Fists of the Dragon. It had the Death by a Thousand Cuts. The trick would be not to cut too deep. A real challenge.

There's some Albinoni in the player – Filippo re della Macedonia. A tragedy in five acts would be good for such a performance. And if he did manage to last the full one thousand, it would be interesting to see how long before he bled out. Hopefully there would be some salt around. Always a good stimulant when working with knives on a live body.

All we have to do is just drive into the open parking lot, out of the rain and–

There's a shadow, flickered across the black top a second ago, just enough to register in the corner of an eye. Movement, people, witnesses. Bad Things.

Change the plan, and quick – but we're already too high profile!

Into reverse and back down to the far end of the parking lot, turn in amongst some other cars. Protection in numbers, make like a tenant who lives here. Kill engine, turn off lights, and see what happens.

Watch the shadow move to a car at the other end, unlock the door and get in – no courtesy light comes on.

That's not right, is it?

Engine starts first time – no stalling from a damp ignition, no smoke from a worn block, licence plate smeared up with something so can't make it out – car pulls out and away – no headlights either.

Slow this down. Count backwards from ten, nine, eight, seven…. Relax the breathing. Now think. If it was Greagson, then we'll have to wait for him to come back. He wouldn't be going far, not with his habit. Just to the nearest dealer.

Only one way to find out. Pop the trunk then get out. Flip the cap down over the eyes; check the stairwell in case anyone else decides to make a surprise appearance. This is not how we planned it – no-no-no – this is the last thing…

Pick up the small toolkit in the soft zip-up case. Something for the lock if needs be, and a pair of pliers for later.

Crouch down, make the body small, and run to the stairway. Around and up to the first floor. Looks like the main door's been forced already – sweet. Slowly open it, come in low and almost close it.

Fuck! The smell is terrible! At least the hallway is clear. So it's down to 204 – make as if we're visiting.

Tap-tap-tap.

Little pig, little pig….

Knock-knock-knock.

C'mon little pig, I can hear your music playing.

Thump-thump-thump!

Believe me, little pig, I will make you squeal for this!

Ear to the door; can't hear any movement. The music's low, not loud enough to miss the knocking. No change of shadow and light at the bottom of the door so no one is behind it.

Okay, if you're not at home when I come a'calling, then I'm going to wait for you in comfort. Get me out of this stinking corridor! *Unzip the tool case, fish out a couple of picks – one large to flip the bar, one small and thin to take the lock down. Gently jigger it one way then the other, feel what catches. Hah! Always trust a landlord to come up cheap. Once I've cracked this, you fucking pig, I'm going to huff, and puff, and blow your whole world down.*

Just line them up and hold them so they don't slip back. Turn the second gently to make sure it fits okay. Good, now a little more pressure to get the catch to release. Hold it there. Now gently open the door. Push it wide and –

FUCK! Say something, say something, say something!

"Hi Wesley. I didn't mean to…"

Greagson on the sofa, facing the door, not even blinking. Blood all down his shirt, eyes glassy. Maybe OD'd and had a nosebleed?

"Wesley?"

Okay, slowly move forward, slowly, slowly, like when we were children. What's the time Mr. Wolf? Still no sign of life. Fuck, he's not breathing!

Okay, okay, slow this all down and take three deep breaths. Two… Three… Better, better…

Right. Didn't think to bring gloves, so need to backtrack and wipe as we go. Check body. Still warm and soft to the back of the hand. Blood down the neck, from somewhere behind the right ear. Smell of gunshot and burnt hair. Small hole, no exit, neat and tidy.

Forget that, we need to call *The Man*. Speed dial 9. Pick up, pick up.... Yes!

"Houston, we have a problem.... Yes, he's here, corporeally but not spiritually.... I mean the fucker's dead, is what I mean! Sorry, sorry, we're cool, we're frosty. Just not what I was expecting when I cracked this crib.... Somebody else killed him.... Didn't see anyone.... No, nobody at all.... Okay, but I thought you wanted me to.... Who? When? Okay, I'm leaving.... Wipe down, then I'm history.... His burner? It's on the table.... Okay, I'll toss it once I'm away from here.... Do you have his address? … Okay, text it to me. Later."

Grab the cell off the table. Backtrack out, wipe the front of the door down with a sleeve – leave nothing to get CSI about. Down the passage to the door and the stairs.

Take it slow, like you own the place and are just visiting to see how the lowlife is.

Hear no evil, speak no evil, leave no evil behind at the scene.... Bottom of the stairs, and wait. Get some night vision back.

Crouch back down and get back to the car, get inside, start up and go.

Once we're a dozen miles away, turn down a side street, yank out the burner's SIM, then dump the crap down the nearest drain we can find.

Head back to home turf. Rain is easier now. Headlights bright in the darkness, traffic increasing, iPod shuffling a little retro drum and bass... Maybe go clubbing, find out where everyone else is hanging, chill a little...

*****

Back in apartment 204, a housefly lazily buzzed out of the bathroom and into the living room. It circled the body several times before it eventually landed on Greagson's neck.

Nervously it tasted the still congealing trickle of warm blood, washed its eyes and wings, then followed the line back up to its source.

9

The next morning I found myself in the guest bed.

During the night I'd woken up on the couch, and dignity had finally gotten the better of me. The suit was scattered across a couple of chairs, but at least I'd managed to get into bed, and not just curl up on top of the covers. Listlessly I looked at the bedside clock and decided it was time to get back into a more positive routine. Almost in a single bound – say two or three – I was up, into a sweatshirt and shorts, then to the top floor where the long gallery houses some simple gym equipment at the far end.

The workout was more spiritual than physical. I needed to do something to dispel the frustration I felt, and the mindless physical repetition gave me a barrier to push against. Anger and frustration were always contributing factors to poor judgement calls, and after visiting Greagson, I had a bad feeling about the whole business.

I started with some free weights, in rapid reps, spaced with stints of five minutes on the treadmill. Cardio-vascular taken care of, it was onto some floor work for the abs and thighs, while a succession of old 1960's pop acted as a soundtrack. Slim Jim & The Heptones, The Vincentte Sisters, and The Raccoons:

> *"Aaaaawwwwww, Honey!*
> *I'll be your dog!*

Woof! Wa-Woof-Woof!
Wa-Woof-Woof! Woof!"

The Raccoons were destined to be the archetypical almost one-hit wonders. Every so often you'd hear their one and only single on the radio, or a new generation would rediscover the dubious joys of garage bubblegum pop. To help celebrate, the reissue machine would knock out another *Best Ever Greatest Hits Revisited*, to suck a few more drops of blood from the desiccated corpse. Still, the song was as catchy as poison ivy, and gave me something to keep rhythm and pace with while working up an honest sweat.

Workout over, I showered, shaved, dressed and preened myself into something I hoped wouldn't scare the wildlife. An hour later, in jeans, Nikes and polo shirt, I was reading the newspaper while half-listening to the sound of water in the canyon below. Usually the noise wasn't intrusive, but the flow had picked up, carrying away the overnight rain. A large mug of coffee, some chilled juice, and a ham and eggs breakfast completed Morning in Shangri La.

In the laundry room annex, off of the kitchen, the washing machine sloshed, chugged and gurgled its way through a mixed load of coloureds. Not only my workout sweats and several days' worth of clothing, but also the bed linen from the master bedroom. I wasn't prepared to sleep in the bed just yet, but at least I was going to make sure it was neat and tidy, regardless. Let's face it; a person can only lick their wounds for so long before even they get tired of the bad taste in their mouth.

The air out on the kitchen veranda was still clear, maybe a touch cooler than a week or so before, but not unpleasant that early in the morning. Even the forecast off the radio said it was going to be a good day.

The Richardsons' dog, having already breakfasted on some of my ham, lay on his side, snoring and growling in his sleep. Every so often his lips would twitch back from his teeth, and his feet would kick out as he chased imaginary things only he would ever see. For an old dog, he was still pretty agile when it came to chasing things. More so when he was awake.

From several stands of trees, Northern Shrikes were declaring their territory, their call distinctive and sharp. Occasionally a hawk would catch a thermal and hang just above the canyon's rim, waiting for something to chance its luck. Nature – the poignant juxtaposition between the beauty of life and the violence of survival.

I refocused and went back to my reading. *The New York Times* was full of international news, and instabilities in various Arabic worlds had taken second place to Afghanistan once more. Occasionally other uprisings and conflicts would break through, and come out on top in the bad news handicap stakes. But, like most of the recent military actions, I was never sure as to what the real agendas were. Even after being briefed and posted into the conflict zones themselves. The Army could be like that, most of the time.

Back in England, having successfully passed the entrance exams and recruiting boards, the Reds & Royals had welcomed me with open curiosity. Dual nationality meant I was neither a true Yank nor a true Brit, and with no previous military background in my families to call upon, I was very much the unknown quantity. Looked on by most of the Army as something of a novelty, the fact I'd spent so much time in the UK as a child and a teenager was a positive advantage. Mom was forever supportive, despite her pacifist leanings, but Dad was furious. He had come up from mid-20th Century Midwest farming stock, where he'd had to fight his way into a college education. Once within its hallowed halls, however, it had entranced him with the abstract and logical joys of mathematics, accounting and economics.

Sadly, as history rolled on, he gained memories of Korea, Cuba and Vietnam. His beliefs were impossible for me to comprehend at the time, so we had never reconciled our differences by the time I'd joined the Army. Done on an angry, resentful impulse, after an argument we'd had concerning the Falklands Conflict. The British called it that, but the rest of the world seemed to call it a War.

Whatever, Dad's politics were certainly not mine, and often my loyalty to my American heritage was subject to question, until the arguments had become bitter and ultimately pointless. But, in retrospect, we all suffer from twenty-twenty hindsight, don't we?

Dad had firmly believed his first born – i.e. me – was destined to follow in the newly-created family tradition: that of banking and high finance. The next addition to the Rhimes household was my sister, Madeline, who was never destined to pick up the financial crown from Dad. He was a product of his time, and held onto the archaic belief which stated that a woman's place was anywhere but the boardroom, and certainly nowhere near money. Madeline, true to her genes, went off into the big wide world, and became a successful finance company director out of spite.

The last chick in the brood was Thomas. He became Dad's pride and joy when he went into finance. It was common knowledge most of his deals had been of the hazy grey, rather than the clear and honest variety, a detail which did little to dampen Dad's enthusiasm.

Mom, on the other hand, always wanted us to fly the nest in as many diverse directions as we felt was our destiny. Born in New Orleans, at the close of World War II, her spirit always gave away her Creole roots, and in photographs from the 50's and 60's it was easy to see why. Bright colours, always laughing or joking, and with the intelligence to talk on many topics of the day, she often gave congressmen a shock when she started discussing politics. It was still at that point in history when Major League American politics was a thinly disguised family-run business. Over the years things have changed. Now corporate-owned lobbyists openly pay for the privilege of influencing congressmen and senators, as to which policies and laws to back.

Towards the end of the 1970s, behind closed bedroom doors, the arguments would flare up. They had kept papering over the cracks for as long as us kids were at home, but once we'd come of age it was only a matter of time.

When she finally walked out, Dad was adamant she would return. But, as months became years, even he had to admit the marriage and the relationship were both dead.

Years later, Mom had admitted she'd left because the relationship had become slowly stifling and destructive – dinner parties, events, constantly being on show as the hostess and obedient wife. So she went off to a new life in Paris, working in the theatre and the arts – back to the world of colour, spectacle, bravado and carnival. She'd kept in touch with us, her children, but had refused point blank to have anything more to do with Dad.

The sudden rush of birds lifting from the nearby trees brought me back into the real world, closely followed by the crunching sound of tires braking on the loose gravel driveway below. Looking over the edge of the veranda I saw a silver sedan had stopped behind my own Ford. The door swung open and Marty Beddows eased himself out, looking slightly awkward due to his leg and his broad shoulders. In my mind's eye he took on the appearance of one of those Saturday morning cartoon characters who had to struggle so far, then, all of a sudden, popped out of the car to a spring-like, wobbling sound effect.

He walked around the car a couple of times to work the stiffness out of his leg while taking in the late fall scenery. When he finished gazing, he turned and started for the front door.

Without looking up, he said, "Peek-a-boo. I see you."

"Come on up, I'm just fixing breakfast." I walked back into the kitchen and deactivated the alarm on the front door. Elizabeth still kept on pushing me to get something more advanced, but when you're already half way down a canyon-side, on the tailbone of the back of beyond, it never seemed worth the effort, or the expense. If it had been good enough for old Uncle Nathan, then it was adequate for what I wanted.

Over by the stove I clicked up a flame, put the skillet back on, and dropped some bacon into the pan. Two slices of white bread on the side. Bacon sandwich; an old British staple. By the time I fixed his coffee – creamer and a spoon of sugar – Marty had silently walked out onto the veranda.

A couple of minutes later I plated up the sandwich, picked up the coffee, and headed back outside again. Marty was already sitting in the other chair by the table. I put the plate and coffee in front of him, motioned towards the roll of paper towels I use as napkins, then sat down opposite him.

He was silent for a while, occasionally picking up his coffee and sipping from it a couple of times as he took in the atmosphere. I figured he'd say what he was going to say when he was good and ready.

Over in the corner the Richardsons' dog barked himself awake with a start. He moved his head languidly to see who had joined us for breakfast. Satisfied, he sneezed, yawned, put his head back down on the deck, stretched all four legs at once, broke wind in the key of F#, then settled back to sleep.

Without taking his eyes off the distant horizon, Marty said, "I swear, Rhimes, you're hopeless as a role model for that dog."

He took the top off his sandwich, picked up a piece of bacon and ate a little before continuing.

"You want to tell me about last night? I know you were over at Wesley Greagson's apartment. Your prints are all over it, and we found one of your business cards."

I looked over the rim of my coffee mug, slightly bemused. "Is that what this is all about? Me hassling Greagson?"

He bit off some more of the bacon, chewed, then swallowed. In the background, above the sound of the turbulent river, the shrikes had started sounding off again.

"No. It's about someone taking Greagson out with a two-two half-load. Up close and personal, behind the ear." He made a gun shape with his right hand, cocking his thumb back like a hammer, the two-fingered barrel behind his right ear.

"Ka-boomba! Mr. Greagson is now an ex-problem. Doc figures it had to have been between eleven last night, and one this morning."

I put my coffee down on the table and looked at him in surprise. "Whoa there, Tonto. He was never my problem, just a potential source of information." In my mind, I ran through everything I could remember about my encounter with Greagson. Part of me wanted to help Marty find who had shot the guy, but another part was keen to prove my own innocence, even though I knew I was innocent anyway. It's a natural reaction to authority.

Marty carefully rebuilt his sandwich, picked it up and said, "You want to tell me what this is all about, Kimosabe?" Sitting back, he took a bite.

"There's not much to tell. I'm still trying to find Preston Llyle, but not having much success."

"Really? You surprise me."

Who says Americans can't do sarcasm? He drank some more coffee, then:

"So how did you get a line on Greagson?"

"Roger Llyle mentioned Preston had an interest in football, so I asked around and turned up a guy called Martinez. He used to handle Greagson and Llyle as part of an exhibition show a while back. He didn't know where Llyle was likely to be holed up, but he did have an old address for Greagson."

"And you just struck lucky? Why was he holding onto an old address?"

"Greagson and Martinez are still in a legal dispute over contracts and obligations. That's why I don't figure Martinez would be involved with a hit on Greagson. The only contracts Mack is interested in are those with advantageous clauses and hefty default penalties."

"So what happened?"

"Nothing, I swear it. When I turned up he thought I was hired muscle, sent to collect an outstanding debt. We ended up getting a little roughhouse and I broke his nose in the process. He fainted, so I did a quick check of the place, but got nothing.

When he came back round, I left him my card, and told him to call me if he happened to run across Llyle."

"So he was in deep to some bookie?"

"Said his name was Geddies. He's either a bookie, or loan shark."

"And that's all you did. Just break his nose and toss the place?"

From behind us, in the laundry room annex, the washing machine gurgled and chuntered its way into the spin rinse part of its cycle.

Looking back at Marty I said, "I still haven't sent the suit to the cleaners. If you, or forensics, want to pick it up and check it for GSR and trace, you're more than welcome."

"And that's everything?"

I felt a little annoyed. "Yeah, that's everything."

I wasn't prepared to talk about the USB flash drive just yet. I wanted to know why it had been so important to Greagson, and why Harrison Tylor desperately wanted to get his hands on it. According to Martinez, in the past they had been thicker than thieves, but now there was obvious dissension in the ranks. I had a feeling the drive would help me, and before I lost it to the authorities I wanted to make a copy of it somehow.

Marty's face remained impassive. It was a mistake to underestimate him, because I knew, from past experience, that his mind never stopped working. Information would be filed and tagged, then brought back to the surface once a connection or a relationship had been established.

Leaning back in my chair a little, I casually added, "Anyway, Greagson's not my interest now. I'm looking for a guy called Bobby Weams, one of Preston's sidekicks. I take it the name...?"

Still with the poker face, Marty said, "Go fish." Which, given the circumstances, I thought was fairly polite.

We fell silent again for a minute or so while he finished the last of his sandwich. I'd given up on my ham and eggs which had long since gone cold and uninviting. Well, to me at least, but I'd never known the Richardsons' dog to be that fussy, or refuse anything I put down in front of him.

Marty reached over, picked up a sheet of paper towel and wiped his mouth.

"You didn't mess with anything while you were there? The front door around the keyhole was wiped clean of prints. When forensics nosed around the lock they found it has been recently messed with. You didn't happen to jiggle the lock to get in?"

I treated the comment with silent contempt. Marty knew I would never consider doing such a thing. To be caught by a patrol was one thing. To be caught by a patrol while in possession of picks was a totally different scenario.

Another fragment of memory surfaced and I relaxed. "Check with security at Orion & Nadler. I called Lindsey Fairfax on a landline, from the front desk, around eleven p.m. Then a patrol car stopped me, and ran a check around about midnight."

"They logged you as a possible weed runner at twenty-three forty-seven, to be exact. With your junker I doubt even you could have made it from Greagson's in such a short time. And anyway, a two-two half load is far too professional for your MO."

I smiled graciously at the backhanded compliment, but kept silent. Hell, I *was* professional, damnit. Sometimes it's just easier not to let on, is all.

The sun was picking up, and it seemed we had done our talking.

Taking a final mouthful of coffee, Marty asked, "You didn't happen to take Greagson's cell phone while you were there, did you? Everybody keeps all sorts of useful information on them these days."

"No. I did a quick check on the address book and text messages, found nothing of interest, so I left it on the table alongside some keys and other stuff he had pushed to one side. Why?"

Marty wiped his mouth again. "It's just that we couldn't find one, and with no working phone sockets in the apartment, I figured he'd be doing his betting via a cell. I don't suppose you remember anything about the address book?"

"Nothing that stuck."

As if listening to a piece of music, Beddows tapped the tabletop rhythmically with a finger. "And you've really had no luck tracking down the Llyles' kid?"

I sighed and shook my head. "Nada. I got nothing from his parents except bad karma from his mother, and raging indifference from his father." Without even thinking about it, I added, "As for Greagson? He turned out to be a dead end."

Marty leaned back and looked up at the clear sky, slowly shaking his head from side to side a little. "C'mon. The boy's just gotta go straight to Hell for that."

10

By the time Marty set off back to the city, the laundry had finished, and it wasn't long before I had it out on lines, strung from one end of the top floor veranda to the other. As simple as it was, it was another act of finality, and it felt good. Uplifting even.

I went out onto the kitchen veranda, and despite my better judgement, scraped the cold ham and half-congealed fried eggs into the dog bowl. With the breakfast things washed and dried, I thought about waking the Richardson's dog, but decided against it. The old adage of letting sleeping dogs lie, had probably been coined specifically for one of his direct ancestors.

I picked up the USB drive from the guest bedroom night stand, slipped it into the pocket of my shirt, and grabbed a casual jacket on my way out.

The Ford turned over without any hiccoughs and within minutes of coming out of the canyon I was headed toward Whiskeytown. From there it was just a case of following several snaking back roads until I reached the outskirts of Saunderson.

From the outset, Saunderson had always been a bit of an anomaly in some respects. It was founded back in 1935 as a camp-cum-village, though post-World War II, the population has steadily grown until had settled at around the 3,000 mark. Part of its growth had been down to the advent of

Disneyworld's success, which had made the founders feel they could've created something equally as profitable.

Their original concept had been to build a town around a theme park with rides. Which was why the Saunderson skyline was broken up by one very large, garishly decorated, fully working Ferris wheel.

Sadly, that's when the money ran out. But the town had shown to the outside world, that here was a place where the spirit of adventure was alive and kicking, and they were forever ready to try their hands at anything. Such enthusiasm caught the eye of business entrepreneurs, so that gradually, over the years, Saunderson developed itself into quite a prosperous, home-grown business community.

Okay, so maybe the annual *Ride the Wheel* ceremony – where newcomers to the town are invited to take an introductory ride on the big wheel itself – is odd, even by Californian standards. But everyone seems to enjoy themselves and, more importantly, the town was still expanding without creating any obvious ethnic or financial divides.

Saunderson itself was built around Main Street, and there was an almost deliberately eclectic mix of building and architectural styles. Everything from pseudo early homesteader cabins, to the ultra-modern four storey Hotel Merrilees, which was built in the shape of a Transylvanian fairytale castle.

Driving into the centre of town, I came off Main and headed down a side street. Another turn led me onto Montague Rise, a crescent-shaped cul-de-sac edged with a series of replica three-story New York brownstones. The big difference between these and the New York variety was they had not been carved up into micro-apartments by so-called property developers looking to make a fast buck. They still retained a lot of the 1890s charm: high ceilings, large picture windows, and good old solid construction. Thankfully, other late 19th Century New York trappings such as poor sanitation, overcrowding, ethnic segregation, rickets and tuberculosis had been allowed to fall by the wayside.

The crescent appeared to be deserted, and I had no trouble pulling up outside a particular house. I locked the car, then went up the steps to a distinctive firebird red front door, replete with highly polished brass trimmings. I was just about to go through yet another buzz-and-wait routine, when the door clicked and swung open, revealing a very empty period hallway.

I stayed where I was. I knew the person I'd come to see, and I wasn't about to move until I was sure it was safe. From a hidden speaker somewhere close by came the sound of girlish giggling.

"Aww, Harrry! You're no fun anymore!"

"Once bitten, Dixie, you know that." Although not visible, I suspected the hallway had at least three or four motion sensors, plus some infra-red trip lines. I didn't need to spray hair lacquer, or blow talcum powder into the air. I knew Dixie, which was more than enough reason to proceed with caution.

Smiling a little, I said, "Can you deactivate whatever it is you're trying out so I can come in? You know I only carry one set of clothes with me."

Again, the girlish giggles. "Ah, but it would be so nice to see you *nekked*." Her voice sent little tingling ripples down my spine, and not all for the right reasons either.

Dixie had been one of my earliest clients, and since then

she'd become a very successful information and data security consultant, with a good reputation. Yet, when she had been starting out, she'd had the misfortune to become the victim of a nasty little blackmailing businessman. He'd initially called her in as a consultant, and had gradually recognised her from some old stag party Polaroids. The photographs came from a time when Dixie was working as a part-time stripper, to help fund her university education. Not the sort of thing a successful business professional wants dragged up, regardless of their gender. And let's face it; we all have things hidden away in our own pasts that we're not proud of.

Whichever way you looked at it, his game was blackmail. It had started out with Dixie first being told to waive her consultation fees. Then he'd gotten her to supply free consultation services for his business friends. At that point she had called me in.

A little bit of background research, and I'd discovered he had a colourful past himself, as a wife beater, with an open warrant in Ohio, for assault and attempted murder. After a little calling around, who should the state police find wandering along a back road, none other than an outstanding warrant.

To me, blackmail was the same as any other bullying, and bullying doesn't have to be physical. The worst is the mental kind, where threats of exposure fester and destroy people's otherwise normal lives.

Not that Dixie's life had been normal. Originally born to bohemian hippie parents, she had been allowed to develop in a uniquely amorphous environment. It was comparable to an extended family, which usually consisted of professors, teachers and other academics. When she'd finally walked out of the chalk dust and bong smoke, her mind had been trained to see connections and relationships in ways that, to me, remained unfathomable. With her natural talents and achievements, it meant instead of her seeking placements, the likes of Berkeley and MIT had actively sought her.

The speaker hummed into life again. "All the toys are safe now, sweet prince, so you can come on up. I'm on the top floor, in the workshop."

Taking a deep breath I walked confidently inside, and didn't even flinch when the front door closed automatically behind me. The light within the hall was a soft cream, and there had been a hint of peach blossom scent added to the air conditioning. Soothing, inviting, and gently relaxing.

At the back of the hallway was a wide, ivory-painted wooden staircase, which corkscrewed the full height of the house. To the side was a metal elevator cage, normally used for moving heavy equipment to and from the top floor workshop. It was tempting, but still mindful of Dixie's fascination with toys and gadgets, I decided to take the stairs.

Outside the workshop, the thumbprint and retina scanning security always proved an interesting experience. They helped to give prospective clients an idea of what Dixie was capable of as well.

Once I'd successfully passed muster, the steel door slid silently to one side, revealing a semi-darkened room. Images and colour flickered around three of the four walls, mainly as the fourth was completely covered with large flatscreen TVs, displaying a myriad of cable and satellite channels. Almost central to the room was Dixie's horseshoe shaped workbench, on top of which sat several more computer screens. Dixie's Ops Commander style chair had been designed to allow her to ride from one end of the horseshoe, around to the other.

I stepped into the room and stood by the doorway so as to let my eyes adjust to the change in lighting levels. In the background came the low hum of the air conditioning as it kept the room, and the machinery, cool. From out of the far, dark corner, Dixie stepped forward.

No matter how she dressed, formal or informal, it was her bright straw-blonde hair which people always described first. Closely followed by her clear green eyes, which have depth and sparkle. She had a quick smile, a humorous disposition, and a dress sense which complemented her figure naturally, rather than bowing to the dictates of high fashion.

Still smiling, she glanced critically at me. "I see no flowers. I see no chocolates. This isn't a social call?"

"Admit it, Dixie. You don't like flowers. As for the chocolates? The merest dream of seeing you again, drove all other rational thoughts clean out of my head."

Dixie fluttered her eyelashes and put a hand to her chest. "I swear, no one knows how to bullshit a lady better than you! Okay, let's can the crap and hand over whatever it is you've bought me."

I took the flash drive from my shirt pocket, and dropped it into her outstretched palm.

"All I know is someone was using this as leverage, and whatever might be on there is important enough to get someone killed."

"Leverage? My, my, aren't you the corporate dog today." She smiled, then became more serious. "So, let's see what there is to see."

She rolled the plastic oblong around in her hands, staring at it intently, as she checked it over.

"Physically, it's a cheap and cheerful Chinese no-brand four gigabyte USB stick." She selected a cable from one of the bench rails, plugged one end into a laptop and the pen drive into the other. Some clickity-clacking on the keyboard ensued, followed by a sudden burst of music from the laptop's small and tinny speakers. Vickery Walsh duck-plucked his guitar, in what had rapidly become his trademark style. Tomorrow it would be someone else with a novel angle to help hide any talent deficit, but for now the fashion was for Walsh.

Dixie wrinkled her nose a little. "Well, there looks like most of an album on this thing. Only the geometry's all wrong. Even allowing for file space and overheads." A manicured fingernail tapped several times on the laptop's LCD screen. "These two files sort of look about right for size, yet the others are way too big. Let me just…."

More clickity-clacking, then she handed the flash drive back.

"Now that I've taken an image of the beast, we can start to play." She turned and looked at me, her voice tinged with a hint of pity. "Sad to say, poppet, this is where you go to MJ's Diner, down on Main Street. I've got some work to do, and you'll only get bored, or in the way. I'll give you a call there in about an hour or two – sooner if this turns out to be something simple."

I couldn't fault her logic, because she knew me too well. As soon as anyone started seriously doing the computer thing, then I tended to switch off. As far as I'm concerned, all technological devices are tools to be used for an end, but some people believe them to be a fashionable end unto themselves.

Grinning like a schoolboy let out of class early, I left her to do whatever it was she wanted to do.

Out in the sun again, I'd walked along several side streets until I got back onto Main Street, and it wasn't long before I'd found MJ's Coffee Shop and Diner.

It was a clean and tidy affair, modern-looking, but in keeping with Northern Californian mom and pop values. Basically they were good coffee and traditional home cooking – the smells of which greeted me when I opened the door and walked in. From speakers near the ceiling, came the sound of a radio turned down low. It had been a news and talk show, which gave the impression of people and conversation, even though it was still too early for the lunchtime rush.

I took a booth by the large front window, sat close to the glass, and glanced through the menu. Too late for breakfast, and too early for lunch, I compromised with brunch. Black coffee, and a grilled cheese sandwich, open face, on whole wheat with ketchup on the side.

The waitress, whose bouffant didn't appear to move no matter how much she nodded or turned her head, jotted it all down, muttering, "Whatever you want is fine by me, honey."

She wore a badge over the pocket of her white blouse, which told me her name was Louisa-May, and from what I could tell she appeared to be chief cook and bottle-washer as well. She looked in her late fifties. Probably still smoked a pack a day despite the taxes and social climate. Drank Manhattans straight up, no ice, in a nearby cocktail bar on Friday nights after work. Loved her husband dearly but still enjoyed the thrill of flirting now and again. Underneath her deep carmine lipstick her smile was warm and genuine, and I smiled back in return, watching as she walked off to start fixing the order.

When she came back, I said, "I don't know how long I'm likely to be. I'm waiting on a call, only it could be in the next ten minutes, or the next two hours."

Again the carmine smile as she poured the coffee.

"You just take as long as you want to, hun," Then she headed back behind the counter.

I slowly cut the toasted slices into quarters, mindful of the melted cheese, then settled down to wait. Watching the traffic, both human and motorised, through the window, I wondered about Preston Llyle, Greagson, Tylor, and Bobby Weams.

Weams was only peripheral, as far as I could tell. Maybe he had just provided the technical know-how – as in the group's pet nerd. Which then begged the question: was it the information which had gotten Greagson killed, or the knowledge of its existence? It wasn't any desperate bookie, or a short-changed dealer looking for revenge. If you had a problem like that, you dealt with it by advertising the corrective action. Black eyes, fat lips and broken bones. Apart from it being a warning to others, you can't collect a debt from a dead man, no matter how much you try. Especially a junkie with a gambling habit.

No, there was something on the flash drive which Greagson had tried to exploit, and which ultimately got him killed. I needed to find either Bobby Weams or Preston Llyle, and soon.

Lindsey Fairfax, on the other hand, was a completely different problem. I wanted to warn her, but didn't have anything except rumours and hearsay. I was getting myself too entangled as well. I had promised forty-eight hours, and here I was, on the fourth day, still working the case. Yet, with no definite conclusion I could put into a report, I was being royally diddled by my own sense of guilt at not having done the job I set out to do. Then again, this had become more than a quickie hunt for a missing person.

Just before midday the short-order cook arrived and covered while Louisa-May took a break. After that, the lunchtime crowd came and went in a regular flow – mothers with baby buggies and cranky infants, white-collars from nearby businesses and casual walk-ins off the street. At the height of the organised chaos, Louisa-May passed by.

"Just got a call from your lady friend. She says you're to head on back as soon as you're ready." Then she went back to her world of refills, fries, pies, and the ubiquitous brown bags to go.

I stood, slipped a five under the coffee cup and some loose change beside it. When I got the chance, I caught Louisa-May's eye, waved my thanks, then retraced my way back to Dixie's.

She was sat in the chair by her workbench, and as the door slid shut behind me, she offered me the chair facing the bank of TV screens. Clearing her throat quickly, she launched into her discoveries as if she were giving a presentation to a gathering of businessmen.

"First, let me give you a little history lesson. Back in the late 1980s and early 1990s, as the Internet was beginning to become widely available, there was always a fear of being prosecuted for pirated music files. These were the early days, when just the threat was enough. But, geeks being geeks, some of them became paranoid about their collections. They developed small programs which camouflaged one type of file within another, and music files were often wrapped into graphics files. So successfully that the graphics file would display normally, until you applied the decoding process and, hey-presto, you had two files where once there was only one.

"It was a neat exploitation, but the dark side quickly worked out ways of turning it around so graphical information could be successfully hidden in other types of files. Everything from industrial espionage through to child pornography. Over the years the encryption programs have become more and more sophisticated, compressing files down so as not to be too obvious there was other material hidden inside.

"What you have on the pen drive is what looks like a collection of twenty audio tracks. What you have in reality are twenty tracks, plus a collection of eighteen frame grabs, and the original two video files they were taken from. The video files only have a short time break between them, so I'm thinking automatic record and save every ten minutes or so. It took a little while to isolate the encryption signatures, but here's what they split out to."

She clicked a mouse button and a series of still pictures came up on the screens, mostly showing two people involved in something which had all the hallmarks of a drugs deal. Packets and bottles of pills in large open cardboard boxes, along with ampoules containing clear liquid. Some of the shots were indistinct, others clearly showed the same two peoples' faces looking directly at the camera.

Dixie gave the mouse another couple of clicks and the video footage popped into animated life. Darkish movements, the video grainy and blurred in places – outside a warehouse – the loading bay lighting flaring across the screen when caught by the camera. The crude, unprotected mic seemed to pick up every rustle of clothing as the wearer moved around. Unmarked cardboard boxes were opened in the back of a dealership-new, designer pickup truck, paintwork shiny and reflective. Snatches of voices came through the noise from time to time:

"…guaranteed to get you humping and pumping…"

"Careful, Bobby! Those are only worth money if they're still sealed! …"

"…okay, to you, a K per case, quality guaranteed. When has The Man ever let you down? …"

"…anything besides the muscle stuff? …"

"…something a little more designer, based on E… you thinking of branching out?…"

"It's Ketamine. Special K"

"Yeah, the stuff vets use to treat animals…"

"Bobby, let the men do the talking here…"

"…mom okay for acid? Only joking! Hey, chill!"

"There's a bag of meds up front, if you want to hold a pharming party?"

"… Okay, so five boxes of booster, a thousand White Doves, two packs of Special K, and I'll toss in the mixed bag of stuff for free. Say six large?"

I'd become so involved with trying to understand the video I hadn't noticed Dixie had moved up beside me.

"It was recorded using a low-grade spy-cam or a stripped down nanny-cam." She was well into her less emotional, technical persona now. "If you look at the unstable picture, the angle, the lens distortion, the low dpi and the poor colour clarity, they're all indicative of a cheap and simple mechanism. I'd say it was hooked up via Wi-Fi, or Bluetooth." She looked at me curiously. "It may have been disguised as a pen, clipped to the top pocket of a shirt, or a cigarette packet. Luckies are a good brand because the simple design allows you to hide the camera lens. The lens isn't going to be much bigger than a piece of fibre optic filament, going by the quality of the finished product."

I squinted as I tried to look deeper into the gritty picture, but the poor quality was made all the more obvious on the high definition screens, and I gave up.

"Is there any way you could clean things up a little bit?"

"This isn't Hollywood, Harry. You'd be amazed at how many people believe movie technology is for real. You can enhance it to some degree, and you can clean it up a little bit, but you can't keep putting into it what was never in it in the first place. You could get a professional lip reader to fill in the soundtrack, and possibly face reconstruction would give you a more positive picture. But apart from that...." Her voice trailed off a little apologetically. "If it helps any, the guy with the camera keeps getting called Bobby. This one here," she stopped the video and went back to the still pictures, "is Preston, and this one," again, flicking through the pictures, "is Harrison. There is a fourth person, right on the edge of vision, very indistinct, but from the soundtrack fragments I'd say it's a woman, rather than a man."

I stared into the screens again, trying to make something out of a fuzzy blob, only they were standing too close to a wire fence, near to a security light which kept overloading the camera sensor and bleaching out the details.

Why had Weams taken the video footage in the first place? What if Bobby was looking to shake down Preston and Harrison? Could that have been what had driven Preston to ground? Maybe Weams had murdered Greagson? Tech geeks could be obsessively possessive over their equipment, sometimes even more than a human-based relationship. And Greagson had admitted to selling the laptop to a fence.

I stood. There was nothing to be gained from running over this again and again. I needed to get back to the office and talk to some people, before telling Lindsey she should forget about Preston, and get on with her life. It wasn't what she wanted to hear, but I doubted she'd want to get involved if she really knew what he was up to.

Turning to Dixie, I said, "I don't suppose you've made copies?"

She smiled. "I'm so far ahead of you, Ace, I'm lapping you for the second time." She held out three CD cases. "The raw files and the stills are on the CD. The video files I've converted to DVD format, and if one version doesn't play on your machine, then the other one will." She tilted her head slightly. "You do have a DVD player, don't you, Ace?"

Taking the cases, I glared at her. She knew me too well. "Of course I have. I'm not a total Luddite." Trouble was I knew she knew I was lying.

She turned me around and, giggling to herself, hustled me up to the workshop door. She did something and the door slid back automatically. Gently she pushed me out onto the landing, and as I turned back to say goodbye she smiled again.

"One day, Ace," she sighed good-naturedly, "I'm really gonna have to tech you up!" As the door slid back in place she put her fingers to her lips and blew me a kiss.

Driving back down the 299 and into the city, I wondered how I was going to break the news to Lindsey. I could do it coldly, just report the facts and let her come to her senses. Even throw in some of the stills, printed off on high gloss paper to help emphasise the finer details.

Or I could break it to her gently. "Ms. Fairfax, as you can see from these covert photographs, the person you love deeply is an unrepentant scumbag." Yep, that ought to do just fine.

I rolled down my window and tried to let the fresh

afternoon air clear my head. Yet the nearer I got to the office, the more antsy I got, and it wasn't long before the Ford's back seat was littered with CDs again. I let the auto-tune run up and down the FM band, but nothing helped distract me from the inevitable. There had to be some way to let her down gently.

Coming into the city's outskirts the traffic was light, but after a short while I found I was getting buzzed by a late model Corvette Z06. Metallic grey and low slung. It had all the hallmarks of the boy-racer club – tinted windows, police scanner aerial, wide tires with alloy rims and spinners. It would slowly come close, then back off, even though the other lane was clear, and I wasn't in a hurry. It was ludicrous to expect my Ford to go afternoon road racing. In comparison to the thoroughbred, my Ford was a carthorse.

The next set of lights changed to red and I pulled into the right-hand lane, blindly stabbing the auto-tune button again.

"And I'm tellin' you people! One! More! Freaking! Time! This is Arnie Jack with the Afternoon Talkback. Don't even think about callin' in if you're a namby-pamby pissant bleedin' heart Liberal 'cos I will chew you up and won't even bother to spit out the bones because there's no bones to spit out! I don't want spineless, I want real, red-blooded opinions and beliefs, an' if you aren't prepared to debate, then get the hell out of my airspace! Today we're talking about the recent hikes in gas prices. Again?! Isn't this why we had all those freaking wars, to protect fuel production and prices? And isn't it true this government can't find their asses with their hands tied behind their own backs? Am I right, or am I wrong – you tell me! We'll be right back, after these announcements!"

The Corvette had kept to the left lane and slowly pulled up alongside me. From the muffled thumping I couldn't tell what was playing on the sound system, only that the bass bins were rippin' wicked, y'all. Old artillery training lectures came back to me, detailing the damage caused by sound wave compression in confined spaces, and I wondered how old the driver would be when their hearing finally gave out. Not my worry. Keeping one eye on the lights I stabbed the auto-tune again. I'm not a bleeding heart Liberal, but even I know Arnie's polarised opinions aren't worth jack. Then the lights changed.

Both of us moved off together, and by the time we were half way across the intersection I realised the loud music I was hearing wasn't coming from the radio, but from the Corvette. Its darkened passenger window had been rolled down, and it matched me for speed. I felt the hairs on the back of my neck stand on end, then an object shot out from the Corvette's open window – a rapid blur of motion in my peripheral vision. Instinctively I braced my hands and arms against the steering wheel and pushed my head back hard against the headrest. Something round and white flashed past my face at eye level, smacked hard into the passenger door post, and ricocheted into the back of the Ford.

No sooner had the missile been launched, than the driver of the Corvette hit the gas and disappeared in a mass of tire smoke and horns from the other cars cut up by the vehicle's escape.

Immediately I twisted the wheel hard to the right, feeling the back of the car fishtail as it made the turn, the tires screaming and smoking in protest as I successfully corrected the skidding.

I yanked the handbrake up hard, unclipped the seatbelt, and had the car door open before the Ford had stopped moving. As I hit the road surface I curled up into a ball, combat rolling over to the curb, before finally throwing myself flat down behind a parked car, eyes closed, and with my hands pressed firmly over my ears.

One Little Indian –

Our small support convoy had just cleared the roadblock checkpoint and was

Two Little Indians –

starting to climb back up the mountain track when two wire-guided

Three Little Indians –

missiles had been fired from handheld launchers from the roadside ahead of us

Four Little Indians –

and both had turned a medical truck and a petrol bowser into one massive

Five Little Indian Boys! –

FIREBALL – wreckage and debris raining down and exploding around us as we crashed into the carnage.

"Are you okay, mister?"

With a convulsive intake of breath I dropped back into reality, and stared at the Nike training shoes of the three children standing around me. No heat, no smell of smoke, no clattering of car bodywork as it fell back to earth.

I stood up and looked at where the Ford had slewed to a stop. The door was wide open and the engine had stalled, but apart from that nothing seemed to be damaged. Even the two-way traffic treated it as just another badly double parked car.

Cautiously I walked over and looked at the back seat. In amongst the compact disks sat a brand new baseball, still shiny and unblemished. Except, across part of it, someone had written in indelible red marker: 'Bang Bang You're Dead.'

As statisticians sometimes point out during election result analysis, there had been a sudden swing in the motivative demographic. This was no longer about Lindsey Fairfax and her misguided affections. This had just become personal.

11

It was 8:20 a.m. in Beijing. Since returning to my office, the late afternoon had passed through a sunset and was moving inexorably into its evening phase.

Across in Window World some people were turning on extra lighting, while others were switching theirs off or closing the vertical blinds. It had turned the building into a giant crossword puzzle grid. Only, one across was starting to look like it was a word with twenty-four letters.

Offices and businesses never wound down and stopped after the working day was done these days. Decades ago, employee evolution had embraced a crazy, competitive work ethic which clearly stated: if you're not working yourself to the bone then you're a failure. People suffered, and their ability to form and maintain physical, social relationships has since been overtaken by the lack of quality time. We are driven by success, strive for it, and are measured by it.

Behind me, in the centre of the desk, was the baseball.

Light and background noise spilled in from the corridor as the office door opened and someone walked quietly in. Closing the door behind them put the room back into semi-darkness. There was the sound of the refrigerator door being opened and closed. Silence. Then the hiss of the top being eased off a bottle of beer.

Interruption over, I slipped back into Window World and

worked on the problem of one across some more. It was a crossword puzzle, but I had no idea what the clues were, which sounded all too familiar of late. I thought about it, then carefully checked the letters off in my head. Twenty-four. One across had to be *microspectrophotometries*. A technique for obtaining measurements of the spectral absorption of a single photoreceptor cell, especially useful when investigating non-human colour vision without behavioural tests.

There was the faint sound of leather against leather as my visitor sat down in the client's chair. The contemplative silence returned, punctuated by the rhythmical metallic tapping of a gold ring against the cold glass of the bottle, and the warmly distinctive scent of Elizabeth's perfume.

I was working on two down – a nine letter word beginning with an S – when she broke the silence once more.

"The first time I fell off my pedal bike was when my dad took the training wheels off. I must have been six or seven. I couldn't work out why something I'd been able to do the day before, had suddenly become impossible. Dad kept on encouraging me to ride the thing, saying 'Get up and get back on the bike, Lizzie! It's the only way you'll learn to ride.' All I remember thinking at the time was 'What the hell do you know?'" She took a pull from the bottle, then carried on. "The point is, I don't really know what you're going through, or how you figure on coping with it, but I'm here when you're ready to talk. It's what you said you wanted to do when you phoned, right?"

Two down. Nine letters beginning with S. Sphincter. Yep. Just about summed it up.

I turned my chair around and faced Elizabeth. In the gloom I could see she was wearing plain black biking leathers which blended with the chair covering. She leaned forward, put the beer bottle on a coaster, then pushed it across the desk towards me. I took a mouthful, pushed it back across the desk, then picked up the baseball.

The logo was undamaged and the stitching showed no signs of having been bruised by any Louisville Slugger. The only blemish was the mark where it had struck the door post, but apart from that, and the red felt tip lettering, it was fresh from the box.

For the second time that day, I explained the situation. Only this time I left everything in, including the computer flash drive, and that I'd told Greagson to contact Tylor, and to tell him I now had the drive. I mentioned the videos showing Llyle and Tylor with a whole host of illegal pills and potions. I still had no idea where that fitted in, but it was all the more reason for Lindsey to forget about Preston, and get on with her life.

At the end of it all, Elizabeth picked up the bottle, took another mouthful, then put it back down on the coaster. "Why do you do it, Harry?" She sounded genuinely curious.

I looked up at her, making eye contact. "You know the saying: walk a mile in another man's shoes…?"

There was a pause before she said, "And?"

"Well, you're a mile away and you've got his shoes. He's not going to come looking for you, even if he desperately wants to."

She just nodded. "Freddy was right. You really are full of it when you're down."

"So much for the psycho analysis." I shook my head in resignation. "How the hell do I move on from here?"

"You already know the answer to that, Harry. You can't make this by defensive play, no matter which way you look at it. You've compromised the evidence against Harrison Tylor, but he doesn't know that. The only other option you have is to go on the offensive and take the play to Tylor yourself. You've got to, for your own protection. Otherwise, once he gets the flash drive, or believes the power you hold over him has been neutralised, he's not going to think twice about killing you. He may even feel he has to, in order to maintain his peer group status."

I was quiet for a while, trying to think of alternatives, but all the time knowing there weren't any. I'd have to use the flash drive as a bargaining chip. Show Tylor it was going to hang on mutual trust. In other words I needed to create the perfect Mexican standoff – and at the same time see if he knew where Preston Llyle might be hiding out.

I glanced down at the baseball on the desk. Looking at the problem in a more positive light, Tylor – or someone – felt I was a serious danger to them, even if I were killed. Otherwise why was I still alive? Looked at another, it showed me just how sloppy I'd become.

Elizabeth was right. I needed to start making an impression on Tylor with some serious, offensive game play. I needed to sort myself out emotionally as well, otherwise the prophesy would be fulfilled, and I'd be bang-bang dead before I knew it.

Ultimately there would come a time when I would have no choice but to take Tylor down. I couldn't trust him not to target me some time in the future, regardless of what insurance I had. The alternative was to drop myself down to his level and kill him. Some days you eat the bear, some days the bear eats you.

Across from me, Elizabeth rose out of the chair. She pursed her lips in thought, then said, "You need to think about our next move. While you're doing that, I'll see what I can find out about Mr. Tylor." Turning, she walked out of my office, quietly closing the door behind her.

In the dim silence, the little green light on the desktop computer twinkled while the coffee maker's red neon power button gently buzzed to itself. I picked up the warm bottle, drained it, dropped it into the office recycling bin, and stood up. Positive thought. Positive action.

I grabbed a mug from the stand, then switched on the office lights. Turning round, I saw the brightness had transformed the office windows into translucent black mirrors, effectively obscuring Window World, as they reflected back ghost images of myself. I poured out half a mug of reheated Colombian dark roast, then went back to the windows. Pulling on the cord made the blinds close, exorcising the ghost of Harry past. At least for the time being.

I needed to somehow get Tylor to come to me on my terms. It would give me the psychological advantage I felt I needed, but I doubted he'd willingly step out of his comfort zone.

I sat back in my chair and took a mouthful of coffee. Oily and bitter, but it helped wash the taste of beer from my mouth.

Movement caught my eye as a dark shadow eclipsed the frosted glass of the office door. Without knocking, Marty Beddows strode in and up to the desk, slamming the door closed behind him. He was wearing a black suit, an angry expression, and was carrying a large manila envelope in his left hand.

"What do you know about Evangeline Mallory?"

I was caught between trying to gauge his anger and where his question was leading. "Nothing. I don't know any Evangeline Mallory. You want to sit down and tell me about it?"

Marty sat and slapped the envelope on the desk. He opened the flap and took out two morgue photographs of an elderly black woman.

"This is the late Evangeline Mallory. She lived in one of those retirement villages down past Connaught, over on the east side. She was supposed to be away visiting family, but her son and daughter-in-law are going through a very acrimonious divorce. According to her other son, she felt it would best if she didn't go see them this year. Trouble is she had a lot of pride and wasn't going to let her family's troubles become the subject of neighbourhood gossip. So she didn't tell anyone, apart from immediate family and a few close friends, about her change of plans."

He picked up my mug of coffee, took a large swig, then worked his mouth for a second or two, trying to remove the aftertaste, before continuing.

"The old neighbourhood watch then gets in touch with the local police. It seems someone with still-functioning short term memory noticed her kitchen door suddenly had a patched up pane of glass. After a few days of nobody seeing nobody, along with some confusion as to whether she was actually at home, one of the regular patrol broke in. They find her upstairs, sleeping the eternal sleep of the dead. She'd been given a helping hand over to the other side. Suffocated. Didn't need a report to tell us that, the pillow was still over her face when they found her."

I was more than a little confused. "What's this got to do with me? I'm telling you, Marty, I don't know her. Gimme a clue or something."

"You've been asking about a guy called Weams? Well, you

just wouldn't believe whose remains we found in Evangeline's kitchen." Beddows pulled out three more photographs and laid them out in front of me.

One was a long shot of a naked body tied to a wooden chair. The photograph was clinical and cold, carefully framed to contain hard facts rather than artistic aesthetics. Left exposed, the flies had wasted little time in settling. The second was a more detailed close-up of the body. I didn't need to see where the hands and feet were bound to the chair, because the signs of torture were still very evident. The third was a close-up of the remains of the victims' face.

I thought about Wesley Greagson, sitting on the broken sofa, his head tilted a little to one side, smugly saying, *"You don't know about Bobby? Preston's little cybergeek?"*

"This is Bobby Weams?" My voice was low and quiet.

Marty sucked on a tooth. "Well, forensics says it's him. Thankfully the patrol found him before the maggots had a chance to chow down and eat most of the evidence."

Purposefully he leaned forward and tapped a finger on the middle photograph, the close-up of the body.

"Doc reckons all the inventive stuff was done while he was still in the land of the living. Some bad puppy had a fun time before curing Bobby of his earwax problem once and for all. He died of a stab wound to the brain, through the ear. Something long, thin, probably circular. The only up-side is, with so much damage beforehand, Doc figures Weams didn't feel the last one coming at all. Neighbours didn't see or hear anything. Mind you, one turns his hearing aid off daily at eight p.m. to save on batteries."

I looked at the photographs as Marty stared down and laced his fingers in his lap. "Thing is," he continued, watching as his thumbs rapidly circled each other. "You start asking about Greagson, and the next thing is he turns up ventilated with his brains scrambled. Then you start asking about Weams, and lo, what the good Lord giveth, some sick fuck taketh away. If I wasn't such a dumb-ass cop I might start asking where you really fitted into all of this."

Looking at him sitting there, I knew he would pull the pin on me without any hesitation if he believed I deserved it. Regardless of our longstanding friendship.

"You don't think I had anything to do with this, do you, Marty?"

He kept watching his fingers intently. "Karrel was all for cuffing you and yanking you down to the station. Itching to get out the rubber hose and knuckle dusters. But I managed to talk him out of it."

I smiled, though felt a little uneasy. "That's mighty kind of you."

Marty went on, without acknowledging my thanks.

"I told him, Hell, Rhimes is too stupid to get involved with something and *not* let us know about it. Hell, again, I said, you start knocking him around, and before you know it you've knocked some sense into him that ain't been there before. After that he's bound to get ideas above his station."

He unclasped his hands, placed them firmly on the arms of the chair and leaned forward a little.

"Don't fuck with me Harry. If you've got something, then you turn it over to us. The days of the Lone Ranger are long gone. Nobody rides off into the sunset any more. Your only redeeming factor is that Weams was killed several days before Greagson."

He got up and left, this time closing the door quietly, leaving behind the pictures of Evangeline Mallory and Bobby Weams' mutilated remains still face up on my desk.

12

For a long time I did my best not to dwell on the photos. I knew the Mallory woman had been an innocent bystander, caught up in the madness when someone had used her kitchen to torture Bobby Weams. From what Marty Beddows had said, it looked like the killer had believed the house had been empty.

Another memory came back from the meeting with Wesley Greagson: *"It's the only copy. I wiped Bobby's laptop before I sold it."*

Poor Bobby really didn't know where his laptop or the files were, and what you don't know you can't tell, no matter what someone does to you. It was a gut feeling, but I was sure Tylor was responsible. Whether he did it himself, or had someone else do it for him, didn't matter. To me he was just as guilty.

According to the desk clock, in Beijing it had just turned 10:05 a.m – 7:05 p.m. local time. It was late and there wasn't any point staying at the office. I put the photos back in the envelope, then dropped the packet in the filing cabinet which held Lindsey's report. The two dead people were strangers to me, but I still felt an obligation to make sure their killer didn't get away.

Coupled with that was Lindsey, and my obligation towards her. My hand hovered before I snatched up the report. Slamming the drawer shut, I felt I'd finally had enough. It had started out as just a quick favour Monday morning – a simple case of tracking down a runaway boyfriend. Now, four days later, it had turned into a nightmare. Time to drop Lindsey – gently or otherwise, I no longer cared – and deal with the threat of Harrison Tylor.

I slipped the report into an envelope and sealed the flap. Folding it lengthways I stuck it in my inside jacket pocket, turned off the lights, and slowly walked to the elevators. Orion and Nadler were in the evening cycle again. Quiet voices and soft ring tones replaced the daytime cacophony. Even the *ding,* which signalled the elevator's arrival, seemed somehow less brusque and intrusive.

Down in the car park, heading towards the visitors' bays, the mix of stale air, exhaust fumes and dampness was comfortingly familiar. I considered driving home, getting a shower and something to eat. Then back into the city to hand over my report to Lindsey. Yet, if I started doing that, I'd start feeling more human, which meant I'd end up making allowances and feeling sympathetic towards her. That would lead me even deeper into the nightmare. No, it'd be less drawn out and lingering to grab some food, call her, deliver the report, then go. That way I wouldn't have time to talk myself out of it.

I took the keys out of my pocket and scanned the bays again. In the background I could hear a heavy motorcycle being kick-started to life.

No sign of the Ford at all.

The sound of the motorbike grew louder, the noise of the engine echoed and re-echoed in the half-empty expanse. Throbbing and pulsing, rather than a rapid burst of acceleration. And suddenly I didn't care about the Ford any more. Instinctively I slipped between a 4x4 and an SUV, dropping into a squat so I wasn't an easy drive-by target. I considered rolling under one of the vehicles, but dismissed the idea. If I got stuck, or caught on something, I'd be an even easier target.

I thought about the safety box inside the filing cabinet, inside which was the snub-nose .38. In the Army sidearms had, to some extent, always been second nature. Back in Civvy Street I'd quickly gotten out of the habit, much to some peoples' chagrin.

Looking at the gap between the vehicles I saw the motorcycle flash past, an indistinct black and chrome blur, the rider not even checking between the cars as they headed for the exit ramp. Maybe it was just an innocent coincidence?

The throbbing sound of the bike engine idling, rather than dying away, didn't make my rationalisation convincing, even to me. I dropped down on my hands and knees, then bent my head to look around the SUV's rear wheel, while still using the back end for cover. I could see the lower third of the motorcycle. One of the rider's legs was outstretched, the boot firmly on the ground to support the massive machine. Was there something familiar about the boot?

Still. Watch and wait. Watch and wait. In the past I had seen snipers completely zone out, totally focussed on their target, conscious only of anything that might affect their accuracy.

The booted foot started to tap the ground impatiently, followed by a slight change of weight. Then a familiar female voice shouted, "If you carried a cell phone we could have called you."

Standing up, I looked towards the leather clad figure. Elizabeth, astride the Yamaha Royal Star, her helmet hanging from one of the handlebars. Thankfully she looked only mildly annoyed.

"We didn't want to disturb you while you were entertaining." She reached into the top pocket of her leather jacket and took out a set of car keys. With a swift flick of her wrist, she sent them spinning over to me, and I managed to catch them without embarrassing myself.

She continued, "We need to start shaking up your routine, so the first thing I've done is retire that clunker of yours. Temporarily, that is. Freddy and I cleaned out most of the personal junk and dumped it in the Chrysler. Freddy even spent five minutes putting CDs back in their right cases before he finally gave up." She pointed to the vehicle next to her. "This is more rugged and reliable, plus it has the space for all the crap you keep. Remember, it's only on loan, not sale or return."

She opened a second pocket and pulled out a glossy black oblong, and tossed that to me as well. "That's a cheap cell phone with GPS. It only works if you keep it regularly charged, and turned on."

I knew she was right, but it still didn't stop me from feeling contrite and angry. Without checking it, I slipped it into a pants pocket.

"One more thing, Harry. There's a nine-mil Browning, with a full magazine, clipped under the drivers' seat. It'll give you a lot more stopping power should you need it."

She picked her helmet off the handlebars, shook back her hair as she put it on, then adjusted it, the visor still up so I could see her face. "All you've got to do now is work out how you're going to deal with Tylor."

She flipped the visor down, kicked the bike into gear, then gently let out the clutch. At the end of the exit ramp she slowed, then eased the Yamaha into traffic.

I looked from the Chrysler to the set of keys in my hand, and pressed the fob with my thumb. Amber lights flashed, and from somewhere came a woink-woink noise.

Moving to the drivers' door I took hold of the handle. With all the confidence of someone who hadn't the faintest idea if he'd just unlocked the car, or armed the alarm system, I tentatively pulled the door open. No ear-splitting noise or bright flashing lights, so I climbed in and set about adjusting things.

As I positioned the drivers' seat, I checked underneath. In a quick-release rig rested a cold, black, automatic. From my army days I was intimately familiar with the Browning, and could still strip it down and reassemble it in my sleep. I didn't bother examining it further. If Elizabeth was happy to provide me with a weapon, then I trusted her judgement. I belted up, started the engine, and headed for the exit ramp.

Out on the street I opened the window and took in some of the cool night air. A quick glance at the steering wheel showed me where the radio's controls were, and soon I was heading down town, listening to a live broadcast of *The Rex Odeon Quartet* performing their *Movie Madness Suite*. Some critics had called it a wonderful homage to early 1960s B-movies. Others said it was nothing more than a blatant rip-off. Usually, most of the audiences were way too busy trying to work out which films the underlying melodies came from, for them to worry about the finer points.

The Quartet were halfway through the second movement, the section where *Psycho Beach Party* merges into *Vampire Frogs of the Bloodlust Planet*, when I finally found a parking space close to Billy Fong's.

I sat for a while with the engine off, lost in contemplation.

All I'd eaten in the last twelve hours had been half a plate of ham and eggs, and a little toasted cheese. I needed something, not only to calm my stomach, but to raise my spirits and my blood sugar level as well. But first there was something I had to do.

I pulled out the new cell phone and dug out the card with Lindsey's number. Tapping it into the phone I put the tiny device to my ear.

The receiver purred once, then a click as the voicemail kicked in almost immediately. I checked the time on the dashboard clock. It was just turning 19:45. Maybe she was screening? Maybe she was held up in an evening snarl-up? Whatever. I let the message play out, then, "It's Mr Rhimes. I've compiled a final report. I appreciate it's getting late, but I would like to drop it off to you this evening." I tried to picture the lobby and whether there'd been any mailboxes, but couldn't. "If it's not convenient I can always mail it to you tomorrow. Could you call me back on this number and we can discuss it further. Thanks."

As I broke the connection I felt oddly relieved that it had gone to voicemail, rather than talking to Lindsey in person. I figured if she wasn't in by the time I arrived at her apartment block, I'd address the envelope to her, then either push it under the main entrance door, or stick a stamp on it and mail it direct. Whatever happened, it would still be up to her to call me if she wanted to take it further. If she did, I'd be happy to recommend other competent investigators who would willingly take the work.

Locking the Chrysler, I walked up the street to Billy Fong's. Already the window booths were full with hungry clientèle. They were eating and casually watching the pedestrians, who in turn casually watched the diners eat as they walked on by. It was one of the reasons I'm not that keen on using booths – they often make me feel like sideshow entertainment. Not what I need when I'm tangling with a bowl of Billy's curried squid. The contents had often been known not to go down without a fight, and that always made it messy.

I opened the door and stepped in – the welcoming sounds and familiar smells enfolded me like an old security blanket. Warm, slightly moist, and with an undertone of cabbage – or, in this case, kimchee.

Settling down on one of the counter stools, I called to Billy for some Shanghai noodles. Billy looked quizzical, then nodded, going back to finishing one order before starting on the next. I closed my eyes, mentally turned down the background noise, and made an effort to relax. It was time to get back to sorting out the Tylor problem.

One possibility, if played right, could produce a bloodless result. Provided I could find Preston, there was always a chance I could get him to turn state's evidence. If he were to introduce the recordings as evidence, it would give them credibility and help validate Preston's potential as a prosecution witness.

If I could find evidence connecting Tylor to the killings of Weams and Greagson, then it would certainly tuck him away for a long time. It wasn't an ideal solution – there were too many ifs in the equation – but at least I could walk away without there being any blood on my hands. For the time being. Depending on how long Tylor was put away for.

But then, didn't cops accept that aspect of their jobs on a daily basis?

I opened my eyes again. I had come out of the office with

every intention of walking away from Lindsey and her quest to find Preston Llyle. Now, it seemed, no matter what I said or did, I was getting drawn into the whole sorry mess all the more. At least, this time, I could justify the lack of a fee. Yeah. That would make a wonderful paragraph or two in the paperwork when I filed for bankruptcy.

Five minutes later Billy came over, carrying with him a steaming bowl of fresh rice noodles. Leaning forward as he set it down, he asked, "There's got to be something on your mind, Harry. Want to talk?"

I looked at him questioningly.

"You didn't make with the jokes. You always make with the terrible car jokes, unless something's bothering you."

I smiled at his concern. "I'm doing favours when I should be doing business."

"If I can help at all, Harry?"

Out of friendship, in Chinese I said, *Dor-tse dai-low*.

Smiling, he replied, *Mmm-sai hak-hay*, then went back to managing the orders. Maybe in a previous life we actually had been brothers. I picked a pair of bamboo chopsticks from a pot on the counter, unwrapped them, then settled down to enjoy my meal.

I'm not sure what initially caught my eye, as I usually didn't bother watching TV much. The reception in the canyon is bad at best, so I tend to stay faithful to the radio. Yet something made me slowly stop eating and concentrate on what was happening on the screen.

The old Zenith was tuned to a local station which had suddenly been put in a spin by breaking news. The outside broadcast team were jockeying for position, which meant poor lighting, hurried shots and odd jump cuts from Mitch, the studio anchor, to Cathy, the reporter at the scene.

"… Isn't that right, Cathy?"

"Sure is, Mitch. Though obviously we haven't been able to interview the neighbour, who discovered the body, just yet."

She was standing off to one side of a large building, itself half hidden in shadows from the street lighting. She held a stick microphone in one hand while her other was making sweeping gestures, emphasising points with short, authoritative movements. Despite the modern technology, the occasional flares as the camera lens caught the building or street lighting full on, made the scene sometimes hard to follow.

Back in the studio, the anchor was feeding her information and discussion points. "As I recall, Cathy, the Shepherdson redevelopment is fairly new. Part of the city's plans for regeneration to help ease the housing problem."

Taking her cue perfectly, Cathy launched into a potted history, which sounded as if it had been culled from an election speech, or some Wikipedia entry. I turned back to my bowl of noodles for another couple of mouthfuls. City politics left me cold. Even Concrete's informal Council meetings were only attended with an element of duress – usually to prevent some of the more crazier schemes from getting through.

Mouth still half full of rice noodles, I glanced back at the screen. The camera had started panning up the side of the building, while Cathy, out of shot, was saying, "…And it was up on the fourth floor, apartment 4C in fact, where the woman's body was found." The picture stopped moving as the cameraman refocused on a shot which showed several windows, and to the left, the faint and faded remains of an old advertising slogan "…*wanna pee!*" It did little to help relieve the constricted feeling I'd started to get in the pit of my stomach as I realised where I'd seen those painted words before.

In the studio, Mitch put a finger to his ear for a couple of seconds while Cathy continued to chatter inanely, recycling what scant details she had. "Can I just break in here, Cathy? We're getting unconfirmed reports that the murder weapon was a bottle of some kind."

"I can't confirm that at the moment, Mitch, but–"

She was cut off by what appeared to be the cameraman's pointing finger coming into shot, and the camera jerkily refocusing on the brightly lit reception area. Through the jerkiness, the screen showed a mass of people and movement around the elevators as an ambulance gurney, bearing a black body bag, was pushed out into the foyer. Like sharks, the smell of blood and death whipped the reporters into a feeding frenzy. The scene became bleached with staccato bursts of white light as photographers desperately fought for potential front page pictures. Then the police took control, and the gurney with the body bag was quickly pushed into the waiting ambulance. The doors were slammed shut, the lights atop of the vehicle flashed, and the siren squawked half-heartedly to help clear a path through the bystanders.

Finally the camera pulled back to frame the station's field reporter. Looking square into the camera, she said, "I'm Cathy Selby, reporting from the recently opened Shepherdson apartments on Carmaline Boulevard, where tonight, an as yet unidentified woman, has been brutally bludgeoned to death, in what is believed to be her own apartment. Back to you in the studio, Mitch."

<h1 style="text-align:center">13</h1>

I don't remember much about the journey home from Billy Fong's. I just put my sticks down, tucked some money under the bowl, then walked out onto the street. In my confusion, I spent several minutes looking for the Ford I no longer had. Finally I had pulled out the keys, and kept pressing the fob until I homed in on the car with the flashing lights.

I drove off, one hand on the wheel while the other slipped a CD into the player. Wilson Rebeauxs' Karolina started in on their *Visions of Death Valley*. Industrial machine rhythms, with additional, heavily distorted, vocals. A cement wall of sound which gave my mind something to bounce against.

The mention of 4C had confirmed it was Lindsey Fairfax's apartment. From what I could recall, there had been little room to swing a cat, let alone exist, and a bottle was rarely ever a weapon of choice. Usually it was snatched up on angry emotional impulse, then used as a club. Contrary to Hollywood, bottles don't smash when they come into violent contact with someone's head. If it had been a frenzied, unplanned attack then there would be plenty for forensics to work on. If it had been planned, of course, then things were going to be different.

Distracted, I touched my jacket and felt the envelope with the report still in the pocket. What had I gleaned from the two times we'd met? She'd struck me as naïve, and perhaps even too trusting. Bobby Weams had been killed because of his involvement with Preston, Tylor and Greagson. Greagson had been killed because he'd tried to blackmail Tylor. But Tylor knew I was the one who had the files, so why go after Lindsey?

And where the hell was Preston Llyle?

I was almost at my turn off to the house when, up ahead of me, a pair of headlights discretely came on. I gently applied the break, slipping a hand carefully beneath the seat. If I needed additional support, the Browning was going to be close at hand. One of the two lights broke away as Freddy turned and headed back down into Concrete, while the other moved slowly towards me, the distinctive lines of Elizabeth's leathers standing out in the Chrysler's headlights. Waving a hand, then turning her motorbike around, she gestured for me to follow her.

We kept the speed low, following the road as it started to drop down towards the canyon. After a couple of kinked and twisting miles, we cut back along a dirt trail which brought us onto the flats on which the majority of Concrete was built.

The dashboard clock showed 21:20, and at that time of night there wasn't much going on down Main Street. Midweek isn't so hot in Concrete if you want to socialise. The best places are either the cinema – situated in part of the old spa complex and run by Cherrie, who had originally been christened Charlie – or Madam Pearl's Bar 'n' Diner, still run by Madam Pearl.

While Elizabeth rode her motorbike around the back of the Star & Belle, I parked outside the main entrance. Turning off the engine and the lights, I shut my eyes and tried to relax. The adrenaline was finally flushing out of my system, and I was starting to feel the tiredness which had backed up behind it. Unbuckling the seatbelt, I got out and took a short walk around the Chrysler to stretch my legs before climbing the steps to the Star & Belle. Through the main door, the soft amber yellow light from the low watt bulbs complimented the '40s-style retro furniture and helped add to the warm ambience. I carried on through the reception area, then slipped around the door marked *Staff Only*. It led into a neat kitchen diner-cum-rest area, designed for the overnight staff, when such had been required in the past. The 1940s theme was made complete with the warm sound of an old valve phonograph playing a Dan Spelling album.

Whereas Elizabeth catered for the outdoor adventurers and backpackers, I knew this was more Freddy's domain. He was over by the original 1870s wood-burning range, stirring something in a pot, the smell of which was driving my stomach crazy.

Even leaning over the stove he came across as being tall and imposing. In fact, if it wasn't for the hint of straw yellow in his close-trimmed beard and hair, and his pale blue-grey eyes, he could have easily been mistaken for an albino. We got along, but I suspected our relationship was based on mutual toleration, rather than from any deep felt respect of each other.

He turned his head, looked at me, made a bleating *Mmm-ma-a-a-a-a* noise, then went back to stirring whatever was in the pot.

From a connecting room, Elizabeth called out a reprimanding, "Freddy, stop that!" before she walked back in. She'd changed out of her leathers, and had decided to go with faded jeans and a red and navy blue checked shirt of brushed cotton.

It was only her hair, and the canvas mules, which stopped her from looking like an extra from some hillbilly hoedown.

Scowling comically at Freddy's back, she went over to an old pinewood sideboard and opened a couple of drawers. She lifted out three placemats from one and a handful of cutlery from the other and handed them all to me.

"You set the table while I sort out something to drink."

Organising the round parlour table made me realise just how much I'd missed the company of friends since the break-up. The easy way we moved around each other, the mutual, complementary interaction, the comfortable silence between us, seemed to highlight my emotional downturn.

Elizabeth poured iced water into three glasses, and set them down in the centre of the table by a basket of yellow cornbread. She helped Freddy bring the rest of the meal to the table, and when both were seated we all started eating.

The stew was thick and rich, the meat and vegetables complemented by the bread, and the three of us were alone with our respective thoughts for a while. To fill the silence, the phonograph's auto-changer creaked and clunked, then dropped another album onto the turntable. Through the comforting hiss of worn vinyl, Susan Naidine's smoky voice told sad stories of betrayal, misadventure, "*and a love gone bad.*"

Halfway through the second track, Freddy slowly broke the silence between the three of us. To no one in particular he gave a brief rundown of his day. He'd set the gun club up with their usual Saturday morning bullet-fest, organised a franks and beans post-devastation lunch, and had arranged for a guy to come out and do the annual furnace and boiler checks. Apart from that it was all business as usual.

Elizabeth dabbed the corners of her mouth with her napkin, took a sip of iced water, then smiled.

"Okay, that brings us to Harry's problem." She looked at me. "Hopefully you've worked out a solution?"

I figured it was now or never. "I'm going to find Preston Llyle and get him to turn against Tylor."

Freddy made a snorting sound, but Elizabeth glared him into silence.

Taking a deep breath, I continued, "I have to keep Tylor from killing me. I have something he wants – those pictures and videos. I need to convince him he's safe, and provided he leaves me alone, then we're not a threat to each other. I've got to make sure he doesn't think I've dissed him too much, otherwise he's going to turn this into an honour thing."

Despite the strain, Freddy remained silent. Elizabeth said, "Okay, makes sense so far, provided you can get Llyle to flip. What if he doesn't?"

"Then I have to take Tylor out, for my own protection, and to stop him dealing in Hell-knows-what."

She looked thoughtful. "How are you going to meet him and convince him you're harmless?"

"I've let him know I've got what he's after. I'm assuming this afternoon's calling card is from him, as he's the only guy I've got real friction with. If I leave myself open, he'll either come to me, or make contact and invite me into his parlour."

From across the table Freddy bleated again, holding out his hand, palm up, to Elizabeth. She pulled a $50 bill from the top pocket of her shirt and placed it into Freddy's waiting hand.

"Don't be such a smug bastard, okay?" Looking over to me she explained, "Freddy bet me fifty you'd play the sacrificial goat. That's why he's been making those noises all evening."

Freddy closed his hand, brought his fist up under his nose and sniffed noisily. "Ah! The sweet smell of success!" He gave his clenched knuckles a soft kiss then put the money into his shirt pocket. Despite my emotions, I felt myself smiling with them.

Later, I helped Elizabeth clear the table, then sat again while Freddy got the coffee. Elizabeth rested her elbows on the table and leaned towards me. "As a favour I can give you some backup for a couple of days. Say until Saturday, eight o'clock. That's as a no-strings favour. After that, I'm going to have to look after our bookings. Sorry, Harry, but without clients, Freddy and I don't survive the winter."

I knew where she was coming from. Still, it was nice of her to do something for me. I smiled a little. "I take it that's not on sale or return either?"

She smiled warmly back at me. "Damn right on that."

Freddy came back with coffee and for a while the three of us exchanged chit-chat and town gossip before it was time to head back home.

When I finally parked at the top of the drive, deliberately blocking the entrance, the dashboard clock read 01:25. It had been one hell of a long day. Tomorrow I was sticking myself in the line of fire to lull Tylor into a false sense of safety. Mmm-ma-a-a-a-a-a.

As I walked to the front door, the security lights came on. From high on the third level, the laundry still hung from the rooftop lines. First thing tomorrow. I didn't have the energy for anything more than a shower and bed.

14

I slept late, until 07:30, and hit my exercise regimen with a vengeance born of anger and frustration. That wasn't usually a good combination to have as motivation, but on something as mindless as physical exercise, I found it was cathartic to simply vent it all in one session.

Showered and shaved, I slipped into a clean pair of jeans and a lemon yellow polo top. It had what was supposed to be a crocodile over the left breast, but to me it looked more like a miniature road-kill frog. Wasn't there a designer label that meant "expensive dead lizard" in some obscure Aztec or Mayan tongue? Mentally debating how I would score on a Rorschach test, I fixed myself an OJ and coffee breakfast, then dropped down to the living room and turned on the radio.

"This is your Morning Coffee Show, and I'm Robbie Moore, the boy next door, telling you we've got the news, sports, travel and the weather, all at the top of the hour. But, before all that, here's Ruth and Terri Anderson to tell you all about having their appendixes removed!"

As the Anderson sisters launched into one of the all-time worst recordings of *The First Cut Is The Deepest*, I contemplated having the boy next door castrated. Apart from the sheer pleasure it would bring to the local community, myself included, it would also help prevent the obnoxious lifeform from attempting to breed with humans.

By the time the song had finished, I'd psyched myself up enough not to put the problem off any longer. It was time to get back to locating Preston Llyle. I'd been tangled up with other things, which had pushed him down the list of priorities. Needing to find him myself, put a whole different focus on things. Leaving aside trying to convince him to go to the city police and make a sworn statement, I wondered just how close the Llyle family was with Tylor's parents. Would influence and family loyalties be a governing factor?

There was the added advantage of Elizabeth. Knowing, for the next couple of days, I would have my own guardian angel to watch over me, certainly took some of the tension out of the thought processes.

The Andersons had segued into the Bob South Ensemble, and their take on the old classic, *Mack The Knife*, when the phone rang. I picked it up, but before I could say anything more than a cursory, "Hello?" the voice at the other end said, "Your carriage awaits."

On cue there was a firm and decisive knocking on the front door. In my ear, Karrel's voice continued, "You're getting your ass hauled to my office."

The knocking sounded again, firmer than before, followed by a muffled voice shouting, "Police! Open up!"

I opened up, then told the two patrol officers to wait while I picked up a fresh jacket. When I was good and ready, I locked up, set the alarm and took a ride into the city in the back of a Crown Vic black & white.

Normally, in less populated country areas, it's not so easy to spot a car tailing you, because every driver was headed in either one direction, or the other. But after a while, seeing the same graphite silver Taurus in the drivers' rear-view mirror, I started to get curious. More so when it kept pace with the black & white as the traffic in our lane closed down to a morning crawl, and other drivers opted for the more free-flowing lane beside us. It looked like a fairly new model and, with the tinted windshield, I couldn't tell how many passengers were with the driver. Then sunlight came in through an open window, backlighting the windscreen. There was a passenger alongside the driver, and both didn't look much like Elizabeth.

Part of me wanted the warm and fuzzy feeling that Elizabeth was also somewhere, watching my back, even though I'd not seen any sign of her. Another part remembered the baseball incident and thought about getting even. Mentally I made a note to pick up the .38 revolver and shoulder rig from the office the first chance I got.

The patrol car finally stopped in front of the white stone Central Police Headquarters building on North Rochester. From the back seat I watched the Taurus make a late left down a side street and disappear from view. I relaxed a little. At least I wasn't going to be the victim of another mid-town drive-by. Hopefully.

The patrol officers waited in silence for me to get out, then drove off again, while I hung around on the sidewalk for a minute or so, searching the traffic. Finally convinced the Taurus wasn't just circling the block, I headed towards the entrance. There was nothing to be gained by just walking off and antagonising Karrel. In fact, I was going to need a sympathetic ally if I was going to successfully use Llyle to put Tylor away. That aside, I was sure Karrel was watching from some vantage point, or had someone keeping tabs on me. If I didn't see him now, he would just call out for another piece of my ass on rye, only next time it would be with a large side order of relish. We might not have liked each other, but that didn't mean we didn't have any respect for each other.

I walked up the steps, and in through the main public doors. The front desk was twelve feet back from the entrance, and several substantial pinewood benches lined the walls. When the morning sunlight shone in through the high windows, the foyer often brought up memories of Sunday church, back when I was a child. The pews, like the pine benches, had been scarred by graffiti and carvings, scratched into them over the years. One of the two payphones was being used by a painfully thin white woman in her mid-twenties. Not so much heroin chic, more a case of the real thing. She was dressed in a tight halter top, which did her small breasts no favours, and washed out low-rider jeans which hung just below the waistband of her lime green thong. Judging from the inflamed state of her navel, her body piercing was fairly recent, and in desperate need of TLC, rather than being displayed for public scrutiny. Bristling with attitude, she glared at me as I walked passed, and asked no one in particular, "Can I get a bit of fuckin' privacy here? Huh?! Can I?!"

I sighed and shifted my gaze along the wall to a cork board with a mass of brightly coloured posters. They were the usual warnings about the dangers of solvent abuse, car crime, and the need for home security. The corner nearest the phone was decorated with business cards for several bail bondsmen and cheap-rate lawyers.

I headed towards the wire mesh and bulletproof glass front of the booking desk, and nodded my head sociably at the silver-haired sergeant.

"Hi, Wendle."

Wendle Reece nodded back without looking up from filling

in some paperwork. "Hi Harry. Go on up, he's expecting you. He's pissed off with you, as per usual." He slipped a hand under the counter and pressed the door release button. "When are you gonna realise, Harry, you don't go poking a bear when you've only got a short stick?"

I looked at him with my best silent movie shock-horror expression. "I'll thank you not to make my sex life public!" Then pushing open the reinforced security door, I made good my movie-star exit and walked into the Headquarters.

Behind me, Wendle shouted out in a tired voice, "You know that's not what I meant, you asshole," which was closely followed by the woman on the phone loudly asking, "Can I get some fuckin' privacy, or what!?"

At the end of the hall was a flight of stairs which switched back on itself, then kicked at an angle before it spread out into a small hallway. From there, the passage led into the Investigations Division of the Major Crimes Unit. It was a large space, with cream-coloured walls, mottled grey linoleum, and a suspended ceiling with fluorescent strip lighting set into it. Despite repeated refurbishments, paint jobs and the general smoking ban, the ghosts of cigarettes past still managed to haunt the building, and would no doubt remain long after the building had been consigned to history. The open plan work area was crowded with a dozen or so desks, carefully positioned so that two officers could share one workstation space. Some had called it an efficient utilisation of space. Others had voiced the truth and called it cheapskating. No one immediately looked up when I entered the area – they had other, more important, things to do and usually never enough time in a day to do them.

On the opposite side was a row of four small offices, and

Marty was waiting for me outside Karrel's. He lifted his right palm up and gave me a slow Sesame Street wave, only his face wasn't wearing the matching smile.

I didn't wave back, just headed towards him as he opened the office door. He waited for me to pass through, then stepped in behind me and closed the door. Karrel was sitting behind the small metal and plastic desk, glowering at his fingers as they impatiently drummed on the desktop. To his right was a portable media suite: TV, video machine and a DVD recorder in a simple sit-up-and-beg style utility cart. To his left, standing with his back to the window, was the imposing figure of Julius DuMont. He was a large black detective, who I had seen around with Marty from time to time. Despite his shaven head and the hints of white in his close cropped beard, I'd watched him perform at a charity kick-boxing display, and knew better than to take his laissez-faire attitude at face value.

With Julius, Marty and myself in the small room, Karrel Johansen appeared almost fragile and delicate – like a fourteen year old in a business suit. But when he spoke, the controlled anger and authority in his voice dispelled the illusion.

"Sit down, Rhimes, and shut up."

Marty moved behind me, took a chair from the corner and put it between myself and Karrel's desk. Dutifully I sat down and waited for Karrel to make the first move.

Looking up from his drumming fingers, he said, "Marty's briefed me on what you've told him, so let's see if you can spin the same bullshit twice. What's your involvement with the Llyle family and Lindsey Fairfax?"

I tried not to look over at Marty, as I knew Karrel was instinctively reading body language, and would be judging my reactions. "Well," I started, then told him about the initial meeting in my office, and the last time I saw her at her apartment, all the time trying to keep track of Karrel's aggressive questions. I mentioned the number of times I'd tried to contact her, and the fact I had originally planned on handing over my report, then dropping the case myself. I left the unfinished business with Harrison Tylor for a later date, once I'd worked out a way of sorting it out myself.

"If you don't believe me then check her voicemail. There should be a couple of messages from me, provided she didn't erase them."

Julius DuMont cleared his throat and gained my attention. "That's one of the reasons you're here now. So how far did you get with finding the Llyle kid?"

"Nowhere. What with tracking down Greagson, and finding out Weams was dead," – Karrel looked sharply at Marty as I carried on – "I've not had the time to hunt the guy down. It's not like she had been paying me for the leg work."

Karrel snorted in disbelief. "You're telling me you took this job for free? Hmmm, lemme guess, she put out to seal the deal?"

I knew it was coming, and I'd tried to be ready for it, but I still felt the surge of anger. "No, she didn't. Unlike your mother."

Karrel gave me a strained grin. "She's got to supplement her pension somehow, so why not with jerkoffs like you?"

There was a rumbling sound from Marty. "K-rist!" It was followed by a heartfelt sigh. "Can we get this pissing contest over with, and get back on track?"

It was what we both needed to clear the air and I sat back in the chair, breathed out heavily, and tried to relax. To no one and everyone I said, "Sorry. Guess I'm getting defensive. I just felt she was a good kid who was in need of a break."

Julius DuMont moved away from the window and came towards me. "Was?"

The tone of his question confused me. "Yeah." I looked at Karrel. "That's what this is all about, isn't it? I saw on the news last night she'd been murdered." I glanced over at Julius, then at Marty for some kind of confirmation, but their expressions were unreadable.

Still confused I turned and faced Karrel again. "In her apartment, last night. Beaten to death, or so the news reporter said?"

"Really, Sherlock? Then I wonder how you explain this?"

On the media suite the television screen flashed into life, showing the ground floor lobby and elevator area of Lindsey Fairfax's apartment block in poor contrasting monochrome. The time code in the bottom right hand corner was spinning faster than a New York taxicab meter, while people jumped and danced across the screen in staccato animation. Karrel's finger stabbed the Play button and the time code froze, then started forward again at its regular pace. For several seconds the lobby remained empty, then two people came into view. The camera was high, giving a slanting viewpoint, but even from that angle I could still make out Margaret Llyle, accompanied by a younger man. The counter sped up, then slowed down again to show the lobby 40 minutes later. The same man appeared out of the elevator, only instead of Margaret Llyle, he was shepherding Lindsey Fairfax out of the building.

Karrel jabbed at the remote again and the playback paused, trapping both of them in a blurry pose. His voice cut across the silence in the room. "Tell me, Rhimes, does she look dead to you?" His thumb went into overdrive on the frame rewind button and the two jerky figures walked backwards into the elevator again. A prod of his thumb and the two of them started to walk out again, only this time Karrel halted the action and zoomed in on the centre of the screen. Lines, definition and contrast all became pixilated, but it was clear there was an irregular pattern across Lindsey's blouse – as if someone had taken a wide paint brush, dipped it into a pot of paint, and flicked it at her several times.

As comprehension finally dawned on me, I said, "So the woman beaten to death in Lindsey's apartment was–"

"Margaret Llyle," Marty Beddows finished off for me.

I turned away from the screen. "How's Roger Llyle taking this?"

Karrel pushed himself away from the desk and stood up. "That's none of your business, Rhimes." He moved around the desk to get closer to me. "Both Llyle and Fairfax are prime suspects and the last thing this investigation needs is you pissing in the evidence pool. So, if I, or Marty, or Julius, finds so much as a single new tippy-tappy footprint belonging to you, we'll shut you down so fast they'll hear the sonic boom down in L.A."

I stood up, nodded sociably to Marty and Julius, then walked out of Karrel's office. Agreeing with the enemy was often the best psychological form of attack, even though it wasn't intentional. I wanted to get away from Lindsey Fairfax and the whole Llyle family, or what little remained of it, and concentrate on Harrison Tylor.

I'd made it half way across the MCU squad room when I heard Karrel shout from his office door, "I'm not kidding, Harry! Don't get involved, because this is high profile now!"

I crossed the other half of the large work area and the hallway in silence, while a dozen pairs of eyes watched me leave.

15

The young woman with the inflamed navel was nowhere to be seen as I walked back out into the sunlight. I stopped and scanned the traffic, looking for signs of the grey Taurus, then realised I was making more of a target of myself. I trotted down the steps to the sidewalk and headed towards the Kincade Building. By the time I'd walked a block, I knew I was being tailed.

He was around five-ten, short cropped black hair, sharp nose and a pinched mouth. He was neatly dressed in a blazer and slacks, which gave him a classic preppy look, though he was certainly in his mid to late 30s. His walk-past-then-hang-back technique was good and I never once caught him making eye contact. But it was his lack of confidence which kept him too close when he should have hung back more and not repeatedly flickered in and out of my peripheral vision.

So, like a pair of bees, we waggle-danced the remaining few blocks down Chancery until we got to the Kincade Building. I walked into the main lobby, taking my time and stopping by the reception desk to say 'Hi' to the security guards. I kept shooting the breeze as I casually turned round to look back and check the entrance. But the guy had more sense than to follow me in. Still smiling and chatting, I watched as he hung back near the doorway, checked his pants pocket for something he didn't have, then walked past the glass doors – disappearing into the general flow of mid-morning pedestrians.

I felt myself relax a little and I waited by the elevators for an empty car to haul me to the sanctuary of the 10th floor.

Stepping into the reception area, I waved a sunshine bright good morning to Michelle. She smiled back and wiggled the fingers of one hand while her other jotted down the details of the new caller in her headset. Darlene looked up from her keyboard, smiled broadly, and treated me to a sentence or two in Sicilian. It roughly translated as my mother was the cheapest whore in the whole of the city, and my father was more renowned for sexually molesting his goats rather than herding them on the mountainside. After that she went back to her typing. In keeping with the cosmopolitan spirit of things, I said, "Grazie!" and walked through the open plan maze to my own inner sanctum.

Closing my office door, I leaned back against it, shut my eyes and let out a sigh. I needed wits and mental clarity if the next part of the dog and pony show was going to be a success.

From the filing cabinet I took the lock box, opened it, unwrapped the Chief's Special from the oilcloth, and did a five-second weapons check to make sure it was okay. I fished out the shoulder rig, slipped it on, dropped the .38 into the holster and made sure the revolver was free and unobstructed by the jacket. I've never felt comfortable with an ankle holster or a waistband clip, and keeping a snub-nose loose in a pocket was just asking for trouble.

The Browning, with its magazine of thirteen rounds, was still under the seat in the Chrysler, but there was no way I was going to go back and collect it. So, for extra insurance, I took out a speed loader, checked the release worked okay, loaded it with ammunition and slipped that into my jacket pocket. The Airweight was only good for five rounds, but speed loaders gave you a time advantage over reloading by hand.

I looked out at the building opposite. Maybe things were different in Window World? Maybe in that reality I was able to settle down, find a simple dead-end job, and coast into old age on a wave of apathy.

Back in the real world, I slowly shook my head. "Live fast, die young; leave a good-looking corpse." And hey, I *was* still young, damnit! Hell, only last week hadn't Darlene called me childish and infantile?

Time to get heavy on some butt-wipe dude's ass!

Or something like that.

Down in the main reception area, I dithered and dallied several times near to the glass fronted entrance. A minute or two of light conversation with the security guards provided additional cover while I casually checked the sidewalk. Nothing suspicious. I started flicking through a magazine from a stack on a side table, walking around as I discovered what joys *Biomechanic Weekly* had to offer. When I'd finished skimming through an article on bio-luminescence as a means of data transference within an organic A.I. construct, I felt I'd advertised my presence long enough.

With no sign of any cruising Taurus, I left the Kincade Building and headed off towards Bicentennial Park. If I kept myself to open, public places, I figured the chances of violent confrontation would be reduced. I'm not anti-violence per se. Just anti-violence when it's used against me.

I made the short distance to the park without spotting anyone obvious, sat on a bench in front of one of the displays, and spent ten minutes in contemplation of a partially coloured mural. It was another conflict piece, though this time it was from a series of scenes found on a shard of ancient Greek pottery. Nude young men with artistically small genitalia competed in energetic sporting or hunting events. Some appeared to be runners or sprinters, others threw javelins at wild boar, and one appeared to be reaching backwards prior to launching a stone from a slingshot.

"That was why he got the nickname Mighty Mouse. His balls had shrunk to the size of peanuts and his dick was like this." Then Martinez had told me about Preston's dangerous mood swings.

So was that what'd happened at Lindsey Fairfax's apartment? Margaret Llyle wasn't likely to have battered herself to death, and there was no way I'd mistaken the woman on the security video. It was Lindsey Fairfax who'd left the building with Preston, and it appeared to be without any duress. Then there were the marks on her blouse. Although I didn't have any scientific evidence, it was a pretty good assumption they were blood splatters. Still, I had a hard time believing she'd been actively involved with Margaret Llyle's death.

So what of the indistinct fourth person in the videos?

I took the new cell phone out of my pocket, flipped it open, and called Dixie's number. Two rings then a recorded message kicked in:

"Leave your name and number after the tone, otherwise I just won't know who to phone!"

"Dixie, it's Harry Rhimes. When you've a spare moment I'd like to talk."

Message left, I closed the phone, slipped it back in my pocket and went back to contemplating the artwork.

About five minutes later my right leg started singing Classy Jay's "Byron Rap."

"I'm a champagne junkie,
It's got sparkle and fizz!
My po-et-tree is real funky –"

With speed driven by embarrassment, I fished out the cell, flipped it open and answered. It was Dixie returning my call.

"What's with the new burner, Ace? If I find out you've been getting your tech from some other sugar bowl, well...," she broke into a throaty chuckle.

That made me smile. Sometimes that's all you need as a pick-me-up. "It's a piece of cheap Chinese junk, Dixie. A guy on a street corner sold it to me for a dollar."

"Ha! You wish! Whatever. You want to know if I can clean up those two video files, right?"

"Am I that predictable?"

" 'Fraid so, Ace. I've been able to scrub some distortion and noise from the sound, but this isn't my speciality. It didn't give us anything new anyway – what's scrunched is scrunched."

"Is there any chance you could enhance the woman? I need to find out who she is – or something about her, at least."

"I can try, but I wouldn't get too hopeful if I were you. When do you want the results?"

"This evening will be fine. I've still got some work to deal with first."

"Well, whatever it is, just be careful, okay?"

"I'll be careful. But, hey, thanks for the concern."

"Just remember, Ace, I don't look good in black." With that she hung up.

I started closing the phone when it started singing again, only this time the caller ID showed as E. I put it back to my ear.

"Hi?"

Elizabeth's voice came on the line. "Isn't it about time you got off your butt and picked up that tail again?"

Reflexively I started to look around the area to see if I could spot where she was. "I didn't know you were with me already."

"Harry, you left your house in a police car. You were tailed by a rental, so no point in following that up. You had an appointment in Central HQ, left, picked up a tail on foot, went to your office, paraded yourself to no avail, then came out to the park. Since then you've been sitting looking at some display, and made one phone call. As long as the phone stays on, I've got you on GPS. All I've got to worry about is the opposition, and your talent for getting into trouble."

I put a hand up, shaded my eyes and looked around, trying to find her.

In my ear she said, "Do you know how weird that makes you look? Do what you need to do to psyche yourself up, but we need to get things moving, starting with that tail you picked up." There was a "bu-bloop" sound and the connection ceased.

I changed the ring tone, closed the phone, and took one last look at the mural. Time to go on the hunt.

16

I spotted the guy as he waited for me on the corner of the Kincade Building. If I'd not known what I was looking for, then I might've easily mistaken his blazer and slacks for regular service staff, or some PA firm uniform. He'd picked a good spot, and was mingling with the few cigarette smokers who haunted the side entrance, using them for cover. His pinched mouth was puckered slightly in concentration as he scanned as much of the pedestrian traffic as best he could. That was my problem as well. For what I wanted to do I didn't need crowds of people.

I walked past the front of the building, heading towards him, and deliberately looked through him as if I was lost in my own thoughts. Then without breaking step, I turned and crossed the street at the corner, the lights, thankfully, in my favour. He caught the move, just in time, and made it across with me. Not bad, considering it was from a standing start.

We carried along Chancery for a block, and I made things as easy as I could. I'd stop every so often to check for keys, take a fake cell phone call, anything to help him keep up, without giving the game away.

After a block I felt it was time to step it up a notch, and ducked into the nearest department store. I mingled with a group of business-suited shoppers who seemed to be on an outing, then came back out several minutes later. It was simple enough to make sure he spotted me before moving on. Disappearing out of his sight would pump some adrenaline into his system, while picking me back up would make him relax and let his endorphins kick in. Just like playing a fish. Give it little line, then reel it in some before you give it a little more line again.

A little further down, and into another store. This time I waited until he'd walked in before I moved out again, deliberately not noticing him. Judging by the frustration on his face, I was getting him into a less than professional frame of mind. I figured the next time would be right.

Almost at the bottom of Chancery, I ducked into a side alley and ran for a couple of seconds to put distance between the two of us. That meant he had to make a snap decision. Either follow me all the way, or let me go, because if I turned around and saw him, I'd be suspicious for sure. I was banking on his eagerness overriding his common sense – choosing to follow, rather than cautiously hanging back.

The other end of the alley opened out into a crowded side street full of panel trucks and flatbeds, picking up and dropping off. I waited just long enough to get my bearings, and to let him keep sight of me, before I headed off through the delivery mayhem. From chaos there is order, but I still ended up weaving around people who were carrying boxes and crates, or pushing clothing rails into the back rooms of stores.

Down another side alley which ran between two windowless buildings, and eventually funnelled out into a small, seemingly forgotten, public square. It was surrounded by 1950s-style apartment buildings, their balconies facing inwards, giving the whole place an arena-like quality. Some of the flagstones were cracked and uneven, and some of those in the shadows were wet and green from leaking air conditioners. In the middle of the square was someone's concept of artistic relief. In the centre sat a disused three-tiered fountain, circled by several weather-worn park benches. At one time someone had tried to turn the fountain into raised flowerbeds, but little seemed to have survived.

I hurried to the back of the fountain, faced the alleyway, and carefully withdrew the .38. Seconds later, the guy came jogging into view, then stopped at the edge of the alleyway and looked around the square. When we made eye contact I stepped to one side. Still holding the revolver loosely down by my side, I waved it a little, allowing the movement to attract his attention and letting him know I had the upper hand.

In a calm voice, I said, "Okay, now step a little closer so we both don't have to shout." He didn't move, so I put my thumb on the revolver's hammer, and slowly cocked the weapon. I had no doubt he was carrying, and for all I knew he might've been more than happy to use it without provocation. But then, if you're not prepared to use a weapon, there's no point in carrying it in the first place. Thankfully he saw sense and moved a little closer.

I nodded my appreciation. "Now, take out your phone."

He looked at me and half smiled. "Aren't you a little old to be mugging people for cell phones?"

"Strangely enough, that's what my therapist says." I continued to smile, tilting my head a little while still holding the revolver down by my side. "She also says I could bang you here and now, and be away before the echoes fade. Now, five will get you ten, whoever hired you really doesn't give a wriggling rat's furry ass-crack whether you make another sunrise or not. They'll just tell someone, to tell someone, who'll go and tell someone else even further down the food chain, that some of the chump bait got eaten by the shark. That's me, the shark. And someone else will take your place."

He looked pained. Maybe I'd offended his sense of worth? Maybe it had been an epiphany for him? Like I really cared? Very slowly he unbuttoned his blazer, and pulled the left side out and away from his body. It gave me a clear view of the inside pocket, and let me see the clip-on holster hanging from the waistband over his left hip. The little black automatic looked mean and efficient snuggled in the leather pouch. With his right hand he carefully dipped into the pocket and came back up with a slim black Smartphone.

"Now what do you want me to do with it?"

I sighed. "Just make the call."

He tried for confused. "Call?"

"Yeah, call Harrison Tylor. Tell him I want to meet up. Today. As soon as possible." I was already feeling a little exposed. I had no doubt we were drawing attention, and while I suspected the tenants didn't get involved with their neighbours' lives, I was pretty sure one of them would eventually call the cops on us.

He started to play dumb again. "Who?" But when I wiggled the .38 down by my side, and slowly shook my head, he'd thumbed the touchscreen several times, tapped on an entry, then carefully brought the phone to his ear.

"Mr. Tylor, it's Michelson, sir. Yes, sir, I am. Yes, we do seem to have a situation. No, sir, Mr. Rhimes is unharmed, at present." Michelson looked pointedly at me, then continued. "He wants to meet with you, sir. I can appreciate that, sir. No, sir, this was not a scenario I could have foreseen. Twelve-thirty? Not a problem, sir. Yes, sir, I'll make sure he is treated with the utmost courtesy. Goodbye, sir."

Crisp, organised, efficient. I suspected my taking control of the situation wasn't going to sit easy with Michelson for quite some time. But he didn't let it show.

"Mr. Tylor will be lunching at twelve-thirty, and requests you join him." He nodded and indicated his outstretched left hand still holding his blazer, and his right hand still holding the cell phone close to his ear. "May I?"

I shook my head. "Just keep 'em where they are." I walked over and lifted the automatic from his hip, popped the magazine and let it fall to the flagstones. Always better to be safe, because by the time you get shot, it's too late to be sorry. Dropping his gun back into its holster, I patted him down quickly, just to make sure he wasn't carrying any other little surprises. Satisfied, I stepped away, picked up the magazine and slipped it into my pocket. With my .38 back in the shoulder rig, I nodded to him. "Okay, now you can put your hands down."

He re-buttoned his blazer then thumbed through the smartphone entries until he found what he was after, and jabbed it with a finger.

"Scoot? Change of plan. Now we've got to deliver this guy to our client. No, he'll call you with the location. I don't know. We're in a square, called…." Michelson looked around for a street sign. "I'm not sure, somewhere off Chancery. Look, we'll pick you up on the corner of Pico and Western. Five minutes or less. Well, if we're not, then just hang around for us, okay?" There was an angry edge to Michelson's voice. Nobody liked it when a plan fell apart.

He slipped the Smartphone back inside his jacket and looked at me expectantly. I turned slightly, pointed to an exit, then dropped in behind him when he moved down the alleyway I'd indicated. It opened out into another side street, which dog-legged us over to Western. Heading towards Pico, it wasn't difficult to spot the Taurus with its distinctive colour and tinted windows. In the back of my mind I felt reassured that Tylor had wanted to see me so readily. If he'd just wanted me dead, then something would've happened long before he'd paid someone to tail me.

As we approached the car, I caught Scoot checking the situation in the rear-view and side mirrors, and I wondered if he would say anything to Michelson later. Somehow I doubted it, if he had any sense.

Scoot started the engine as we got in – Michelson in front, and me in the rear – then gently nosed the car out into the late-morning traffic.

He drove carefully, all the while cheerfully tapping his fingers against the steering wheel in time to some song playing inside his head. He seemed a few years younger than Michelson, his dark hair fashionably long over his collar and ears, but professionally feather cut and not cheap. He wore a lightweight off the rack two-piece suit, white shirt and plain coloured tie. Coupled with his office junior persona, I didn't think he would've looked out of place at a corner hot-dog stand, or in a queue at a local deli. Picking up sandwiches to go, to be eaten al-desko while he answered the phone or updated his Facebook page.

The more we moved out to the suburbs, the easier traffic became. I settled into the back seat and watched the scenery go by in an attempt to relieve the boredom. Failing dismally, I tried conversation.

"I take it you guys work for Harrison Tylor?"

Michelson remained predictably silent, but glared at Scoot when the younger man said, "No. We're private, like yourself."

"Really?"

"Yeah, we're from Sacramento. Mr. Tylor reckoned you might know someone local, so he went out of town for – hey! Stop that!" The car swerved a little as Michelson tried unsuccessfully to rabbit punch Scoot into silence.

Admitting defeat, Michelson sighed. "Ah, what's the use. Yeah, Tylor hired us to keep tabs on you. He told us you were up to something – though didn't say what – and we were to follow you around, note where you went, who you saw. Just regular stuff like that. We picked you up this morning."

"I know. I saw you tailing the black and white, then lost you when they dropped me off at headquarters."

Scoot smirked a little. "See, told you he'd made us."

Michelson glowered out of the passenger window. He looked crestfallen and dejected. I didn't have the heart to tell him I'd clocked him as he'd tailed me from headquarters back to my office. Nor did I mention the fact he'd been goofing off somewhere when I'd left again, despite my best efforts to let him see me heading to the park.

I patted him gently a couple of times on the shoulder. "If it's any consolation, I didn't make you until I was coming out of a store on Chancery. That's why I cut down the alley and ambushed you in the square."

He smiled weakly. "Thanks." He knew it for what it was, but accepted the compliment all the same.

Still tapping his fingers to the silent melody, Scoot said, "Things would've been different if we were back in Sacramento, Eddie. He never would have seen us there." Turning his head slightly towards the back, he added, "Ain't that right, Mr. Rhimes?"

"Right on the money, Scoot." I let some silence happen, then asked, "Would one of you mind telling me where we're headed?"

Michelson nodded and Scoot said, "Mr. Tylor is having lunch at some golf course. Said for us to drop you off so you and he can talk business."

17

Some golf course turned out to be the Norwood, one of the more exclusive clubs the city had to offer.

Built in the late 1920s, in the heart of the city's greenbelt, it managed to retain and preserve all of its Great Gatsby charm. That, plus a solid reputation and first-class pedigree meant it could successfully ignore the upstart modern culture of instant celebrity. You wouldn't find the Norwood playing host to any flavour of the week rap artists, or the latest winner from some phone-in reality game show.

Myth and legend said it had initially been built on the same foundation stones as Las Vegas; bribery, corruption, and Syndicate money. Post-Prohibition, and with its past successfully sanitised, it had continued to cultivate an ultra-select membership. Most came to the links to relax, and maybe do a little private, off-shore, wheeling and dealing.

Such was its power and influence, that several political dynasties had successfully risen, Phoenix-like, from the ashes of failed campaigns. Some, no doubt, by the time the players had finally made it to the 19th hole.

When we pulled up to the barrier, Scoot picked up an oblong black Smartphone, opened an app, and keyed in a combination of numbers and letters. The guard stepped up as Scoot powered the window down and presented it to the guard. He checked it over, pulled a laminated tag from his top pocket, handed both back to Scoot, then raised the barrier. Hanging the new tag from the rear view mirror, Scoot dropped the car into gear and headed towards the clubhouse.

A few minutes later he'd located an empty bay in the visitor's section of a parking lot which looked to me like it took up a couple of acres, at a conservative guess.

Michelson, having found his place in the script once more, took control of the situation.

"Stay with the car, Scoot. I'll deliver Mr. Rhimes, collect our money, then we're out of here." He opened the door, adding, "We're not running a taxi service." He stepped out of the car and half-slammed the door shut behind him.

Scoot started tapping his fingers on the steering wheel again. I caught his eye in the rear-view mirror. "Don't worry, he'll get over it." I slipped my hand into my pocket, took out the magazine belonging to Michelson's automatic, and dropped it into the top pocket of Scoot's jacket. Scoot just smiled and carried on tapping something in six-eight time. I got out and followed Michelson as he headed towards the clubhouse.

Inside, we cut across the foyer without arousing interest from either Security or the club staff – another testament to our apparent invisibility – two men dressed in smart casuals, purposefully heading somewhere. Through a set of mahogany panelled doors, and we were into the club's informal dining area – an expanse of tables covered in starched white linen and decorative centre pieces of alternating silver and crystal.

The lunchtime crowd appeared to consist of the successful and self-confident, dressed in designer one-offs and custom ensembles, which advertised their wealth, even to the most casual of observers.

Mixed in amongst the membership was a generous smattering of arm candy, both male and female. Looking demure, they knew how to laugh in all the right places, though I suspected they were not entirely oblivious to the dangers of swimming with the old-school barracudas.

Off to one side, some of the large floor to ceiling glazed panels, which formed part of the far wall, had been folded back, allowing access to the decked area and the lawns. The opening gave a clear view of the surrounding landscaped countryside, and the golfing greens beyond, giving the room an almost marquee atmosphere. Off in a corner a string quartet played light classical pieces – Italian and frothy, like the cappuccinos the waiters carried on silver trays.

Michelson had a quiet word with one of the staff stationed by the main door and, as the quartet struck up an energetic rendition of Strauss' *La Viennoise*, we carefully snaked and weaved our way through the room and out onto the decked area beyond.

Harrison Tylor was seated at a table towards the edge, away from the lunchtime crowd. With his back to the clubhouse, he had a clear view across the well-kept lawns which were separated from the greens by a thick screen of trees, shrubs and undergrowth. Sitting beside him was an attractive young woman. She had the charisma of a fashion model, around 18 or 20, her make-up applied skilfully, hinting and highlighting rather than garish and dazzling. She was trim and fit, though not overly muscular. From her demeanour and the way she smiled she appeared to be confident, but the smile was superficial – looking into her eyes was like looking into the heart of an ice cube: cold and brittle.

She was wearing a designer open-neck blouse, its gentle,

golden amber colour complementing her complexion, and a crisply pleated matching skirt. It was effective, given her slim figure, and gave her a refined and coquettish schoolgirl appearance. The only thing which seemed incongruous and out of place was the distinctive tattoo half hidden in her cleavage. The stylised three entwined letter P's and the teardrop of blood – the gang mark of the Piederbeck Pussy Posse. Now disbanded, the Triple P's had been one of the first all-girl gangs to make the front pages of local and state-wide newspapers. Their history of violence and dealing was formidable, and to find even an ex-gang member at Harrison's table had me curious. In the past, it had always been the Posse who had called the shots.

Tylor was dressed in a sliver green polo shirt, graphite grey cotton slacks, with his tailored club blazer slung around the back of his chair. His tan was genuine, going up into his light brown hairline, and the skin tone helped show off his orthodontist's handiwork when he smiled. Not quite 30 years old, and already living the life of the idle super-rich.

The waiter guided me to a seat set across from Tylor and his companion, while Michelson leant forward, whispered something into Tylor's ear, then stood back, expectantly. There was no mistaking his uneasiness now. He wanted to be back in Sacramento and working on the next fee-paying job.

As I sat down, Tylor dismissively held out a long white envelope towards him. Torn between opening it and counting the money, or just pocketing it in good faith, Michelson hesitated, then pushed it into his jacket pocket. Watching Michelson's back as he left, I briefly wondered whether he thought the humiliation was worth the effort.

Tylor, his teeth white against his tan, turned back to the

table, stood up and offered his hand. "A pleasure to finally meet with you Mr. Rhimes."

I stood, reached across the table and shook hands, locking our thumbs and applying a firmer than usual pressure. If we were going to start posturing, then I figured it best to get in the first shot.

Round one over, we both sat down again.

Before I had a chance to speak, Tylor started playing host. "Ah, where are my manners? Let me introduce you to Valentina Melo."

I made eye contact and smiled. "My pleasure."

The young woman nodded, but didn't smile, seemingly going back into the contemplative silence she had maintained since I had arrived – her lips moving fractionally in time with the music coming from the main room.

Tylor rested his forearms on the table, clasped his hands together and leaned forward a little. In a slightly conspiratorial tone he said, "She's a project of mine. Her parents were beaten and hacked to death when she was still a little girl living in Cartagena, Colombia. As far as I can gather, they were mistaken for informants by members of a drug cartel. About ten years ago she managed to stow away on a number of freight and cargo ships, finally making it to Miami, where she became involved with the Hispanic gang culture. However, a few years later she turned up here, on the run because she didn't like having sex with a particular gang leader." He turned his head to look at her, "Did you."

For the first time since I'd met her, Valentina's expression changed. A seemingly innocent smile turned the corners of her mouth upwards, adding small dimples to her cheeks.

Still looking at her, Tylor continued, "She was halfway

through giving him a blow job when she cut his cock and balls off. To keep him quiet she stuffed them in his mouth and choked him as he bled to death."

She looked down at the tablecloth and said quietly, "It's true." Her expression was wistful, as if reliving a happy childhood memory, while the tip of her index finger lightly caressed the silver butter knife by her side plate.

Tylor turned back to me. "Well, with a calling card like that, she was immediately welcomed into the Triple P's. SAGE finally closed them down, back in oh-nine. I encouraged my father to think of Valentina as a worthwhile social project – rehabilitating her back into society and giving her a second chance in life. Not forgetting all the good-will publicity that such philanthropy usually generates. Are you ready to order?"

All I'd eaten had been the light breakfast, and while I didn't make a habit of dining with hyenas and coyotes, I figured the least I could do was screw a meal out of him before things got too hot.

Without looking at the menu, I said, "Certainly. I'll have a small Caesar salad to start with."

Tylor made a casual hand waving gesture and a waiter immediately approached our table. Without breaking eye contact with me, he said, "Two small Caesar salads, and the whitebait starter for the young lady." As the waiter headed back into the main restaurant, Tylor smiled a little apologetically. "You'll have to forgive Valentina, she's still a little feral when it comes to her tastes in food."

Pleasantries over, he leaned forward again, suddenly cold and business-like.

"I understand, from a late friend, you have something I want. What better than to have lunch and conduct our business in a civilised manner."

His arrogance was getting under my skin. "I don't consider drug dealing to be civilised." Memories of friends and associates whose successful careers had been destroyed by alcohol, cocaine and other addictions, fuelled my anger. "Quite the reverse, in fact."

Still staring at me, Tylor replied, "How very righteous. Especially considering your extensive combat record." He waited for me to reply. When I remained silent he continued, "Actually, I consider myself to be entrepreneurial!" He spread his arms wide – the irritating smile back in place, matched by a strange energy in his voice – as if he were a salesman making a pitch.

"Look at it out here, Mr. Rhimes. There's space. There's money. And there is a driving peer pressure for people to live a lifestyle they believe tells the rest of the world they are Successful, with a capital S! Such people don't want the ordinary, the regular, or the commonplace. No. What they want is something exclusive. Which is where I come into the equation. I'm a professional Go-To man! If you want it, and can afford it, then you come to me to get it! Satisfaction guaranteed! Let's face it, Harry, out here even granny has her own meth lab in the backyard shed. No, the only thing with any real market impact is something the locals can't grow or manufacture themselves. Exotic recreational designer compounds. And as my clientèle consists of the rich and exceedingly bored, then just like any other successful business venture, my chosen market is ripe for exploiting."

Tylor's confidence annoyed me. I considered my actions, then decided it was time to wrong foot him to see how he reacted. Smiling almost as ingratiatingly as he was, I carefully pointed to my jacket.

"May I?"

"Be my guest!"

Slowly I reached inside, took out the computer flash drive, and placed it in the centre of the table, unmistakably black against the starched white of the tablecloth. Smiling again, I said, "I think this is what you're looking for?"

Tylor's face showed confusion for a second, then the smile was back in place.

"That is a copy, right?"

Matching him smile for smile was getting painful, but I smiled back all the same. "Nope. This is exactly what I picked up from Greagson." Without pausing I took a gamble, "He wasn't all that happy to give it up, I'll say that."

"So it was you who shot him?"

"No, not my style, but–" Just then my thigh started to make a chirping noise. I looked apologetically at Tylor, then pulled out Elizabeth's cell phone, flipped it open and put it to my ear.

Elizabeth said, "Ready on your signal, Harry." Then the line went dead. Short, sweet and to the point. Except I had no idea what the hell Elizabeth had planned.

Too late to back out now. I slipped the phone back into my pocket. "As I was saying, I didn't kill Greagson. Someone put a .22 into his skull, but not me. After all, why shoot the messenger?"

Tylor looked thoughtful. "Why indeed."

Now I was as confused as Tylor obviously was. If we hadn't shot Greagson, then who the hell had? No time for that, I still needed to impress on Tylor the futility of trying to kill me.

I rested my left elbow on the table top, forearm upraised, my hand clenched into a fist. "There are three very good reasons why you shouldn't come gunning for me. One," I raised a finger, "I have more than one copy of the pictures, held by more than one person, in different locations, near and far. Email is a wondrous thing, after all." I paused for dramatic effect, then deliberately raised a second finger. "Two. Despite the incident with the baseball–"

Tylor interrupted me with a smirk, "That was fun. I wish I'd seen your face."

"Shut up. Again, two. Despite the incident with the baseball, I don't know of anything between us which would require any kind of revenge killing. Anything like that would be detrimental to both of us, expensive in money and manpower, and probably attract the attentions of the law."

Tylor nodded a little, as if conceding the point, which was a good sign. Now for the clincher.

"And lastly, three." I held up my third finger in line with the other two, and almost instantaneously two red dots of light appeared on Tylor – one on his forehead, the other on the left side of his chest.

Ignoring Valentina's sharp intake of breath, I continued, "If I really wanted to take you out, you would be face down on the table with a bullet in your head and another through your heart for good measure. By the time the cops arrived, my sniper team would be long gone, and you would just be another victim of some tedious little drug feud."

Sniper team? I had no idea who might be behind the second targeting laser, but if Elizabeth trusted them then that was good enough for me.

At Valentina's surprised gasp, Tylor's body had become tense – his left forearm immediately raised, hand open, in a rapid halting gesture. His head moved fractionally as he looked down at the tiny circle of red light, bright against the light green of his polo shirt. Deliberately he closed his eyes, then opened them again, as he carefully regaining his composure.

Looking over his shoulder and into the crowded dining room I spotted his two-man support team, one at a table to the left, the other off at a table to our right. Both young men were wearing similar style blazers to the one Tylor had draped casually over the back of his chair. The pair had rapidly stood up, drawing attention to themselves from several nearby tables, their movements frozen in the act of reaching inside their jackets as if to take out their wallets. They looked across at each other then slowly sat back down at Tylor's hand signal.

It was time for me to wrap it up and make an exit.

"Do we have a deal? If you've any sense then you'll have done your homework on me. You know my word is good, and my vengeance mighty."

Valentina turned her head away from Tylor and looked directly at me. With just a hint of a smile and a soft, gigglish laugh she started to sing part of Handel's *Messiah*:

> *"King of kings!*
> *Forever and ever!*
> *Hallelujah!*
> *Hallelujah!*
> *Ha-lay-lu-jah!"*

Her voice caught me by surprise. It sounded deeper and fuller than when she had spoken before – almost masculine – and I watched her for several seconds to see what she would do next. Originally I'd started this without any real plan, but now I had an uneasy feeling the situation was getting out of control. In the background I could hear the quartet's melodious tones as they fingered out another piece. This time it was Tchaikovsky's *Waltz of the Flowers*. During my childhood in Britain, there had been an advertising campaign for a chocolate bar, which had used the music to an irritatingly good effect. *"Everyone's a Fruit and Nut case...."*

Valentina just smiled and went back to silently stroking the silver knives by her side plate. Turning back to Tylor, I asked again, "Do we have a deal?"

Remaining calm, he pursed his lips as he weighed up the pros and cons. "You have a good reputation for keeping your word – a bit of a novelty these days, I have to admit – and in my line of business the wrong kind of attention can be fatal. If the videos are as incriminating as I've been led to believe, then yes, it would be advantageous to ensure our mutual survival. If they're not incriminating, there's no call for a feud."

"My reasoning exactly." I felt I had time for one more question, then I needed to get the hell away. "I'm still trying to find your buddy, Preston Llyle. I don't suppose you have any idea where he might be?"

Tylor gave me one of his cherubic smiles. "None at all. Maybe you should ask his mother where he is. Oh. Wait. I think I see a problem with that...."

I wasn't sure if he'd deliberately trailed off for effect, or the arrival of the starters. Either way, after the waiter had placed the salad in front of me I stood up, careful not to block the lasers, nodded politely to Valentina, then turned to Tylor. He was frowning in an exaggerated, cartoonesque way.

"You're not leaving us so soon, are you?"

"I'm just going to walk away. Once I'm clear, the sniper team will retire. But only when I'm clear."

I started to turn, about to walk off the wooden decking, when Tylor said, "Are you sure you don't want to take a doggy bag with you. Ha! Doggy bag! Bow wow!"

I turned my head to look back at him, but he was grinning inanely at me. Valentina, her hands arched above the plate the waiter had put in front of her, seemed to be more absorbed with holding a whitebait between her thumb and forefingers of both hands. Slowly she pulled the tiny fried fish apart, then almost shyly put both pieces into her mouth.

I stepped off the decking and onto the manicured lawn, trying not to appear hurried or anxious to get away from Tylor and his unsettling girlfriend. To help confuse things a little more I veered off to one side, around a clump of shrubs, and came back into the stand of trees from behind.

Elizabeth stood with her back to me, while on the top plates of two sturdy tripods were mounted the telescopic laser sights. Off to one side was a bag I knew contained her Remington 700 XCR – a very effective, compact tactical rifle.

Without turning around, she said, "The tripods are ex-thrift store, but these sights are too expensive to lose. You take the right and I'll take the left. Ready? Go!"

The on-off switch was clearly marked, and within seconds both sights were back in their protective cases, tossed into the bag with the Remington. A quick visual sweep of the immediate area to make sure it was clean, then we rapidly moved off, working our way through the overgrowth of greenery which kept the clubhouse grounds separate from the links.

Further along the boundary we picked up some more camouflage in the form of two golf bags and an electric golf cart. It might not have been the fastest getaway vehicle, but it certainly blended in.

Over the hum of the electric engine, Elizabeth asked, "How

did it go?"

"As well as could be expected, considering they both need professional help."

Elizabeth looked at me sharply. "Is that a yes, or a no? I need to know, Harry, because we can still turn around now and take both of them out of the equation. Two shots, Harry, before it's too late."

I knew she was serious. Common sense always dictated that, when it came down to personal survival, you ensured you had nothing which sounded like a maybe or a no. Only an emphatic yes ensured the continuation of the species.

"Okay, it's a yes. But...."

"You know how I feel about 'buts,' Harry. How big is this one? And don't even think about it, because I swear to God and your maker, I *will* put you in traction."

"I figure it's good for now. A year? Two years down the line? I'm not sure. When the Llyle kid gets put away, Tylor has the gang connections to make sure he becomes a statistic. Hell, there was even an ex-member of the Triple P's at the same table. It's in Tylor's long term interests."

"So all we've done is bought you some time? Great!"

I could tell she wasn't impressed. An awful lot now hinged on finding Preston Llyle and getting him to turn on Tylor. If he did, then maybe the D.A. wouldn't put up too much opposition. Perhaps even cut a deal when it came to his mother's murder. Especially if it netted Tylor and his organisation.

We trundled onto the back edge of the parking lot and left the cart in a nearby bay. Elizabeth put her bag in the back of a nondescript dark green 4x4, got in behind the wheel, and waited for me to buckle up.

As we pulled up at the security post to hand back the Visitor's ID tag, Elizabeth looked over to me. "You know I can't cover you after tonight, don't you?"

"I'll be okay. I'm not completely defenceless."

"Really? You don't say."

The security guard tapped politely on Elizabeth's window. She wound it down, handed back the tag, waited for the guard to tap her name off his iPad, then we headed off towards the 299.

18

After a while, the peppery silence between us finally got to me.

Still staring at the road, I said, "Look, I'm sorry it hasn't worked out totally the way I'd planned it. I didn't intend to screw things up, and I really am grateful for all your help in keeping my sorry ass alive. And I'm sorry for getting you mad at me."

Elizabeth finally cracked a smile and sighed in good natured frustration. "Just once, it would be nice if you took the easy route when it comes to sorting out a problem. Harry, I love you more than any of one of the half dozen brothers I often wish I never had, but sometimes you can be so damn infuriating. And you know damn well I can't stay mad at you for long. But I just wish, Harry, I just wish, for once, you listened more to your head, and less to your crackpot homespun moral code. Or whatever the Hell it is you live by."

I tapped a finger against my lips a few times. "When you say you can't stay mad at me for long, just how long are we talking about here? Y'know, on average?"

She laughed and cut loose with several expressive expletives, then punched me on the arm with her fist for good measure. From there we both lapsed into an amicable silence, and to help ease the boredom, I turned the radio on. Predictably it was tuned to a retro station. Big band dance music of the '40s and '50s. I put the volume down low and stretched out a little of the tension. When I'd finished, Elizabeth reached across and patted my forearm a couple of times. Sometimes all it takes is the smallest of gestures to make the world right again.

As the sound of *Teddy Stone and His Scintillating Strings* oozed from the car stereo, it was a mercifully short time before we parked up at the top of the track leading to my house. We did a quick check of the grounds, found nothing suspicious, so Elizabeth said she would head back to the hotel.

Settled in the 4x4 again, she wound down the window, a look of resignation on her face. "I'm not going to say be careful. You're not stupid. It's just, sometimes, I don't think you want to accept the inevitable."

I tilted my head to one side, closed one eye, and looked at her quizzically. "Would you really have put me in traction?"

She put a hand on my chest and gently pushed me backwards. "You bet your sorry ass."

I stepped back off the roadway and up onto the scrubby verge as she drove off, then watched her red tail lights flashing on and off as she headed down towards Concrete, and the Star & Belle. I looked out over the canyon at the late afternoon sun – feeling an autumn edge to the breeze. I doubted Tylor would try anything, though I was going to be careful for the next couple of days. Or at least until I'd located Preston.

The Chrysler was still at the top of the driveway, and rather than leave the access blocked, I rolled the vehicle down to the parking area. Before I got out I reached under the driver's seat and unclipped the Browning. Despite being in the car all day, the metal was cold and the grips felt clammy, psychologically still damp from the sweating palms of previous owners. Out of nowhere I thought I could smell the supple brown leather and olive green canvas webbing, mixed in with the acrid smell of the firing range, and the sound of the Range Sergeant's voice.

"Treat this weapon as you do your own. Keep it clean, safe, and test fire it regularly! But remember. Although you might not be a Catholic, in the Army, a negligent discharge is a punishable offence!"

Years later I'd read in the regimental newsletter that Sergeant Major "Shady" Lane had been killed in Bosnia. In trying to defend refugees in a church, he'd been caught in crossfire between the Serbs and the Croats.

"In the Army, Sir, you don't make friends. You only make acquaintances."

Turning the automatic on its side I popped the magazine out, then put the weapon on the passenger's seat. With a finger I checked the magazine spring as I thumbed out all thirteen rounds. They were new and relatively unscratched, not some old firing range stock which had been passed around several weapons before coming to me. I reloaded the magazine, slipped it back into the Browning, and cocked the slide. The fourteenth round jumped out, bounced off the backrest and landed safely on the passenger seat. The British Army officially frowned on keeping one up the pipe, but what you did in the field was not always strictly by the book. I reloaded the magazine with the loose round then re-clipped the automatic back under the driver's seat. With the Chief's Special in the shoulder rig still under my arm, plus the five extra rounds in the speed loader, I felt I was carrying more than enough personal firepower. Worst case scenario, there was another .38 in the gun safe in the house. And, hell, wasn't it my Constitutional Right to shoot first and ask questions later?

I walked quietly back into the house, checked through the mail, then went into the guest bedroom I'd taken to using. I was feeling less and less uneasy about returning to the master bedroom, but I'd not really had time to start moving things back. As I slipped my jacket onto a hanger and put it back on the rail, I noticed a bulge in one of the other jackets hanging up. It was the envelope containing the report I had been going to give to Lindsey. I flattened it out and put it on the bedside cabinet. That could wait. I just wanted to switch off the world and forget about life in general. I changed into shorts and a running top, pulled on some nondescript trainers, then went up to the makeshift gym.

Sixty minutes of non-stop workout against *Crotch*'s last album, *Sludgemummy* – "A veritable feast of speed-death-metal at its most nihilistic" according to *Rolling Stoned Fanzine* – left my desire for mindless exertion fairly well sated.

Showered and changed, I picked up the envelope and headed up the stairs and into the kitchen.

Napoleon was right when he said an army marches on its stomach, but it often does its thinking over a good cup of tea. I put some water in the kettle, set it on the stove to boil, and by the time the tea was brewed and poured, I was starting to consider my next moves.

I had just gotten to the part where we all lived happily ever after, when I realised I couldn't see any sign of the Richardsons' dog. I pushed open the glass door and looked around the veranda. I assumed it was down to his age, but all I'd ever seen the dog do during the day was sleep. Always in the same spot, and always in the shade created by the herbs and potted shrubs I kept in the far corner. He was never a day dog – he always preferred to do his hunting and roaming during the cool of the night.

I walked out onto the deck and called him a dozen times or

more, checking up and around the back of the house, and visually scanning the other side of the canyon as well. Still no sign of him. There was no way of telling when he'd last slept over by the railings. I tried thinking back to earlier in the morning, before the patrol had come knocking. Had he barked at their arrival?

But the more I tried to remember, the more I kept coming back to Harrison Tylor saying *"Ha! Doggy bag! Bow wow!"* as I'd crossed the golf club lawn.

I went over to railings and tried to see if he was visible near the water's edge. Again, nothing.

I started to drum my fingers on the top rail. I wasn't totally sure if Tylor possessed the cojones to physically hurt the Richardsons' dog. If anything had been done, then it had been put in motion before he and I had come to our mutually agreed impasse. Not that such thoughts made things all the more palatable for me. Far from it. But I had to acknowledge that, up to the time of our non-aggression pact, anything had, quite literally, been fair game. Only it looked like Tylor had taken advantage of better intelligence and had started to escalate things sooner than I'd thought.

I looked back at the corner. The rosemary and coriander appeared undisturbed – the accumulated windblown dust still in place around the base of their containers – and there appeared to be no marks or signs of a struggle, or any sign of blood on the wooden decking. I put the Richardsons' dog on a mental list of names, next to Bobby Weams, Evangeline Mallory, Wesley Greagson and Margaret Llyle.

You know my word is good, and my vengeance mighty.

I went over to the sink, splashed my face with some cold water, then grabbed a dish towel and dried myself off. I couldn't help feeling a touch melancholy as I picked up the envelope with the report in it, went downstairs into the living room and poured myself a small measure Armagnac.

Turning the radio on, I put the volume low, sat down and started to read through the material again. In the background the DJ played some "drive time easy listening" for those people stuck in the Friday evening chaos.

Before long I was down to the section concerning Jacqueline Llyle's death. It was obvious, despite using several forensic procedures; the time of death had been screwed from the start. Heated pools maintained body temperature after death, highlighted discolouration and bruising, which could well have occurred days before, and destroyed most trace evidence with chemicals. At least the pathologist had confirmed that the water found in Jacqueline's lungs was identical to that in the pool, so she was relatively still in situ when the 911 call was phoned in.

I was halfway down the third page when something finally pinged. I flipped back to the start and, instead of skimming through the cast list and introduction, I ran my finger down the lines until I spotted what I was looking for. Back when the incident had happened it had been a County Sheriff's call, rather than a city boundary one. So most of the investigating officers' names meant little or nothing to me. Until I found the name of Julius DuMont on the list. Not only was he down for the Scene of Crime, but his name appeared for follow-up reviews over the years, even though he was now a part of Karrel Johansen's Major Crimes Unit.

It was coming up to 16:30. I took a gamble, picked up the phone and rang Wendle Reece on the front desk. It rang several times before Wendle picked up and automatically launched into his enthusiastic, but well-worn spiel.

I let him finish, then said, "Hi Wendle, it's Harry Rhimes."

Immediately his tone changed to one of suspicion. "Oh. It's you. What can I do for you, Harry?"

"Can you pass a message to Julius DuMont? Ask him to call me back on this number." I gave Wendle my home number. I had a copy of my case notes, so discussing it over the phone wouldn't present any problems.

Wendle checked his screen. "You're in luck. Looks like he's not logged out yet, so he should be around. How urgent is this?"

"Difficult to say. Tell him I'd like to talk about Jacqueline Llyle."

"I'll pass it on."

I thanked him, then put the cordless handset back in its cradle. I wasn't sure where talking to Julius might lead, but I figured if anyone could give me a handle on the family and the boy, it was him. I stretched my legs, took a sip of Armagnac, and let it sit on my tongue for a short while – warming it through before letting it trickle down my throat. Feeling it glow inside told me it was time to eat.

Back up in the kitchen I put together some salad leaves, a French-style vinaigrette dressing, and tossed in a few cherry tomatoes for colour. The refrigerator brought forth half a cold roast chicken. Breaking off a few pieces I threw them into the bowl and mixed it up. It was light, fresh, home-made and green, therefore it had to be healthy, right?

Through the glass doors the setting sun was throwing up a backdrop of warm orange and rose, which helped lift my spirits a little. It was one of the few things I seemed to share with Dad – a fascination with nature. After he'd moved us all to London, he'd never been able to settle in the City. So, with each successive move, we seemed to go further and further into the suburbs as the years went by. All the houses had been rentals, and I had to admit that most of the places had been decidedly quirky and odd. Corridors and landings would suddenly have two or three steps to the next level. Or there would be rooms up in the eaves, with tiny round or diamond shaped windows and low sloping ceilings. Ideal places for imaginative children to let their fantasies take flight.

For Dad, though, going out into the countryside was his, then later my way of escaping the pressures of day to day living. Nature had helped when it came time for me to combat the mental chaos and battle stress of field ops and, later still, in coping with Post Traumatic Stress Disorder.

The sound of the kitchen phone broke into my reverie. I picked up the handset and, retreating into the safety of humour, said in an over-the-top Vincent Price voice, "Harry Rhimes – Investigator of crimes."

Dixie's infectious laughter came down the line. "Ha! You need some better material than that, Ace! Whatever, I've got some good news and some bad news – which do you want first?"

Still in character, I said, "Oh, why is everyone a critic? Do your worst, madam. Do your worst."

"Ah, one hundred percent, sweet cured ham on the bone. Whatever. The good news is, I was able to clean up some of the images. Bad news is, I've still got bupkis on the fourth person."

Nothing like a dead end to knock you out of the fun zone and back into reality. I sighed heavily. "I don't suppose there's any more of the good news?"

"Well, there's perhaps a scooch more. Wherever the deal

took place, it was protected by Pellman Security Services. You can see one of their big signs tied to the chain link fence. Pellman are owned by LBE – that's Llyle Business Enterprises."

In the scraps of video it had been Tylor making the sale off the back of a truck. The boxes hadn't looked heavy or awkward, otherwise Bobby Weams wouldn't have been able to move them around as easily as he had done, let alone lift them off the back of Tylor's vehicle. He'd been carrying the camera on him, so if he'd loaded them straight into another car or van, it would have been recorded as he moved the stuff around. Which meant, wherever the deal had taken place, Preston had to be storing the stuff on site – otherwise why would Tylor have gone out there. Which meant Preston had free and easy access. So, maybe, it was a place he felt no one would think to go looking for him?

"That certainly helps, Dixie, believe me. It's opened up a whole new can of ideas. You wouldn't happen to have a direct number for Roger Llyle, do you? I've got one for his personal secretary, but I'm betting that's now off-limits to me."

"Every queen geek has her nest of followers. I'll get one of my cyber-minions on it. Call you back."

Smiling, I put the kitchen phone back in its caddy, finished the chicken salad, then headed down into the living room. The drive-time slot had given way to the regular Friday evening news and sports review hour.

"...which seems to be similar in nature to the recent track-side fracas between Kathy 'Balls of Steel' Shepherd, and Vicky 'The Eraser' Cockbill. Footage from the event will be viewed by a disciplinary board next Monday. And now, one more thing to worry about: Bubonic Plague. It seems a West Texas hunter caught the disease from a flea-infested rabbit he shot, while out camping in the backwoods. A simple course of antibiotics and he was as good as new. Apparently, it says here, the last recorded case in Texas, was way back in two-thousand and four. Can you believe it? Penny! Bring us a little sanity – what's the weather going to be like this weekend?"

"Well, Carl...."

I kicked off my shoes, picked up my drink, and laid down on the couch with the envelope in one hand and the telephone down by my side. Time to go through it all again.

19

I was in that no-man's land between sleep and wakefulness, when I heard someone at the door. I went to the intercom and thumbed the button. "Who is it?"

"Lieutenant DuMont. I understand you want to talk about the Llyle case?" Then, as if to clarify which one, he added, "Jacqueline Llyle, that is."

I released the deadbolt and opened the door. "Come on through."

Julius DuMont closed the door behind him and followed me into the living room. Frankly, I hadn't expected the personal touch. I indicated one of the easy chairs as I crossed to the stereo and turned it down.

He eased himself into the armchair. "One of guys from Narcotics and Vice is off sick, so some of us are helping out with their surveillance. I'm just killing time before my stint. Plus, I've been wondering when you'd get around to talking to me."

As I sat back down on the sofa, he continued, "Marty said you'd pick up on the Jacqueline Llyle case. Either from the family or old newspaper stuff."

I relaxed. "Did he say anything else?"

DuMont's mouth curved up on one side, amused at my fishing. "You mean about the case? No. He did say I should use my own judgement though, whether I should talk to you or not. I still don't know why you and Karrel keep slugging at each other, but that's your problem, not mine. Your message said you wanted to talk about the Jacqueline Llyle case. Now, I'm still heavily involved with Margaret Llyle's murder, which is off limits." He looked at me with a wry smile. "So provided we keep the conversation to the cold case, then we won't be upsetting the Chief, will we. I take it you've still not found the boy?"

I shook my head. "He seems to have disappeared completely. If it wasn't for the security footage and seeing him with Lindsey Fairfax, then I would've said he was dead somewhere."

"The last time I saw him in the flesh he was just a teenager. Every other time I've talked to him has been either through the family lawyer, or the rare phone call. Anyway, you said you wanted to talk?"

I reached across the coffee table and handed him the package with my notes and report in it. "This is everything I have so far."

Julius settled back and shook the paperwork out onto his lap. As he leafed through the pages, I watched him for any reaction. There was nothing until he came to Elizabeth's input, which included a précis of the sheriff's report. He pursed his lips. Without looking up, he said, "Do I ask where you got this from?"

"Not really. Though I trust the source enough to know nothing's been compromised in regard to the cold case investigation. Apart from it still being open, what's your interest in it now? You're no longer with the County Sheriff." Out of curiosity I added, "What made you move from County to City anyway?"

"I come from a long line of Afro-Caribbean farmers. I'm your genuine, ethnic, third generation sod buster." Without raising his head, he looked up at me. "Back then, after the riots down in L.A., I was a public relations wet dream come true. The city chiefs made me a much better offer than what I was getting at the County Sheriff's Office. To a young guy with a family? You do the math." His gaze went back to the report.

I was still curious. "What keeps dragging you back to this? Other cops would've just dropped it and moved on by now."

"So maybe I'm not like other cops. What keeps dragging me back is the way she was found. Originally, being new to County, and this being my first real case, I kept feeling there was something not right somewhere, but it was hard to say what seemed out of place with the whole thing at first."

He put the papers back into the envelope and handed it back to me.

"After a while I finally got a handle on it. It was the fact she was found nude, but with no evidence of any recent sexual activity. She wasn't an unattractive young woman, but according to friends and house staff she'd never been one for casually flaunting her body. When I interviewed her stepmother, Margaret appeared cold towards the girl, saying Jacqueline had resented her from the outset, and communication between the two of them had been minimal at best. I doubt Jacqueline's trust in parental relationships was helped any when her birth mother finally abandoned her. Angel Llyle left her daughter with Roger while she went off to pursue an already failing modelling career. Not good for anyone's self-esteem."

He concentrated and thought back over the case.

"There was only Preston's word about the second person.

No one else had seen anything because they'd either been off shift, or stood down by Jacqueline herself. He said he only caught a fleeting glimpse, and his description was fairly vanilla. It could have fitted a whole host of kids Jacqueline knew at the time."

I decided to change direction. "What about the drugs? Did she strike you as someone who would use them out of need, or maybe out of spite towards her parents?"

. "Consensus was she would sometimes dabble. Ecstasy now and again, and the occasional High School joint. A rare upper if she was cramming late for an exam. But all the incidents which came to light were on a sociable level, as far as we could tell. Just fashion. Peer pressure can do strange things to kids."

I nodded in agreement. "At least you were able to keep working the case."

Julius held up his hands resignedly. "It's been cold for over a decade now. I get the feeling no one's interested in it any more. Not even the media"

"Jacqueline's not an angle I've been working on, but if you want to brainstorm what you've got?"

Julius nodded. "Okay, give me your feelings on the Llyle boy. Do you see him taking an empty wine bottle and beating his own mother to death?"

"I know he's prone to fits of violence, but Margaret made sure he kept to a regular therapy program. Some rehab to get him off the steroids he was hooked on."

"What makes you say that?"

"Nobody's pressed any charges for assault, have they?"

"Not as far as I know – nothing like that on his record, at least. A couple of minors, but apart from that he's pretty clean."

"What if I told you he'd severely beaten a guy when he was on an exhibition football tour?"

"And?"

"The guy's name was Andy Newhart. Llyle used a deodorant can tied into the end of a towel and just laid into the guy. Apparently the argument was over who walked out onto the field first. After the incident Margaret stepped in, calmed the Newhart family down, and promised to put Preston back into therapy."

Julius looked thoughtful. "Okay, so he's not as clinically stable as he could be, but do you think he was like that twelve years ago, when Jacqueline died?"

I started to get into the mood. "You mean what if Preston was a pre-teen psycho?"

Julius shook his head. "Nope, I don't buy it. Okay, personality, mood swings, they could be down to all the sports junk he's taken. But consider this; if you're going to put him in the role of Jacqueline's killer, then why the obvious lack of violence, whereas violent outbursts appear to be his preferred M.O.?"

I took a sip of my drink. "He didn't need to. The drugs wiped her out. All he had to do was just wait. Dragging her body out of the pool, the attempts at resuscitation, they could have hidden other signs of bruising or a struggle."

Julius shook his head. "Sorry, I still don't buy it. Any violence would be emotionally chaotic and immediate, rather than controlled, precise and premeditated."

"So you believe in the unknown boyfriend then?"

"Not at all. I think he's a total fabrication from the start."

"Based on what?" My curiosity was tweaked.

"A gut feeling. Something should have turned up at college,

or letters, or texts, emails even – some other evidence like that. She was isolated at home, yet even her best friend knew nothing about any love interests – long, short, or just casual." He was starting to become more animated. "What I don't know is why? Supposedly he was the one who brought the drugs into the house. Yet we traced the weed back to a local guy who used to sell on some of his parents' stash for comic book money. He swore blind he never passed Jacqueline so much as a toke, let alone enough for a couple of joints apiece. We only made him because he broke down during the initial interview. Apart from that everyone's alibis seemed to check out at the time."

"But you still make Preston for the murder of Margaret?"

"With his history, and what you've just told me about his violent outbursts? I'd say he's looking to be the favourite in a one horse race. Unless you think Lindsey Fairfax did it?"

I shook my head. "Not from what I've seen of her. Admittedly, it isn't much, but no, she doesn't strike me as the type. At least, not for that kind of physical violence." Of course, she might have goaded Preston into committing the murder, for whatever reason, but I left that thought unspoken. If Julius DuMont was as good a cop as Marty had implied, he would keep an open mind until hard evidence pulled him in one direction or another.

Julius checked his watch. "Time for me to head back."

As he eased himself out of the chair, I stood up, unsure as to who had gained the most from our meeting, but all the more happier now we'd had it.

Outside, watching him drive off into the twilight, I caught sight of the moon against the darkening sky. Ghostly, but full. A wolf's moon.

"Don't you run, little lady,
Don't you scream and cry!
For the Wolfman is coming...
Time to say, bye bye..."

In the psychobilly days of the late 1980s I would have paid good money to own any of The Arcadians' privately pressed records. What price now that vinyl was making a comeback?

With an involuntary shiver – no doubt due to the chill in the air – I turned round and went back into the house. As I closed the door the phone started ringing and I managed to catch it before the voicemail started in on its spiel.

"Hi!"

"Back at ya, Ace!" It was Dixie again. "Numbers, numbers, numbers. It took a little time, but Roger Llyle is one very private item, so don't blame me if these are no longer connected."

"Fine. Give me what you've got."

"Ah, be still my beating heart! Okay, pen at the ready?"

She proceeded to give me three possible contact numbers.

"I can't vouch for any of them, Ace. A guy like Roger Llyle knows how to keep himself private."

"It's more than I hoped for."

"Don't speak too soon, Ace. They might just turn out to be dead ends after all. Call me if they are, and I'll see what else I can dig up which might be useful to you. Whatever. You take care, you hear?"

"If I can't be good then I'm always careful."

She sighed. "Ah. If only that were true! Take care all the same."

"I will. Talk to you later, Dixie."

"Later, Ace."

I hung up, then hit the first one on the list. No answer. However, the second proved good. It rang several times, then a divert clicked in, and after a couple more rings it was picked up. A familiar Southern accent came on the line.

"The Llyle residence. Good evening."

Steadman's precise tones were welcome – at least it proved I had the right place.

Mustering all the diplomacy I could, I said, "Good evening Steadman, this is Mr. Rhimes. Is Mr. Llyle in?"

Steadman paused for a fraction of a second. "May I enquire what the call is about, sir?" Well, at least I still rated a sir, even though the previous meeting had not been of a smooth and pleasant nature.

"You can tell him it concerns his son."

"Very good, sir."

I was put on hold. When the sound came back it had the distinctive hollow openness of a speakerphone. In the background I could hear Roger Llyle's voice telling Steadman to bring him a little closer, then, "Mr. Rhimes. It seems you are more resourceful than I thought." Llyle coughed loudly and cleared his throat. His breathing sounded laboured, and there was a wet, phlegmy edge to his coughing.

"If you like, I can call back later." I didn't want to, but I felt obliged to make the offer in view of the old man's health.

"I'm rather surprised you were able to call me at all, Mr. Rhimes. No matter, no matter. Steadman tells me you wish to talk about my son. Have you been able to locate him?" There was a note of concern in the old man's voice, something which hadn't been there at our first meeting.

"I've not been able to track him down exactly, but I wanted to talk to you in regard to one of your business concerns –

Pellman Security Services – owned by LBE.”

“You’ve lost me, Mr. Rhimes. What has a security service got to do with Preston?”

Over the next ten minutes I talked about the video and the anonymous warehouse where the deals took place. I mentioned the murders of Bobby Weams and Wesley Greagson, and how I felt the two were related – though I didn’t mention Tylor’s name. Maybe later, if I thought the old man could help put him away. For now, though, I needed Tylor to think he was safe and secure.

“So you see, Mr. Llyle, I wanted to ask if it was possible to have a list of sites Pellman are supervising in the local area.”

There was a long silence at the other end. I could still hear Llyle breathing heavily as he thought things over. A little impatiently, I said, “Look, it’s in both our interests for me to find him and turn him over to you. That way you can wrap him up with a good legal team, rather than the city police having him before your lawyers can shut things down.”

Some of his anger coloured his reply. “Your concern for my family is very touching, but let us both stop with the pretences. What do you stand to gain out of such an arrangement? Are you looking for me to hire you? Is that it?”

I tried to keep my own rising anger out of my voice. “I’m already hired, Mr. Llyle. However, I believe your son knows the whereabouts of my client, Ms. Fairfax. I’m pretty sure if you and I work together on this, there will be less chance of Preston hurting someone else.”

Llyle considered the information. “Is he really that unstable, Mr. Rhimes? Do you feel he would actually attack Ms. Fairfax – perhaps even kill her? From what I saw this afternoon she seemed pretty compliant in following him when she left the scene of Margaret's murder." Another break as he cleared his throat, then, "I identified Margaret's body this afternoon, along with the people on the security footage. They haven't released anything to the media yet, but those jackals already know about the video. Journalists only seem to be interested in sensationalism and scandal – anything but news itself."

"So, do you think your son is guilty of murder?"

Llyle let out a long sigh. "Mr. Rhimes, I have no idea about anything when it comes to Preston." He cleared his throat again. "Okay, what is it you want from me?"

I relaxed a little. "Thank you. First, I would appreciate a list of warehouse sites which Pellman Securities have been involved with recently. I'm working on the basis that I'm looking for somewhere within easy reach. But, at the same time, somewhere that's infrequently used or even abandoned.

"Secondly, I'd like to pass over a DVD which you can pass to your lawyers. It contains a video of Preston, plus others, involved in some drug dealing. I'd like your lawyers to consider using that material to Preston's advantage, in encouraging him to testify against the others involved."

"What's to stop me from just destroying it?"

"Well, it helps to prove Preston's somewhat questionable mental state, so it should help in bargaining with the DA. You're a very astute man, Mr. Llyle. You know there's nothing to be gained from *not* passing the information on to your legal team. I take it that's still Spencer, Hartman and Spencer? They seemed pretty efficient the last time I was warned off."

"Ah, my apologies about that. That was Margaret's doing. Personally I was all for just ignoring you. I figured you would get bored soon enough, but she is–" he corrected himself, "*was*, an advocate of an attack being the best form of defence."

Another moment of heavy breathing, then, "Come by the house tomorrow morning, around ten o'clock. Steadman will see to the arrangements. Now I'm afraid I have to leave you. It's late, and old age can be a very demanding mistress."

I smiled at his humour, "In your case I very much doubt it."

There was a hint of amusement in his voice. "Are you sure you're not looking to be put on a retainer, Mr. Rhimes?" Then, obviously moving his head away from the phone, "Steadman, we're done here."

Steadman switched back to the handset. "If you could let me have the details of your vehicle, sir, I'll see to it house security is properly briefed for the morning."

I told him the Chrysler's details, agreed ten o'clock would be fine, then dropped the handset into its holder.

I picked up my glass and started to sip my way through the remains of the Armagnac. Through the closed patio doors, moonlight limned the edges of the furniture and deepened the shadows in the room – almost making the world seem black and white. If only things were really that simple. I emptied my glass, put my head back against the sofa, closed my eyes and started to think about Margaret Llyle.

As my Aunt Ginny used to say, Margaret Llyle was all "new coat and no knickers." From what little I'd seen in person, and various accounts in the press and on television, Margaret had not been a good self-publicist. In fact there was a lot of her past which appeared to be supposition rather than fact.

In Roger Llyle she had been lucky. Love might well be totally blind, but I doubted Roger would have let himself be coerced into something he didn't want. Maybe it was her assumed gold-digger past which had made her ferociously protective of her son. He was, after all, an alternative route to Roger's money. That would help explain why her relationship with Jacqueline had been so strained. Was it due to stepmother-hood, or something deeper? And with both Jacqueline and Margaret now unavailable for comment, it would be forever open to conjecture.

One of the few constants was Roger Llyle's ability to be emotionally impervious to it all, though I doubted the accident had been responsible for that paralysis as well. He had been lucid, sharp, almost predatory on the phone.

That left Preston and Lindsey. Somehow they didn't strike me as simply a failed relationship. Maybe Lindsey pushed Preston into killing his mother because Margaret had been adamantly against her? If she'd played on his insecurities and inferiority complex, then maybe she'd wound him up enough to have another explosive, violent outburst?

I looked at the clock by the stereo system. It was heading toward midnight. As I hauled myself up off the sofa, I could feel a slight ache in my thighs, shoulders and biceps. Next time, perhaps not so aggressive in the gym. I walked outside and stood on the pathway running around the base of the house. The moon was high and full. A wolf's moon indeed – gibberishly gibbous.

Resisting the temptation to throw back my head and howl in frustration, I stepped back inside and carefully locked up for the night. I went to bed feeling tired and uneasy. There were things in the back of my mind which refused to come up above the mists. I didn't know what the hell they were, but I was damn sure they were important

20

I didn't immediately drop off to sleep as I'd hoped. The Bad Fairy had escaped from its jar and every time I closed my eyes my mind would crash and stumble through one failed relationship after another. Whenever I tried to make logical sense of it all, I wound up defending my actions and rewriting the break-ups with a stream of *If Only I Had Said*s. I still didn't want to pick at the scabs of the most recent failure, but I suspected it would still come down to the same root cause. Too much compromise and not enough two-way communication, for fear of destroying what little was actually there in the first place. Tiny shards of anger and resentment had festered like septic cactus barbs which wouldn't clean and heal, unless cauterised by the fire of explosive rejection. And that always brought me the escape route of Mom and Dad.

Part of me condemned Dad for not letting go. I tried to remember how I'd felt when I'd heard Mom had left for Paris, but kept coming up against an emotional void. For some reason I'd deliberately hidden those memories from scrutiny behind a mental brick wall, unable to recall them even now. Why hadn't Dad realised Mom had stopped loving him? He couldn't see her frustrations, nor understand how his successes seemed never to be enough for the both of them. Mom wanted to be successful in her own right as well.

Had either of them been wrong? The question presupposed

one of them had been right. Yet both, in their own minds, thought that what they were doing was for the best.

In contrast, the arguments between Dad and myself always seemed to have their foundations in politics, or so I thought. Sometimes, though, I wasn't so sure they were not just the result of antagonistic defiance on my part.

After several hours of tossing and turning I decided I needed some additional medication to help me relax and drop off to sleep. Usually I sleep in the raw but even so I threw on a cotton robe for the sake of modesty, grabbed a couple of pills from the bathroom, then headed off to the kitchen for some tea.

I didn't bother putting on the light when I got to the doorway – the full moon was bright enough to see by – but I stopped almost as soon as I'd stepped over the threshold. There had been the faint sound of loose dirt and stones trickling down onto the wooden planking above my head. A short pause, then the soft sound of someone landing lightly on the veranda decking above.

As quietly as I could, I headed back into the guest bedroom. On top of the chest of drawers was the shoulder rig. I pulled the .38 out of the holster, cocked it, then went back to the kitchen.

Crouching down, I mentally cursed the clear sky and bright moonlight, as the sound of movement came again. This time closer to the edge of the wall, still carelessly scattering gravel from the rocky canyon-side as they moved down onto the kitchen level. In a rush of adrenaline I padded across the kitchen floor, and took cover against the wall by the patio door frame. Still crouching, I raised my free hand up and flipped the lock back, then stood up, yanked the door open, and jumped out onto the decking – landing in the classic legs spread posture, arms outstretched in front of me, both hands holding the .38.

"Hold it right there!"

It took me several seconds to realise the revolver was pointing into empty space. Movement drew my gaze down towards my bare feet.

From just below groin height the Richardsons' dog looked up at me with his one good eye, his lips curled back from his teeth, and a low, aggressive growl in the back of his throat.

Instinctively I took a step backwards, half surprised and half relieved to see the dog had finally returned from whatever it had been up to. In reply, he looked up at me with an imperious, screw you expression on his face, then audibly broke wind.

I made safe the .38, dropped it in the pocket of my robe, and wondered what had made the damn stinking dog decide to adopt me, and not some other poor bastard further down the canyon. Turning around I went back into the kitchen, opened the refrigerator, and took out a bowl of ground steak. Pulling off a large piece, I went back out and dropped it into his food bowl. As my heart rate slowed down to a more regular speed, I headed back into the kitchen. The dog sniffed the air then lazily padded over the decking towards the bowl. He looked at the food, then at me, then back at the food, this time licking his lips.

I glared back at him, doing my best to sound angry. "Yeah? Well, don't get used to it, pal. Tomorrow you're back dining with me. Sloppy Joes, and liking it."

His head went down into the bowl and his tail started swinging slowly from side to side.

Driving out here with Harrison feels totally wrong tonight. Been here too many times. *It's not going to be safe for much longer, kitten. We keep coming to the same place and someone will see us; remember us – they always do.*

       When the enterprising burglar's not a-burgling
       (Not a-burgling.)
       When the cut-throat isn't occupied in crime
       ('Pied in crime....)

Always used the truck for deliveries, but this isn't a drop. This is a meeting, so I get to drive the Lexus.

Lonely, bad-sad place. No life. Sometimes those lights on the fence posts come on when there's nobody here. This is a land of ghosts and vengeful spirits – clink and clank – groaning night noises, voices in the wind. When it's safe it's Halloween, when no-one is allowed to hurt us. All fun and make-believe – trick or treat, Daddy? Treat-treat-treat!

But this isn't All Hallows Eve.

And the moon is full. Big, bright, moon. It's a magical tragical moon tonight. It has the power of change – the power to raise the dead. But once they're dead you can't kill them any more. No matter how much you try, you can't make them stop doing things. It's not like they will give you candy when it's all over... Stop this! It isn't real!

Skin feels strange tonight. *Inside is a jerky, twitchy tension, even biting a thumb – hard – doesn't stop it.* Not like it used to. And the feel from Harrison is all wrong. *He's got attitude, but it doesn't sing right – it's all off key, painfully loud in the angry section. Mad, bad, and ready to blow.* He didn't hesitate when he met Pres. Just followed him in through the gap – *didn't even shut the doors behind them. Dark. Evil.*

Not evil, kitten! Kisses are nice! C'mon, give your uncle a kiss. And there. And there. And….

Too much flat ground – no place to hide behind, no place to vanish into. They'll all see what you do, where you go. Tension building up, crackhead twitchery – like jammed out on crystal – gotta chill, gotta ease down and get my head back. Can't get *Il Trovatore* out of my skull.

Chi del gitano i giorni abbella?

La zingarella!

But he's been gone too long. He says, "Wait here and don't get involved" *– but he shouldn't have gone into the place on his own.*

Should never have listened to Preston.

His eyes are empty and he has no soul to lose. Not anymore. It's already lost to the wind and the Devil, child, remember that!

Should never have come out here. Should have made him come to us. Home ground is safe ground. But here is all wrong, wrong, wrong!

Damn-damn-damn-this! Can't stand the waiting, got to do something, got to know what's going down.

Find the lever, pop the trunk. Now gently slip out of the car and sneak round the back. He's here somewhere – where are you, where are you?! Ah! Unzip the leather tool case and there he is! "It's the rubber grip that makes it non-slip!" *Take out a roll of tape and a couple of small rubber wedges, slip them into a pocket. Now, close the trunk quietly so no one can hear. No one but those already dead.*

Down, down, down, down, down.

Amongst the dead men!

Stop it!

Slip Mr. Longshanks *up the sleeve – but not too far. He's got to be easy to reach if he's going to work his magic. Cross the cement and tarmac to the side of the warehouse. Bars on windows, so no chance of getting in through there. Warehouse seems dark inside, but there's just too much bright light out here – too much moonglow.*

Preston's car is parked up by the side door. Looks familiar somehow – somewhere recent, but can't think with so many other voices in here. Must concentrate!

Take the cap off the tyre valve. Now, slip Mr. Longshanks *out and push down hard. Hissing sounds so loud! Like a big, black lizard in the jungle, curled up on a stone. One more for luck. This way Preston can't chase us and catch us – and so we keep ourselves safe and sound, kitten.*

And now is the time for all good little children to be in bed. Childish thoughts create fear, and should be banished. Tuck yourself in tight and go to sleep.

This is our time.

Okay, up by the side door – check the bottom to see if there's any light behind it. Last thing you want is walk into somewhere occupied. Nothing visible. Good. Gently try the handle. Slowly, slowly, slowly. And in. All clear. Out with the tape, ease a strip off, and tape up the door catch. Rule One: ensure you can always get out faster than you got in.

Seems pretty well lit from natural light. Windows not too good but the light coming through the gap between the front doors is more than enough. Boxes and cases over to the left and along the far wall near the main doors. They have to be here somewhere. People don't just vanish, unless you want them to.

Blind door off to one side. Plywood, standard lever handle. Put an ear to the door – nothing heard so far.

Work the handle, and into a corridor. Wedge it open this time – no need to be discrete inside. Move towards the light from the glass half of a two panel door at the far end of the passageway. Careful – don't be seen looking through the glass. It's a packing area, pre-creased cardboard sheets that fold into boxes. Small card table off to one side – Harrison and Preston around it. Some woman sitting on the floor over by the corner – looks half asleep, or high.

Voices – muffled through the door. Push gently, slowly, open it a fraction, let more sound out. Slip a little rubber wedge under to hold it in place, Preston's voice clearer now.

"Wesley tried the same shit with me, too. Said he had something which would knock me out of my inheritance. So I paid him a visit."

"You shot him?"

"As best I can remember. You know how things get hazy when I get angry. At least that's what my therapists always wanted to hear in the past."

"But why the hell did you go and kill your fucking mother? She was keeping us in financial bliss. Anything to spite your old man, you said. Then you go chill her. Just think of what we could have done with that kind of money, Pres? Set up a real organisation which would've hauled in a hundred thousand on a monthly basis – hell, no, make that on a weekly basis. Now it's not even academic!"

"That's where you're wrong. I killed her because I was sick and tired of all the nagging, the controlling, and the manipulation. Did you know she kept the other tab of acid you gave her? All sealed up in a little Ziploc bag, so as not to smudge your fingerprints. She kept saying we had to look after each other. But she only meant herself. With all that childhood mental abuse, is it any wonder I finally had a psychotic break? I've had enough therapy to know how to fake one, and half of Mom's doctors wouldn't even recognise a true sociopath if one were to punch them in the face. What assets I've accumulated are mine – clean and legal – the law can't touch them. That's why I want those files destroyed."

"You're totally fucking nuts, you know that?"

"That's the whole idea. And when I'm finally cured, all the assets come back to me. I won't be the first person to pull this off, and I doubt I'll be the last, either."

"Well, if you think you're on a home run with Wesley down and out, think again. I had a meeting this afternoon with someone who left me this little trinket."

"Bobby gave this to you?"

"No, some smart guy called Rhimes. We did lunch, and this was the topic of conversation. He's looking for you as well, you know that?"

"I don't understand. I thought this was all under control? I thought…."

"Well, he said he had a copy, should he ever want to use it."

"But you said this was all under control. You said you could fix it without any hassles – and I end up having to sort Wesley out."

"I didn't know about this until yesterday."

"Yesterday? I thought you said you found out over lunch?"

"For Christ's sake, does it fucking matter?! You're just going to have to put your plans on hold for a while – at least until we deal with this new problem."

"That's not possible! I need Lindsey here as a witness to my mother's death, but I still need to do one more thing before I turn myself in."

"What? Turn yourself…. You really are totally fucking insane!"

"You're screwing everything up, Harrison! Why couldn't you have just taken care of things like you said you were going to? You've totally screwed everything!"

Okay, stay calm, just ride the – Fuck! Where the hell did Preston get the crowbar from?

"Okay, Pres, calm down, just calm–"

That sounded like bone snapping. He's down, on his knees, Preston smashing into him with that metal bar – arms, head, chest – kicking him as he rolls over – blood on the walls, the floor. The woman in the corner – she looks totally ripped on something, doesn't know what the fuck is happening. Preston picking The Man *up by his jacket then throwing him into the corner – body looks like it's made of rags and stuffing, limp and bleeding.*

It's a Raggedy-Andy! All floppy!

Go back to sleep, child! There's nothing for you to see here!

But I wanna-

GO!

There's nothing we can do. The Man is down and gone. *Need to get out, back to home turf.*

Stay calm and backtrack down the corridor, through the main warehouse, and out into the moonlight – *bright, damnit!*

Now, start the Lexus and let's get the fuck out of here.

21

Window World was tinged with the remains of a bloody sunrise. In the reflection, the large disk was tiger striped with dark fingers of cloud. It looked primordial and inviting, in a reassuring kind of way, which part of me found comforting. Soothing even. But what was the old Boy Scout saying? "Red sky in morning; Sailor take warning?" That was all I could remember, so what the warning was about had always remained a mystery to me.

Leaning back in my office chair, I sipped black coffee in the hope it would clear some of the lethargy in my head. I couldn't put my finger on exactly why, but I felt out of sync with the world.

After the Richardsons' dog had returned, I'd gone back to bed and slept the sleep of the righteous until around 05:30. Still keeping with the gym routine, I'd worked the treadmill for 30 minutes, then showered with water as cold as I could take it. Finally I'd changed into one of my remaining clean suits, slipped a tie around the collar of a freshly pressed white shirt, and I was good to go.

I'd raided the refrigerator, fixed breakfast for two, washed up, locked up, then drove the Chrysler into the city.

Once parked, I'd taken a swift walk back up the exit ramp, grabbed a bagel from the corner deli, then headed back to the office. Darlene and Michelle's weekend replacement had only just started doing her nails, and my ever-cheerful, "Hello there," went unacknowledged. I'd simply shrugged my shoulders and carried on regardless. It was her loss, not mine.

I'd then trekked across the vast expanse of the Orion & Nadler open plan desert – alive with people, but devoid of emotion – turned the corner and had successfully made it to the safety of my office base camp. I'd fired up the coffee maker, dumped the warm deli bag on my desk, then from Lindsey's file I'd pulled out one of the disks Dixie had given me. I looked at the contents of the clear plastic case in my hand and marvelled at an alien technology which could so easily trap a fragment of history under its plastic skin. Well, alien to me at least.

Maybe one day I'd become infected with the desire to own more and more complex pieces of technology, buying into the built-in obsolescence of the 21st Century gadget mentality. But until then....

I'd put the disk in a plain white mailer bag and slipped it into my jacket pocket. The next quarter of an hour was spent just sipping coffee, picking at the bagel, and contemplating Window World.

As always, it had nothing to tell me. No solutions to offer, nor any philosophical insights to impart. It was just a point of focus while the caffeine kicked in and I slowly came back up to speed with the real world. After a while I decided there was nothing to be gained in hanging back longer than I really had to.

With the Browning in the Chrysler, I put the Chief's Special and the speed loader back in the safety of their cabinet. The Browning was far more imposing, and sometimes all it took were Hollywood theatrics to keep control of a situation, without it turning into a shootout. But you still had to be prepared to pull the trigger, without hesitation, when the time came.

Once I'd safely eased the Chrysler into the morning traffic, my right hand delved into the chaos on the passenger seat. It resurfaced and fed its prize into the dashboard's waiting maw. Lights blinked, the display flashed, and over the top of a passionately vocal crowd *The Dog Ends* started in on their standard headlining set:

"It's so good to see so many of you regular tossers here at the Grope and Wanker! Here's a little ditty dedicated to the lot of yer!" The mixing desk overloaded as the crowd let rip with a cheer, and the lead guitarist slammed out the opening chords to their signature piece: *Miss Handshandy's Blues.*

It felt strange heading to the Llyle estate again. Tuesday I had left under a cloud, with my name on a list. Yet here I was, Saturday morning, heading back like a prodigal son – though I doubted I'd be welcomed as such.

As city gave way to country, I thought back to my own father, and his reaction when I had been seriously injured on patrol. Field medical had patched and stitched me back together as best they could, then flown me back to the UK – the army hospital at Woolwich. Dad had been waiting for me when they finally wheeled me onto the ward. As I looked at him sitting by the bedside that first day, I began to realise just how distant we'd become. Both of us stubbornly placing ideals and personal beliefs above our emotions, for fear they might be perceived as weaknesses. After centuries-long minutes of silence, he had taken one of my hands in both of his and squeezed it, shaking a little as he did so, and I finally had a glimpse of his love and the fear he had for my wellbeing.

It was the only glimpse I ever got, and as the days turned into weeks, the life-long frictions and aggravations between us had quickly resurfaced like old and welcome friends.

Back at the concert, *Miss Handshandy* had given way to several of the band's more recent songs, and before long I'd found the tarmac driveway leading up to the Llyle estate. Pulling up outside the massive gates, I killed the engine, but before I had a chance to unclip the seatbelt the gates started to swing outwards. Yep, it really was a different appointment entirely.

This time, when I parked the Chrysler off to one side of the main drive, careful not to disturb the gravel too much, Steadman greeted me out on the stone steps. He looked freshly pressed and his accent was still as southern as a plate of grits.

"If you will be good enough to follow me, sir." There was none of his previous uncertainty – he now knew my place, plus Roger Llyle had called me back into the fold, which had made me respectable and clean once more.

Through the main doorway and the guard with the detector wand stepped forward. Without breaking his stride, Steadman waved him away, muttering a slightly irritated "Not now Michael."

Michael just nodded, accepting the breach of security without any argument and even offered a polite, "Good morning, sir," to me as we passed. It appeared Steadman held more authority than I had originally gave him credit for.

We passed through the door to the inner sanctum, and Steadman led me into a library which looked to be about the size of my living room. Once there, he'd then left me alone to gaze lustfully at the shelves lining three of the walls. The books showed all the signs of wear and use – of being loved and cared for over the years, rather than just bought by the yard to fill up shelf space. I toyed with the idea of taking one off its shelf and flicking through it – but the door opened and Steadman wheeled Roger Llyle into the room. I waited while he closed the door, then took up his regular position behind Llyle's wheelchair.

Roger Llyle's breathing appeared to be worsening, and the tremors in his hands were more pronounced than before. Whether it was just from agitation, medication, or a combination of both, it was impossible to tell. The only thing for sure was that his health was obviously deteriorating.

He took a laboured breath, exhaled, then said, "I'm not one for hollow pleasantries, so if you don't mind I'd like to get down to business. I take it you have the disk?"

Reaching into my jacket pocket I extracted the white mailer. "The DA doesn't have a copy of this, or even knows it exists, so I'd appreciate it if the source remained confidential."

Llyle snorted a little. "I've no problem with that, Mr. Rhimes, believe me."

I figured that was about as close to a handshake as Llyle could manage. I reached over and gave the package to Steadman, who dropped it into a pouch on the back of Llyle's wheelchair, his face as blank and emotionless as his body language.

I looked questioningly at Llyle. He took a breath, then broke into another bout of hacking. Steadman started to move forward, his top pocket handkerchief out and ready, but Llyle shook his head dismissively. When the fit was over there was a faint look of triumph on his face.

"My apologies. The stress has exacerbated things a little." Like passing an accident on the Freeway, it was difficult for me to turn my head away and not look at the wreckage.

He took another couple of breaths, then said, "Now, I understand you're still in the employ of Ms. Fairfax. You doing this work for free?"

"She's paid me for two days, but the clock's been stopped and restarted so many times even I've lost count."

"Which has always been one of the many pitfalls of altruism when it comes to business arrangements."

Reflexively I brindled inside. The last thing I needed was an introductory lecture to *Business 101 – Discarding Your Moral Integrity*. I had received more than my fair share of those, in the past, from Dad.

"Whatever, Mr. Rhimes, I understand you were contracted to find my son, and to pass on his whereabouts to Ms. Fairfax. I, too, want to make use of your services in regard to locating my son. Once you've found him, you can then inform me of his whereabouts – for a one-off payment, naturally – so I can talk him into turning himself over to the family lawyers.

I mulled it over. An extra phone call to Llyle would actually help me with my own plans.

"Okay, sir, I'm comfortable with that, and we can discuss a price later. However, in order to progress the investigation I need access to that list."

Llyle nodded in agreement. "Give it to him."

Steadman reached back into the pouch and pulled out a brown padded envelope. As he handed it to me I felt the circular edge of a computer disk. It meant I'd have to stop by the office to use the desktop, but at least that gave me ready access to the Internet and maps.

Llyle looked at me, his gaze steady and meaningful. "That contains a list of the assets, within a fairly large radius, but still local to the area. Pellman are covering them in their capacity as a physical security specialist, even though some of the assets are in the process of being sold. I have informed their management that they are to give you their fullest co-operation in the matter of finding my son, but only regarding him and nothing more. If needs be, both you and they will defer to me, and I will make the judgement call as to whether or not your request is valid, or just fishing."

I slipped the brown envelope into my jacket pocket. "Sounds fair enough."

Llyle seemed to relax a little, almost as if he'd been worried I wouldn't consent to his control of things. "Tell me, Mr. Rhimes, what do you hope to gain by going through with all of this for Ms. Fairfax?" He sounded genuinely curious.

I tilted my head slightly to one side. "Have you ever heard the expression, walk a mile in another man's shoes?"

22

The drive back to the office had been uneventful. *The Dog Ends* had finished their marathon set with an encore of *Licking Chicken Licken* as I parked back under the Kincade Building.

Up in my office, I turned on the workstation, logged on, loaded the disk, and clicked the data to the screen. Rather than just a list, it turned out to be a massive spreadsheet detailing company names, assets protected, call-out times, locations and contact details.

Call me old fashioned but I hate reading off a screen, so with the printer fully loaded with paper, I hit the print icon and left it to its own devices.

As the print off started to stack up, I took a peek at Window World in the hope it would distract me for a while. But it wasn't as calming as usual. If anything, the reflected sun was harsh and cold, like a metallic barrier, rather than warm and inviting. With no ready diversion I kept coming back to the fact that Preston was still a loose cannon – something which still niggled at me. With his unpredictable nature, I wondered about his ability to be seen as a credible witness. Llyle's legal team would coach him as much as they could, but there was no guarantee Tylor wouldn't wriggle out of it on a technicality.

Maybe Elizabeth had been right all along. Maybe we should've turned round, gone back and taken Tylor out when we'd had the chance. It would've certainly solved all my problems, and taken some of the crap off the streets as well.

Turning back from Window World, I aimlessly surveyed the desk while I waited for the printer to finish. The desk clock said it was 16:25 in Beijing, and the phone was flashing to indicate I had voice mail. In the rush to access the Pellman data I'd neglected the rest of my usual office routine, and I automatically pushed the buttons which awoke the electronic female voice. She told me in emotionless tones there were three messages for me. I picked out a fresh pencil, flipped to a clean page of the legal pad, then pressed the Play button. Maybe this time was going to be my million dollar client.

From the speaker came a rustling noise, followed by what sounded like a caricature of Lindsey's voice. Slurred and disoriented, as if only just awake, yet compelled to tell me something before she drifted back to sleep again.

"Hello?... Hello, hello? Who's there... ha ha... Mmmm. Leave a message after the Tony? Who's Tony? Hmmm... There's something I have to tell you, Mr. Rhimes. It's about Preston, and his mother. Yes.... That's it. Oh. No. No, it isn't, because I haven't told you yet, have I? Ha ha...." She groaned and fought unsuccessfully to half stifle another yawn. "Hmmm.... Preston says I should tell this to the police when they come, but you're like the police, aren't you? You're a detective, your card says you are, so it will be okay to tell you, won't it?" Another break, then, with an edge of concern, she said, "Oh, hold on, he's started bleeding again."

There was the sharp sound of the handset missing the base several times before the line went dead and the recording stopped.

I sat staring at the speaker before I realised the menu was flashing its three choices – Save, Delete, or Call Back.

Without hesitating I tapped Call Back and snatched up the receiver. The ringing tone purred in my ear, but after about the twentieth purr I gave up and put the receiver back in its cradle. I checked the time of the messages – they were all within fifteen minutes of each other, and all from the same number. Tapping back to the message menu I pressed Save, then Play to get the second message.

"Hello Mr. Rhimes, it's me again. I've stopped him bleeding, for a while at least. He's all wrapped up, so it's okay for now. Wellll, not that okay as he's not breathing too good, but...." She took a deep breath and sighed heavily, like a little girl who knew she had to do something, but deliberately kept on putting it off. "But I've still got to tell you something important. Preston was at my apartment. He didn't tell me he was coming over, as it was a surprise. He brought along his mother. No. No, that's not true. She came along with him, or did she bring him along to see me? I don't really think he wanted her to be there, somehow. She kept talking as if I wasn't there, and he kept telling her to keep out of things. It wasn't going to be like the last time. Back then it was all different, so Preston says. But Margaret was angry at me. She kept saying I wasn't going to be the.... Well, the person who was going to take Preston away from her. As if! He was the one who came looking for me to start with!" There was indignation in her voice. "He was the one who kept chasing me. That's why I wanted you to find him when he suddenly stopped. We had made plans together, and his mother kept on interfering with things."

Her voice dropped, as if imparting a secret. "He was ever so furious to hear your messages on the telephone. He wanted to know why I'd hired you, why I hadn't just left things alone. He said he no longer trusted me because I'd been trying to spy on him. That's when Margaret started to laugh at him. She was laughing and saying that Preston was hopeless at organising things – that he had never been successful because he was weak when it came to the hard decisions. That's why everything had been left up to her. She was the one who finally sorted Jacqueline out."

She went quiet for a while. Then in a half whisper she said, "That's when he hit her around the side of the head with the bottle. Not just the once. He kept on and–"

"Message length exceeded."

I looked up sharply as the flat voice of the answering machine broke into the stream of Lindsey's conversation. Quickly I pressed Save, then Play again.

Lindsey's voice came back into the office. It had lost some of its emotional edge, seemingly more colder and factual now, with the sound of her fear coming through in her careful delivery.

"I think we got cut off, didn't we? I'm supposed to be telling you all about Preston, and how he killed his mother, aren't I? That's what he wants me to talk about. She kept on taunting him about something. Money? She said Preston should just let her have the money, then everything would get better. Only…."

Her voice trailed off into silence. I tapped the volume button a couple of times, then hurriedly turned it down again as her voice came booming out of the speaker.

"He didn't know when to stop. When he hit Margaret the first time she was knocked sideways in the chair. After that he just couldn't stop hitting her. They don't break like they do in the films – did you know that? In films they're made of sugar, and…."

She drifted off as if distracted by something, then, "It really was awful, Mr. Rhimes. Preston didn't say a word, and Margaret just sort of lay there…. Blood was everywhere by the time he had calmed down and stopped." She exhaled heavily. "Hold on, he's bleeding again. I need to make some more bandages…."

There was a banging noise as Lindsey put the receiver down onto something hard. Then in the distance the sound of a door opening and closing, followed by what I assumed was Preston's voice.

"What the fuck do you think you're doing?"

There was a muffled reply from Lindsey, followed by Preston's irritated voice again, only much louder this time.

"Forget it, he's dead. There's no point in you doing all that Florence Nightingale crap!"

From the speaker came the sound of footsteps getting closer to the receiver, then, "What the fuck's this? Are you calling someone? Is this still fucking working?" The handset was picked back up and the sound of his voice was loud, harsh and angry.

"Hello? Anyone there? Hello?"

There was a second or two of atmospheric noise, then the connection was finally broken.

23

The silence was deafening. The printer had finished spewing out pages long before the messages had ended. I looked down at the legal pad and the blunt pencil in my hand. The pages were a mess of words, taken down as fast as I could write. Hurriedly I tore them off the pad, arranged them across the desk, then set about making sense of them with the aid of the saved recordings.

Several replays and a dozen sheets later I had what I felt was an accurate transcript. I wasn't sure just how admissible it would be. Lindsey had sounded as if she was totally loaded on something, or the shock of recent events had traumatised her into a protective fantasy world of her own construction.

I re-read the transcript through one more time. How much of it was true and how much was fantasy remained to be seen, but at least I knew she was still alive. Unless Preston couldn't control himself when he'd found her using the phone. The coldness in his voice had been quite startling after concentrating so long on Lindsey's.

But she'd been adamant Preston needed her to tell the police about what had happened in her apartment. Why? Obviously Preston had set a game plan in motion and needed Lindsey's verbal statement to implement it successfully. He might be crazy, but I'd never thought of him as stupid – and I had the feeling he'd been engineering things for quite some time.

Which just left the person who Lindsey kept saying was injured and bleeding. When Preston had arrived on the scene there had been no doubt in his insistence that whoever it was, was dead. But still bleeding? In her confused state, maybe Lindsey was imagining things?

Another rapid scan through the transcript revealed no names or hints. The only sure thing was the person was male – He's dead was as specific as it got, but there was no denying it was all pretty inconclusive.

I went back into the phone's menu and pulled up the messages section again. The three saved messages were lined up neatly on the phone's display, alongside the times they were received, and the number they had originated from. I scribbled the number down, then went back to the computer. Spreadsheet still loaded, I keyed the number into the search facility. When it finally finished sorting for matching phone numbers I'd struck lucky, and printed off the highlighted details.

The number belonged to a block which had been allocated to a warehouse complex, last used by an Internet shopping business. The company had never really boomed and had finally gone bust several years before, due to the flood of similar services. Pellman had been brought in mainly because they were already running security operations for most of the other units which made up the complex. Preston had probably waved his ID and pulled the Boss's son routine to get the site security guards to leave him alone. Sometimes, when you're that far down the food chain, it's easier to just go with the flow than to try swimming against it with the rule book in your hand. Plus, with Preston inhabiting the warehouse, it would serve as a deterrent against others deciding to make use of it, thus making Pellman's job a damn sight easier.

I Google-mapped the best route and sent it to the printer while I tried to mentally picture where the directions took me. Failing dismally, I grabbed my jacket, picked up the print off from the stack, and made my way toward the elevators.

I jabbed at the call button several times in rapid succession – feeling a thread of agitation and tension building up in me as I waited for it to arrive – and looked across to the Reception desks. The weekend receptionist was still engrossed in filing and doing her nails. Compared with her, Darlene was far more efficient and professional – but then I suspected Darlene's nails had been retractable from birth.

By the time the elevator arrived I was starting to feel a little wound up, and my melodramatic parting of, "I'm just going outside and I may be some time," finally made her stop and look up. In a very truculent manner, she wrinkled her nose and screwed her face up in an attempt to give me what she probably thought was attitude. All it did was remind me of a crumpled tissue smeared with cheap, drug store make-up. Her supposedly superior sounding put-down of, "Like, *what* did you say?" was thankfully terminated by the elevator doors closing.

Back in the Chrysler, I cleared a space on the passenger seat and put the printed sheets within easy view should I need it. SatNav is a wonderful thing, provided you're prepared to program it, and trust it not to leave you jammed up a dead end alleyway it believes is a shortcut. I checked the gas, then sped up the exit ramp and out into the late Saturday afternoon traffic, this time heading south along Chancery, then onto Pico and the opposite end of Springfield – heading east again.

City turned into residential, turned into not-so desirable

residential, then turned into clumps of warehouse and storage units. A flat, dusty grey wasteland with the occasional truck or van for a sign of life. Some of the businesses were still shipping goods, or stocking up for the coming week. Others had ground-floor windows boarded up, while some of the upper floor windows had panes of glass missing or broken – probably the result of bored, target-practising kids.

The directions were taking me to the fringe of the industrial area – the wire fence boundaries edging onto scrubby flatland and single track roads. I slowed down and slowly cruised the area, looking for an easy access in and out of the clusters of units.

Rounding a corner, I suddenly stopped and backed up slowly. There it was: a neat little foreign sports car parked discretely between one of the main buildings and a shed or ancillary building. Rust-streaked pipes and old metal air ducts went across the gap from the side of the warehouse into the ancillary at roof height, and the small building's windows were caked with dust and filth. The sports car appeared just washed and waxed, and from a distance, looked more like a Porsche than a BMW. If I had been going any faster, I wouldn't have spotted it out of the corner of my eye.

I didn't want to go in through the main entrance if there was an alternative around the back, so I drove around the perimeter one more time – conscious of the noise of the Chrysler's engine, loud in the desolation. There was a side entrance, through a double set of gates, held together with a chain and padlock. It looked impressive but I suspected it would snap if I decided to ram my way in. But that was going to be the last of the last resorts.

At the back of the complex was another flat white cement

area, plus a single side door, set almost on the corner of the building. From the distance it looked old and weathered, and I was willing to bet Preston kept all his comings and goings via the front to give the impression of occupancy. This was going to be it.

I pulled the Chrysler close up against the wire fence, angling it so the front wheels were turned out. Unclipping the Browning, I gave it one final check, then slipped the safety catch off and carefully put it in my inside jacket pocket. Not ideal, but it would keep the weapon safe while I climbed over the fence.

The front wheel made a step up to the hood, then an easy climb onto the Chrysler's roof. From that height, getting over the wire fence and dropping lightly down the other side was even easier. How I was going to get back to the car would be another insurmountable problem I'd just have to surmount, but I'd figure that out when the time came.

With the Browning back in my hand, I walked to the door and gently touched it, feeling it rock back and forth a little too freely in its frame. There were no signs of any forced entry so I gave it a gentle tug. It started to swing open, and a check on the door frame showed the strike plate had been taped over. Curiouser and curiouser, said Alice.

I pulled the door further open and slipped in as quickly as I could. With no lighting, and dirty windows, the interior was dim and dark in places. I waited several seconds and let my eyes adjust before I moved off again.

Discarded metal shelving racks stood haphazardly around the main warehouse floor. Some were still stacked with collapsing or broken cardboard boxes, other boxes were new, still sealed, and piled up in their own little section. Above was a gallery-style mezzanine, the offices dark and uninhabited, and even the silence sounded mournful and abandoned.

I turned my head and caught a slight halo around what I thought was a panel, but as I moved closer I found it was a simple flat door, faced off with plywood. I looked down at the cheap aluminium lever handle, then traced the hinges on the opposite side. The door opened outwards, onto the massive stockroom floor. I put my ear to the flat surface and listened intently, counting the seconds off until a full minute had passed. No sound of anything moving. Still, better safe than dead. I shifted the Browning to my left hand and flattened my back to the wall, opposite the door handle. If anybody was going to start shooting, I didn't want to be the perfect target framed in the doorway. Carefully reaching out with my right hand, I gently pushed the lever, then slowly tried to open the door.

Locked. Just what I didn't need.

I took another look at the door and the frame around the handle. It was the usual, One Size Fits All, regardless of the hole it had to fill, and it had come up short by about a quarter of an inch.

I walked over to the shelves, searching as I went for anything I could use as a pry bar. In amongst the rubbish dumped nearby I found a couple of broken wooden slats, about three feet long and four inches wide, probably broken off a forklift pallet. I went back to the door and, using a touch of brute force, managed to wedge a piece between the frame and the edge of the door at handle height. Gently I put my hip against it and applied some force. The slat had a little springiness, but not enough to stop it from putting pressure on the door frame and flexing it slightly. I took hold of the door handle, pushed down, applied pressure with my hip again, and gave the handle a forceful tug towards me. With the gap and the sideways force of the lever, it was enough. There was a sharp snap as metal jumped over metal, and the lock popped free of the door frame.

The door opened into a narrow, unlit passageway – the only light coming from a pane of clear glass in a door at the far end. Cautiously I moved towards it. As I got close, I dropped down below window height and listened hard for anything which would give me some idea of what lay beyond. Nothing. I pressed my ear against the wooden door panel. Again, nothing.

I thought back to basic training, and Sergeant Lane showing a group of us Sandhurst sprogs a simple leather wallet, which he'd opened to reveal two chromed steel mirrors.

"So, not only do I have eyes in the back of my head, but with this little device I can quite easily see round corners without getting my loved ones shot off."

Slowly I edged myself up the wooden panel and looked through the corner of the glass. On the other side, the room was a mess. Slumped over a table, with her head across folded arms, Lindsey seemed to be asleep. On the floor, close by, was a very battered and damaged Harrison Tylor. He was laying awkwardly, his body arranged in a strange parody of the casualty prone position. Blood had pooled around his rag-bandaged head, and one of his legs was splayed out at an unnatural angle, clearly broken in several places. His face was a mass of puffy bruises, nose shattered and misshapen, while a stomping foot had badly damaged a cheek bone. It was obvious he'd been bleeding from his nose, his ear, and the matted dark mess which used to be the back of his head. Some of his once-perfect teeth had cut through his lower lip, and two lay in the congealed blood like miniature mah-jong tiles. It looked like Preston had choreographed a pretty extensive ballet de la mort. I waited, watching his chest, but there was no sign of any movement. There was no sign of Preston Llyle either – and I wasn't sure if that was a good, or a bad thing.

With the gun butt, I tapped several times on the wooden door frame. No obvious reaction from either of them. A little harder. Still no movement. Okay, if I was going to take it further, I'd have to assume it was safe ground and proceed accordingly. An examination of the door confirmed it opened inwards, which made breaking it open all the more easier. People often make the misguided assumption that Hollywood is correct, and you can just kick a door open with one swift heel to the lock. It's also a quick way to break some of the bones in your foot.

Bracing my right shoulder against the door, I pushed down on the handle so only the locking bar was still engaged. Gently at first, I started rhythmically rocking back and forth, applying more and more pressure to the door each time. After a few seconds the wooden frame gave up, cracking along the grain before finally splintering, while I still held onto the handle, stopping the door from flying open and bouncing on its hinges.

Still being cautious I dropped down into a crouch again, then let the door swing slowly open, the Browning ready.

Nothing.

I stood up, crossed to the small table and immediately checked Lindsey's neck for a pulse. It was slow, but regular. On the table was a collection of small, amber brown bottles with assorted prescription labels. They were scattered in and around half a dozen bottles of supermarket branded Sparkling

Spring water. Behind her, on the floor, was the broken remains of a telephone. Looking up I could see where it had been thrown against the wall. At least Preston had taken his anger out on that, rather than Lindsey. It looked like she'd just been sedated, rather than overdosed, though I had no idea how I was going to revive her enough to get her away to somewhere safe.

Asleep, with her face relaxed, she looked more elfin and tomboyish than when we'd first met, despite the puffy smudges under her eyes. The things we do, and put ourselves through, for love. I touched her hair gently with my fingertips, and wondered what she'd ever seen in Preston Llyle.

I checked back on Tylor. As far as I could tell he hadn't moved since I'd entered. I knelt down beside him and tried to find a pulse in his neck. At first I couldn't be sure, but his body felt warmer to the touch than if he'd been dead for any length of time.

With two of my fingers pressed firmly against the side of his throat, I started to wonder what his chances of survival were. The state of his injuries, the obvious loss of blood – I considered how it might be a merciful release for both of us if I were to apply a little more pressure for a while? With the heavy discolouration of the contusions and bruising, two more finger marks on his throat, or the sole of a shoe for that matter, wouldn't stand out as having occurred any later than the rest.

But doing that would put me down on his level. And what was to say he wouldn't die in the back of the ambulance on the way to the hospital. Just another DoA statistic.

Still on one knee, I put the Browning on the floor, and took out the cell phone. As I flipped it open to dial 911, something made me stop immediately. It was the icy coldness of a gun muzzle pressed against the back of my neck.

Then a familiar voice behind me said, "This is where the games end."

24

My concern for Lindsey and the preoccupation with the battered state of Tylor, had distracted me. I should've secured the perimeter and kept an eye on the only point of entry. Yeah, and if wishes were fishes, I'd have a whale of a time.

Preston Llyle kept the little .22 automatic close to the back of my head as he swiftly scooped up the Browning from the floor. Switching to the 9mm, he moved back and dropped the .22 on the table, next to Lindsey Fairfax's head. The Browning's wider grips made it awkward for Preston's hand, and he flexed his fingers repeatedly, trying to get the butt to sit more comfortably. I figured, given the short distance between us, even if he'd decided to just let one loose, the bullet was bound to find some part of my body to stick into.

He moved in close behind me and pulled the cell phone out of my hand.

"Somehow I don't think you'll be needing this."

Keeping it open, he edged over to the table and proceeded to smash it on the corner half a dozen times, shattering the case and screen, before he was satisfied it was useless.

"Oooops! Clumsy me."

Then, in one violent motion, he hurled the wreckage into the corner. It landed alongside the broken remains of the office phone.

"Now lie on the floor, face down, or little miss Sleeping

Beauty here gets one of your bullets in the back of her head."

I thought about pushing him, but the coldness in his voice, and the expression on his face, stopped me. As I complied he pulled a chair from the table, placed it in a clear spot between myself and the door, then sat and silently looked at me.

He'd not changed that much from the photograph. A little older, and there was an unsettling wildness about the eyes, as if there was some manic energy he was only just managing to keep in check. He'd kept himself in good shape. There was a proportional correctness to his physique, rather than an imbalance, which usually singled out the more hardened gym junkies. He was wearing a T-shirt advertising a fishing holiday down in the Florida Keys. A sketch of a large marlin jumping out of the water with a fishing line running from its mouth back to a luxury motor boat. The T-shirt was matched with a pair of washed out blue jeans – designer distressed holes around the thighs and knees – and a pair of air-sole sports shoes, which was why he'd been able to creep up on me.

I tilted my head to one side so I could see him more easily. "I don't suppose there's any chance you'd let me up so we can at least talk this over?"

Preston continued to stare down at me, remaining silent, his hand still flexing around the butt of the Browning. This wasn't how I'd pictured it would go, but it seemed time to start my pitch.

"I don't know what all this is about, but I'm prepared to listen. If we can work something out between us, I know your father has a legal team standing by, and they'll do the best they can for you."

He smirked. "Somehow I don't see me simply walking away from all of this. As crazy as it sounds, that would be one of the bad case scenarios. Especially as I make the body count four so far."

"Four?" I figured it three, including his possible involvement with Jacqueline's murder.

Again the smirk. "Why, yes." He counted them off on his fingers. "There's Wesley, my sainted mother, naturally, then poor Harrison over there. Oh, and yourself, of course."

I needed to gain some time, especially in view of his last comment.

"So why did you kill Greagson? It's hardly in the 'All for one, and one for all' spirit, is it?"

Preston leaned forward, still keeping the large automatic aimed in the region of my lower back. The tip of his tongue flicked between his lips a couple of times before he replied, "I see you've done your homework, but we went our separate ways several years ago. Especially with Wesley's gambling addiction. When he couldn't afford to keep himself out of debt all the time, he resorted to cheap and crude extortion. But you know all this. Harrison said you took the files from Wes and tried to shake us down with a similar routine."

"What?" My surprise was genuine. "Did he tell you that?"

Preston nodded, the hint of a grin raised the corners of his mouth. I tried to sound confident.

"Did he tell you I gave him the pen drive with the video files on it? Did he tell you we'd already agreed on a truce, because life's too short for me to keep looking over my shoulder all the time?" Then a thought struck me. "He didn't try to set you up to kill me, did he?"

Preston shifted uneasily on the wooden chair. Emotionally unsettled, his body rocked gently back and forth several times. I tried to add a touch of camaraderie into my voice.

"When I got the drive from Greagson, I told him to tell you and Harrison I wanted a truce. All I wanted was to find out where you were, tell Lindsey, then forget the whole damn lot of you. Mack Martinez told me where I could find Greagson, and talked about the three of you as well. But Wesley thought I was working for you or Tylor, and that's how I got dragged into this mess." Okay, so maybe I embroidered it with a fringe of white lies, but there was more than enough truth to make it sound plausible. I pushed at him again.

"Was Tylor setting you up to kill me? He was the one who had your friend Bobby Weams killed. Is that why you beat the hell out of him?" Sometimes playing on an educated guess can pay dividends.

Still rocking back and forth, Preston looked confused. "He.... No.... Yes, maybe.... Look, it doesn't matter now, does it!"

I kept at him. "Did he tell you to kill your mother, too?"

Leaning forward angrily, Preston's personality immediately changed. "My sainted whore of a mother got exactly what was coming to her. She deserved it for everything I've endured for the last twenty-six years. She taught me the only way is to take what you want, when you want, whichever way you can. She even thought poor Lindsey was a threat to the honey pot, even though she never was."

"But what about your engagement to her?"

"Non-existent. Lindsey believes what she wants to believe. I had no intention of marrying her, if that's what you want to hear. As long as she tells the police how she saw me kill my mother in her apartment, then I don't particularly care what happens to her after that. I still don't know why you took the case on anyway."

As calmly as I could, I said, "So why did you kill Margaret?"

His face reddened in a sudden flare of rage. "Because she was getting in the fucking way! All she could see were her handouts, and that stupid will of his. I'm supposed to inherit a piece of the Llyle fortune when I reach forty. That's fourteen years I have to wait to get some of what's rightfully mine! I couldn't keep living on mommy's loose change and pocket-book handouts! Forever having to beg and borrow to live and do business. How much respect do you think that got me?"

I tried to slow him down a little. "Probably not much, especially if people around you knew of the situation."

"Oh, there were only a few who knew, and most of those are dead. Except you, of course. I need Lindsey, but you're not essential."

There's nothing like the threat of your own death to make you stall for time. "But I'll be able to help you cut a deal with the D.A. I can help your legal team, if nothing else. I talked to Martinez, so I know about the steroids and the mood swings."

"Ah, you see? That's the sure-fire power of advertising! Okay, so maybe I did do some boosters when I was younger. But I'm not stupid, I knew the risks. The whole experience made me realise how much of a market there was for them. You hang around gyms and, sooner or later, you see the locker room dealers in action. Hell, I was even selling some of the stuff to so-called professional coaches and personal trainers. And business, I might add, was always good. Especially with the uncertainties of Internet transactions. No guarantee of quality or the goods even turning up. Plus the problems of credit card fraud and identity theft. I made sure my buyers believed I was using my own goods. That way people were happy to accept the stuff as genuine. If I was prepared to use it, then it must be the real deal."

His confidence returned and he started to brag. As I was trying to buy as much time as I could, I let him carry on.

"Once I'd come off them, I found throwing a little tantrum now and again usually got me what I wanted. That was the purpose of the therapy sessions over the years. Throw a fit, do the therapy, get the reward at the end of it. It got me a 'not to be messed with' reputation, which suited me just fine."

"You mean the whole thing's been a scam? You've been faking it?"

"Not initially. About the last seven to ten years. You see, if you study up real hard – something us stereotypical jocks are not renowned for doing – and go to a couple of inexperienced therapists, you get all the information you need. Three or four hundred dollars to an obliging orderly, and you can have copies of as many real cases as you want. After that, the rest was easy – or child's play, depending on your brand of therapy. I think I can safely say, even without your help, I pretty much have a Temporary Insanity plea in the bag, don't you?"

The more he'd relaxed and confided in me, the more his grasp on the Browning had eased, until it was finally pointing off target, somewhere down towards my shoes. But I still needed a plan, no matter how basic.

Stalling for more time, I said, "A good prosecution team will start punching holes in your fantasies from day one. Couple that with assessments and forensics, and I don't see you beating a multiple murder rap."

There was that smug grin again. "I stand a very good chance of getting away with it, just as others have in the past. They've set the precedents and rulings, and courts are loathe to go against such things."

From my position on the floor I tried to look cynical and disbelieving. His tongue flicked over his lips several times in contemplation before he went on.

"Consider this. I had an overbearing mother and never knew my father as anything other than a cold and emotionless figure. The one real consolation was that he treated both Jacqueline and myself with equal distaste. Jackie and I got on together quite well, oddly enough, and it was a little sad to watch my mother get away with drowning her in the pool. Margaret was the one who slipped her the acid tab. Then Mommy Dearest waited until Jackie was seeing cute little bunnies and squirrels, fed her some more Vodka, helped her to undress, then slid her into the pool. Hell, Jackie was so totally off her face and out of it, Mom didn't even break into a sweat when she held her under."

He paused to parody a sigh of contentment. "As Mom was already fucking the family doctor – doggy style as I recall, the last time I walked in on them – there were few worries about getting me off the scene for a while. Of course, once he'd been fool enough to do it the first time, it was easy to squeeze him. All he had to do was keep the paperwork coming, recommending me for assessments and therapy when situations called for a little vacation. All due to the suspect state of my mental health."

He was slouching back on the chair, legs spread as wide as his grin, as he basked in what he believed was his own success. I still hadn't thought of any way out of my situation, but it didn't stop me trying. "I still don't get it. Why go through all this? Maybe I'm missing something?"

"With people out of the way I stand to inherit a damn sight more than if Margaret and Jackie were still alive."

"I hate to be the one to break in with bad news, but you can't."

Preston sounded overly smug again. "Can't what? Can't inherit due to not being able to benefit as a result of a crime or a felony? But I'm going for Temporary Insanity, and under the law I can't be held responsible for any of my actions." He pursed his lips. "I was originally playing for an Irresistible Impulse plea, but the legal vultures closed that off years ago. I've studied the M'Naghten Test, and the Section Twenty-five-B test. I figure I can get around the sub-clause hurdle, on the grounds of personality and seizure disorders. The addiction angle as well." He leaned forward toward me. "And believe me, I've been practising this role for a very long time."

The cold tone of his voice made me realise he wasn't leading me on. He seriously believed in his ability to kill, and get away with it. Lindsey would add credibility to the image of his madness, and because of her relationship with Preston she would be marked down as a suspect witness. It had all the making of reasonable doubt already, regardless of Preston's groundwork.

Preston chuckled to himself. "There's still one more act to go, then the whole show's complete."

Before he could say anything more, our attentions were diverted. From across the table came an odd snuffling sound as Lindsey moved her head into a more comfortable position. It didn't distract Preston as much as I'd hoped. Keeping his eye on me, with his free hand he reached across and gave her hair a tousling.

"Hello, Princess. Time to wake up." Lindsey stirred, but still seemed heavily sedated. "Come on, Sleeping Beauty. That's a girl. Time for you to start earning your reprieve."

I felt it was worth another appeal in order to gain more time now that Lindsay was starting to add to the distractions.

"Do you really have to kill me? I've already said I'm prepared to testify for the defence, rather than the prosecution. The fact I've been hired by your father makes me a tainted and suspect witness to the prosecution anyway."

He looked me in the eye, his expression unwavering and unblinking, his voice cold and steady. "Oh dear. Did you think you were going to be the final act? Ha! Hardly! You're merely just the interlude bell – the one which tells the audience there's five minutes left, so chug down your drinks and get back to your seats, for the finale is about to begin!" The undertone of amusement vanished, replaced by a burst of hatred. "In what I hope the papers will call a fit of psychotic rage, I'm going to blow my father's fucking brains out!"

Groggy and confused, Lindsey slowly sat up, repeatedly shaking her head to try and clear it. I didn't know what Preston had given her, but it certainly seemed effective. It was then that things got out of control.

As she tried to push herself to her feet, she staggered and fell forwards onto the small table, sending it into Preston and knocking the Browning out of his grasp. I immediately saw my chance. I put my hands on the floor to push myself up, but my right hand went into Tylor's half congealed blood and slipped out from under me, sending me back down onto the cold cement. It gave Preston time to recover, but I was already moving, crab-wise, towards the Browning. I'd almost reached it when Preston snatched up the chair and slammed one of the legs down onto my left hand.

There are times when events adopt what they call a crystal clarity, and the realisation of bones breaking was one of those moments. The pain would follow shortly, but adrenaline and fear kept me from immediately feeling anything. It gave me time to act.

I freed my hand and used the chair to pull myself to my feet. As I came up I yanked the chair up with me, trying to catch Preston under the chin with the back rail. He pulled his head back, tugged the chair out of my hands, and threw it across the room. I looked for an opening so I could deliver a good right jab to his chest or stomach, but as I started to swing I heard Lindsey say "Harry?"

It was enough to distract me and the jab glanced harmlessly off him. With an ineffectual left hand, all I could do was follow through with the swing and try to move away from him again – leaving myself wide open. Out of the corner of my eye I saw him bend down, snatch the Browning up in one hand, then rapidly down again close to Tylor's body, for the blood-covered crowbar. In one anger powered backhand movement he swung the crowbar, catching me on the side with full body momentum, and I felt a stabbing pain in my chest as one of my ribs gave way. The force of the blow put Preston off balance, and he staggered back a few steps, dropping the crowbar and pulling the Browning close up against his chest, preventing me from grabbing it off him. Over by the doorway I caught sight of the .22 automatic. It was no match for the 9mm when it came to range, but this close up it was a no brainer. If I could make the first shot I could kill him, or at least seriously cripple the bastard.

I charged past him, trying to knock him off balance, but as I stooped down to pick up the automatic with my good hand, the 9mm discharged behind me and the glass pane in the door shattered. I tucked my head down further and snatched up the small weapon, doing a forward roll into the corridor. Behind me another wild shot went off and the bullet smacked into the stud wall by my face.

Keeping low, I scrambled as fast as I could and shoulder-charged the far door. My ribs exploded in pain from the impact, but I had no time to think about it as the door bounced back on its hinges – only the protruding locking bolt stopped it from shutting completely behind me.

Slipping the automatic into a jacket pocket, I tried to sprint across the warehouse floor, heading towards the mass of shelving and the cover of the boxes and crates I'd seen earlier. Behind me I could hear Preston crashing through the door, but I was too busy trying to focus on getting away and desperately trying not to focus on the pain throbbing in my left hand and ribs.

I almost made it, too. But I tripped over some debris scattered on the floor, effectively tangling around my feet. At the same time something kicked me in the head – knocking me to the left – and from behind me I could hear Preston's triumphal whoop of joy and the resonating echoes of the Browning letting loose another shot.

At which point, as Raymond Chandler's characters so poetically observed, the blackness came up from below and swallowed me whole.

25

I was a cow. I've no idea why a cow, but I was a cow. I knew I was a cow because it was raining and I was sitting down with my legs tucked up, keeping the grass dry under me. What helped confirm it was the stinging pain of the branding iron close to my ear, and the smell of burnt hair. I tried to go back to sleep, but I kept hearing the milkmaid's sing-song voice.

"Time to get up. Time to get up. It's time to get up, Mr. Rhimes."

The rain stopped, once the bottle of Sparking Spring had emptied, though it took Lindsey a moment to realise her haphazard waving of the bottle was no longer splashing water on my face.

As I regained more of my senses, I realised the branding pain was coming from a groove in my scalp just above my right ear, the result of the near miss from Preston's lucky bullet. The majority of the sledgehammer throbbing, though, was coming from the back of my head where I'd struck the shelving on my way down.

I looked up into Lindsey's blankly smiling face. Judging by her eyes, she was still circling at thirty thousand feet, though going by her less-than-sleepy demeanour, she was at least starting to make a landing approach towards reality.

Memories realigned and I had a sudden feeling of

foreboding. Without trying to move, I kept my voice down low. "Lindsey, where's Preston?"

She made an exaggerated frown. "He's gone to the party, and he's not taken any of us. Not you. Not Harrison. And not me."

"Party?"

"Yep! He's gone home to have a party. He drove off…."

I wasn't sure if she'd stopped to think, or if her train of thought had just pulled into a siding. Encouraging her back, I said, "Drove off?"

"He drove off about ten minutes ago. I have to stay behind with the two of you."

She yawned, her mouth opening wide, and when she finished she looked at me expectantly. In her condition, it wasn't going to be safe to send her looking for help on her own.

"Okay, tell you what I'm going to do. I'm going to go and talk to Preston, and see if I can get him to change his mind. How does that sound?"

She smiled, so I smiled back. I didn't want to dwell on what her mental state would be when this was all over. Now for the more complicated part.

Getting to my feet was an interesting experience. Not only due to my damaged ribs, but judging by the swelling and discolouration of my left hand, I figured whatever was wrong with it was not going to be nice, either.

Standing up beside me, Lindsey yawned long and loud again, and a thought struck me. I leant on her for support and hustled her back into the packing room as quickly as I could. Tylor still lay motionless in the pool of blood, but Lindsey had put the table back on its feet and gathered up most of the prescription drugs. She'd arranged them neatly in order of bottle height, which made me wonder just how close she was to adding OCD to her list of achievements.

As I picked up each one, I realised the collection of prescription medications was pretty random and eclectic. Muscle relaxants and anti-inflammatories, to arthritis relief and industrial-strength painkillers – even an assortment of anti-depressants and tranquillisers thrown in for good measure.

Picking up a bottle of Percodan with my good hand, I put the base of it in my mouth and finally managed to twist the childproof lid off. I emptied the contents onto the table and sorted out what looked like half a strong dose, in the hope it would still be enough to numb the broken hand and ribs, without inducing any drowsiness. For good measure, I put a handful more into a pocket, then dug out a couple of jumbo sized Valium and swallowed them as well, on the grounds that it would still be better than nothing.

I looked over at the useless remains of the phones by the far wall, and wondered if there was any advantage in trying to find another telephone connected to a working outlet. Harrison Tylor was no longer a threat, and Lindsey was still away with the fairies. Plus, the longer I left it, the more chance there was of Preston succeeding.

I sat Lindsay down in the chair. "I want you to stay here until I can get some help. Okay?"

"Okay…. Dokey…."

Considering what she'd been through, it was the best I was likely to get.

Satisfied she'd stay put, I went back across the main warehouse floor. In my condition, there was no way I was going to make it over the chain link fence, so I headed for the main entrance. I was banking that Preston, in his rush to kill his father, hadn't stopped to lock the doors and entrance gates behind him.

Trying to shoulder the sliding door to one side left me momentarily seeing vivid white flashes until the pain eased back. But after steady pressure against the rusted metal, I stepped out into the late afternoon sunshine. Over by the fence, the large metal gates were wide open, and from around the side of the building I could see the tyre marks where the low-slung Porsche had left at high speed.

Time to hurt some more. I closed my eyes, psyched myself up, then wrapped my arms around my broken ribs and did my best to jog. Following along the perimeter fence, I found the Chrysler, tugged the keys out of my pocket and fumbled one-handed with the fob until I'd managed to unlock the car. Shoving them in my mouth, with my good hand I opened the door, gripped the steering wheel and hauled myself into the driver's seat. Key card in the ignition, I kept the door open while I belted myself in, then reached awkwardly across and pulled the door shut with my good hand. As I put my feet to the pedals something caught in the back of my throat, and I tried unsuccessfully to control a fit of coughing. The pain in my chest bit like a nest of angry dragons every time I hacked, and I had to fight back a wave of nausea.

"This is Charlie-Victor. Medivac departing this location, now inbound, two PAX. ETA Xray-Sierra, one zero, repeat, one zero minutes, over."

Looking down at my chest I caught the metallic smell of warm blood, and saw the thin piece of shrapnel sticking out of what had supposedly been protective Kevlar. Over the sound of the main rotor picking up speed I heard a voice say, "You're going to be okay, Sir. Just hold still while this takes effect." Then someone unscrewed the top of my skull, delved in, threw a switch and simply turned out all the lights.

I shook my head to clear it, and opened all the windows to let in some fresh air. Cursing the lack of field medics and their morphine cocktails, I prayed the painkillers would pick up the slack soon. Anything to dull the pain from unbearable, down to just mere agony. Tentatively I cleared the back of my throat and spat into my hand. No blood, which was a relief – so probably just cracked ribs rather than broken ones.

Wiping my palm on my trousers, I started the engine, tugged the Chrysler into gear, then pressed down hard on the gas. The car shot forward, tyres squealing, and I had to fight the wheel hard to make it safely around the perimeter fencing. More rapid footwork between the brake and the gas, and suddenly I had to make the turn onto the access road, without totalling the Chrysler in the process. As I straightened the car I realised several CDs and the Google map print off had been thrown across the car and were now around my feet. I looked down and tried to clear things with my left foot, felt the wheel jerk as it caught a pothole, then heard the loud honking sound of an air horn. Looking up I saw I'd bounced over into the oncoming lane, and a rig carrying several shipping containers was telling me to move back over. I yanked the wheel to the right, then left again so as not to end up wrapped in someone's security fencing.

As I navigated the car around the convoluted maze of the business units, I realised just how desolate the place was. With the cell phone and landline out of commission, I figured my chances of finding someone on a Saturday afternoon were slim to anorexic. Lindsey would be okay, provided she stayed put, but Harrison Tylor was a different matter. Like Preston, Harrison Tylor was now more use to me dead than alive. What I needed was for someone to call Marty Beddows or Julius DuMont – even Karrel if he was in – so they could sort out Lindsey while I tried to deal with Preston. No dead father, no insanity plea.

Out of the business park, I headed north until I picked up the 299, then headed east and put my foot down. Hell, if a patrol stopped me it'd make things easier to get a message to someone. Provided the patrol guys would actually listen to me in my medicated state.

As luck would have it – or not, in this case – I had a clear run until it came time to turn off onto the back roads which led me out to the Llyle place. Even though the painkillers had let me tune some of the agony out of my head, trying to stay on track and dodge the worst of the road surface was jacking my tension and anger levels way up high. Bringing my knees up under the steering wheel and keeping the car roughly on course with my thighs, I pulled out a couple more Valium plus another white Percodan. With my tongue, I worked up some spit, tossed the pills into my mouth and hoped I could still swallow without gagging.

Pills successfully down, I went back to driving one-handed as fast as the road would let me. As I checked the rear-view mirror, I caught sight of the sun as it sank down into a rich and colourful sunset. It looked very much like one of Mom's early paintings. She would put a colour on the canvas, then stare off into the space between the sun and the horizon, regardless of what style she'd chosen to paint in. "It's not about motivation or talent, it's about doing and learning. That's what really counts."

The dashboard clock said 17:27. I was driving as fast as I could manage to the Llyle estate. That was the doing. All I needed to do was work out where the learning came in.

As I began to feel the buzz from the medication, I started purposefully humming a Nightshades instrumental, *Freight Train to Nowhere.* With my foot pressed on the accelerator, I was ready to hoot like a train, when up ahead I saw the sign for the Llyle turnoff. I tapped the brake, turned the wheel, then immediately hit the brakes again. The Chrysler skidded to a stop, throwing up a shower of dirt and stones in the process.

Parked almost across the black tarmac driveway leading to the high walled entrance was a familiar 4x4, bearing a rent-a-cop logo across the hood and doors. Preston's Porsche lay almost on its side in the storm gully alongside the driveway. Judging by the tyre marks, the Porsche had taken the corner too fast, fishtailed, and spun around before landing solidly in the ditch. From where I was sitting, apart from the scratched up paintwork and a broken headlight, the car looked fairly unscathed. The windshield was still intact and there was no obvious signs of blood on the light coloured trim, or the driver's seat. It seemed Preston was still alive, though his father might not be.

Looking further up the driveway, I saw the sandy-brown uniforms of the two security guards, Tweedledum and

Tweedledee. They were headed back from the main gates, both cautiously watching the Chrysler, and viewing it with suspicion. Tweedledee made a show as he unclipped the cover of his holster. Given my somewhat dramatic entrance, I would've certainly done the same. You never get a second chance to fire the first shot.

When they reached their vehicle, Tweedledum took a security clipboard from off the back seat, while Tweedledee maintained solid and unwavering eye contact with me, his fingers resting lightly on the butt of his sidearm. I made no attempt to get out of the car, just kept my right hand on the steering wheel where they could see it, and the rest of my body still. The right hand looked okay, but the left looked like a mini-mart blueberry muffin – yellowish with unappetising blue and mauve smears showing through the skin.

With a tap of his finger, Tweedledum found the Chrysler's details, said something to his partner, then threw the clipboard onto the back seat again. As they approached, I rolled down the window and tried to sound casual.

"Have either of you seen Preston Llyle? He was driving the Porsche."

Both shook their heads, but Tweedledum looked worried. "We've only just arrived ourselves. Saw the Porsche, then went up and tried the gate intercom. No reply from that, and no joy raising house security on the radio, either."

Tweedledee tapped the Bluetooth in his ear. "An' the cell phone signal around here is less than friggin' useless, so we've not been able to dial into the house either. It's their company policy to have a two-man team on at the weekend to monitor the cameras and keep check on the perimeter. Someone should have picked up on us by now."

Seemed like my first impression of the two guards had been way off the mark. I looked at the pair of them. "Okay, we've gotten ourselves a situation. The only comms we have is your radio?"

Tweedledum pointed to the small transceiver clipped high on his chest. "Clear link back to our Ops."

"Okay, tell them we need police assistance and an ambulance to this location. There's an armed intruder, Preston Llyle, who may have already shot and killed his father. They also need to send some assistance to a warehouse, here." I reached down and pulled out the Google map print off from underneath my feet and handed it over. "There's at least one, possibly two, injured people at that location, who are wanted by the Major Crimes Unit. Get them to tell 911 to contact either Martin Beddows or Julius DuMont, as this is all connected to a case they're working on."

As he started calling it in, I looked at Tweedledee. "Do you guys have an access code to the house?"

"Sure. We were about to use it when you showed up." Then he added, "Seriously? The kid's gonna blow his old man away?"

"You better believe it. Okay, listen up, here's the brief in a nutshell. Once we're through those gates we'll have to play it by ear. Preston Llyle's armed with a heavyweight 9mm automatic and a maximum of eleven rounds to play with. I'm guessing the lack of response from the house means he's already taken out the security, so it might be less – but worst case says eleven."

I turned as Tweedledum came off the radio.

"They're relaying it to 911 now. I heard you say the Llyle kid's armed and gunning for his father. What else you got?"

"He's pretending he's nuts – trying to get off murder by copping insanity – so expect the unexpected. Shoot to maim if at all possible." Still, for all I knew, Preston had already killed his father, and was waiting peacefully for the police to come along and arrest him.

Tweedledee just nodded. "Fine by us – you're the boss."

It didn't surprise me that they seemed more than happy for me to take charge. If there was a major fuck-up, then it would be my ass getting reamed at any subsequent hearing, not theirs.

Scant minutes later, with the Double Ts riding point in their 4x4, we headed up to the main house. Even before the vehicles pulled up, I could see the main door. Wide open and with no apparent movement within. Nothing I hadn't expected.

I climbed out of the Chrysler as best I could, but managed to jar my heel, which awoke the dragons in my chest again, letting me know the pain was fighting back. I pulled out another white Percodan and wondered if chewing it would get it into my system faster than just swallowing it. I worked some spit up, closed my eyes, stuck it into my mouth and swallowed it down.

When I opened my eyes again, the Double Ts were out of the 4x4 and were using it as cover. As I came over, Tweedledee looked down at my left hand.

"Shit. You sure you're safe to carry on with this?"

Tweedledum offered a second opinion. "Wow, man. Even from here that looks nasty."

If I'd had any sense, I would've waited for the police. But

over the past few hours this had moved onto a totally personal level, and not just about me. Tylor could rot in Hell, but Lindsey deserved something for what she'd been through. From somewhere cold and emotionless, I said, "He's killed at least three other people, and hurt a lot more. He owes me; big time."

Tweedledee made eye contact, then pulled open the back door of their 4x4, reached in, and came out with a wide roll of duct tape. "I hear ya, buddy. Couple of strips of this'll keep it safe for a while."

With my arm bound up in a makeshift sling, the three of us took stock of the situation. Still no movement from the entrance hall, and a quick check on the windows showed no one visible was watching us.

I felt in my jacket pocket and came up with the dinky automatic. It looked deceptively ineffectual in my hand, and effeminately petite in comparison to the Glocks the Double Ts removed from their holsters. But needs must when the Devil drives, and a .22 could be just as lethal – Wesley Greagson bore testament to that.

Okay, time to put a plan into action.

I nodded towards Tweedledee. "You know where the security guys are based?"

"Sure. Round back of the main house, near the kitchen and the laundry room."

"Okay, I want you to run a quick perimeter check, and if you can't find a way in through the back then make one. I need someone to check on the guards and staff. If any are still alive, then get them out the way you got in. If they're too badly injured then secure the area and make sure they're out of any danger."

"Got it."

As he crouched down and moved off, I wondered how long it would be before the cops arrived. Too long. "Okay, you and me are going in through the front."

I did my best to cushion my ribs as we worked our way up the steps and the main door, but before we'd made it over the threshold, both of us saw the security guard, Michael, off to one side, sprawled face-up on the floor. A short distance away was his tazer, the metal darts still imbedded in his shirt.

To the rear, the door leading into the house was wide open. I thought about the layout beyond. There were no fancy twists or turns, and maybe no staircases, either. With Roger Llyle in a wheelchair, moving around the house meant ramps and elevators. Apart from that, I knew nothing. If there'd been time I would've found one of the house guards and made use of their knowledge. But on that count I could only assume the worst, and damage limitation meant locating Preston as fast as possible.

I nodded towards Michael, and said in a low voice, "You check him over, make sure he's okay. I'll go on ahead and make sure the corridor's clear."

"Understood."

I carried on through the doorway, into the main house, and hadn't gone far when I heard muffled voices in an angry exchange. The sound of heavy coughing told me Roger Llyle was still alive, which helped explain Preston's rising volume as I moved nearer to the study door. It would certainly stand me in good stead with the D. A. if I could help prolong what little natural life Roger Llyle had left. Nobody likes prominent citizens murdered in their own homes – especially ones with powerful political connections.

I turned the study door handle. It was locked. On the other side I could hear Preston's voice clearly, ranting and screaming, on the verge of hysteria. Given the choice, I would rather go for a cold-blooded sociopath, than for some overly emotional psychotic.

I considered throwing myself against the solid-looking wood panels and frame, but the sound of Tweedledum's low voice stopped me.

"The guy took a lot of volts from that thing, but he's breathing regular so I guess he should be okay." He looked at the study door. "If you want in quick then it's going to have to be the both of us."

Riding on painkillers, tranquilisers, endorphins and adrenaline, I couldn't see a problem. Which was why I was surprised when our first attempt failed to break through. Thankfully, Preston, still in full rant, didn't seem to notice the noise above his own. We stepped back, then slammed at the door again. This time the frame finally gave up resisting, splintered, and the door to the study sprang wide open.

Caught by our own momentum, we burst into the room together, and I felt myself losing my footing as we tumbled through the doorway. Before I hit the floor, I took in Steadman, Preston and Roger Llyle.

Steadman was in his usual position, behind Roger Llyle's wheelchair. Preston, full of emotion and built-up resentment, flecks of spittle at the corners of his mouth, stood in front of Roger. He was holding the Browning at arm's length, the weapon turned sideways, gangsta style, the muzzle of the automatic pointed directly at the centre of the old man's forehead. Roger Llyle appeared tired and impassive, unconcerned as to the events happening around him, while Steadman seemed his usual, disinterested self.

Our sudden entrance cut Preston off in mid-rant, and caused him to turn towards us in surprise. As the Browning swung round in our direction his hand jerked violently upwards as he fired several rounds towards the top of the doorway.

Immediately Steadman yanked the wheelchair backwards with his left hand as his right moved behind him and grabbed an ugly black bodied automatic from under his jacket. Without pausing, he snapped off two quick rounds at Preston.

For a split second, there was a look of confusion, failure and frustration on the young man's face. Then the right side of his head exploded as the bullet exited, spraying bone fragments, blood and brain matter into the air. The second shot, aimed lower, smashed into Preston's side, the entry blossoming poppy red through his T-shirt. The force of his turning, plus the awkward size of the Browning, sent the weapon from his hand. It bounced off a rug, skittering harmlessly into the corner of the study, and I knew Preston Llyle was already dead before his body started to fall to the floor

At last it was over. The painkillers had finally given up the fight, and with no strength left, so had I.

As I lay face down on the carpet with my left arm strapped and pinned under me, the pain from my broken hand and cracked ribs took me to a new level of physical experience.

In retaliation to the overload, I mentally threw myself over the cliff of consciousness, and gleefully let the blackness swallow me up a second time.

26

When I finally made it back to the land of the living, I found myself in the main entrance hall, sitting on the floor, with my back against the wall. Next to me, Michael – the security guard – was still unconscious. My gaffer tape sling had been removed from my arm, and someone had taken my jacket off and laid it down between the two of us. My tie was missing, and between passing out and waking again, someone had ripped the top three buttons off my shirt. Not that I cared. I was still buzzing along in my own little cocoon, just watching the world go by. Kneeling down beside me, the paramedic angel administering to my injuries had close-cropped blonde hair, a round face, and a Hollywood disposition. His reassuring smile was tooth-perfect. He cleaned up the bullet wound in my scalp, then used a handful of butterfly bandages plus some superglue to close the raw edges together.

As he pulled more packets from the large medical bag beside him, he said, "Ah, you're back with me again. Guess you already know the state you're in, huh?"

I was going to say something, but he held up a hand and stopped me.

"Don't worry, the worst is yet to come. But let's see if we can take your mind off it for a while."

He went to work on my right hand and deftly fitted a peripheral cannula into a vein on the back of it, securing it with surgical tape as he went. Loading several syringes, he connected the first to the peripheral port and eased the contents into my system.

"This is to stop you puking when the good stuff goes in." He connected the second and pushed the contents into me. "And this is to distract you while I go to work on that." He pointed at my left hand.

Somewhere in the haziness – between deftly straightening, splinting, and finally taping my hand up – Julius DuMont glided out of the organised chaos as casually as a shark patrolling a reef.

Still looking at me, he asked Blondie, "Is he okay to question?"

The angel glanced up at the badge hanging over DuMont's breast pocket. "You're kidding me, right? He's pumped to the gills with morphine, and before that he was stoked on some other crap, so you know anything he says will be inadmissible."

I worked the dryness out of my mouth. "I'll be fine, I know this guy. Anyway, someone else could probably use your help for five minute while I talk to Julius here."

Picking up his bag, the angel reluctantly agreed. "Okay. But as soon as we get some more transport out here, you're on it."

When he'd gone, Julius took out a compact digital recorder.

He shook his head sympathetically. "You know you look like shit, don't you?"

"I do my best."

He hunkered down, putting the recorder on the floor between us. "Before I forget." He took the white mailer from his coat and showed it to me. "Roger Llyle said to give this back to you."

I waved my right arm a little helplessly in the direction of my ruined jacket, then waited while he carefully slipped the envelope into the inside pocket. The mailer hadn't been opened. He continued, "He said it's no longer required. You didn't tell me Roger Llyle was a client of yours."

"He," I tried to re-evaluate things as best I could. "He came up, sort of at the last minute."

"Well, I guess that's between you and him."

I could tell from his tone he wanted to know more, but I was in no fit state to chance my luck.

To distract him, I said, "Back at my office there's a transcript I made of three voicemail messages. Lindsey Fairfax managed to get to a phone before the Llyle kid destroyed it."

"She tell you where she was?"

"In a way, yeah. I did a trace on the number through a couple of databases, Googled the location, then headed out to get my hands on Preston, and to make sure Lindsey Fairfax was okay.

"You didn't think to call us with any of that information?"

I smiled apologetically. "Guess I got swept up with the excitement of it all. But, hey, I got the security guys to call you, remember?"

"Quite a few people are going to remember, Harry. Maybe not for the reasons you're hoping for, but they'll certainly remember."

There was an undertow of suspicion in his voice, but I looked down at my shoes and continued where I'd left off.

"Anyway, when I got there I found Lindsey was sedated and Harrison Tylor dead." Mentally I crossed my fingers in the hope he hadn't survived.

DuMont nodded. "And?"

"And I ended up talking to Preston. He told me about how

Margaret Llyle had killed Jacqueline. She came back to the house after Roger had left, slipped Jacqueline the LSD and vodka, then held her head under the water." I stopped to see how he'd take that news.

"That tallies with what Roger Llyle's already told us. Seems Preston was adamant about their roles in the incident. Always had my suspicions, but never any hard evidence. They've turned over something in a Ziploc bag to forensics, but it'll be days before anything comes back from the lab. He say anything else?"

"Only that he was leaving witnesses to help back up an insanity plea. That's what kept Lindsey Fairfax alive."

"That helps explain why he only shot one of the house security team. Had him tie the other up first, then killed the guy. The rest of the weekend staff were locked up in one of the pantries off the main kitchen." He let some silence come between us, before adding, "Anything else you want to talk about while we're at it? I've already interviewed the two external guards, McKenzie and Parnell. They say you turned up already battered, not long after the Llyle kid."

I deliberately looked over DuMont's shoulder. "Is that you, Mom? Haven't seen you in ages. You want to talk to me in private? Okay." I closed my eyes and allowed myself to drift into the cotton wool which had successfully kept the pain at bay. It worked. Dumont patted my leg, turned off the recorder, and stood up.

"I'll let you get some rest. But, in case I forget, thanks for your help in regard to Jacqueline. It'll be good to finally mark the case closed."

I just nodded and kept my eyes shut, letting another wave of happiness wash over me while Julius swam off into the background hubbub again.

I stayed floating for a while, until the sound of a gurney trundling past made me look across the room. The sight of the body bag, with a security company cap resting on top of it, brought me back down to Earth. Walking beside it was a guy I took to be the second house security guard. They had barely left through the front door when another gurney came out from the main part of the house. It was more anonymous, though it was flanked by a couple of uniformed officers. Preston's final exit. In its wake came a bunch of people I recognised as being Major Crimes guys. One broke away and stood over me like a large, black thunderhead.

"K-rist."

"Love you too, Marty. Love you too."

I felt the toe of his shoe bang against the sole of mine several times.

"Don't you dare pass out on me, you asshole. What the hell is all this? Jeezus-fecking-Christ, Harry, why didn't you tell someone what was going down?"

I felt emotionally hurt. "It's only been six days, Marty. I didn't know it was going to get out of control and messy. It was supposed to be a simple hide-and-go-seek...." I heard the apologetic tone in my voice. I didn't like it, but hoped it would placate him.

"And what's this crap I'm hearing from the security guard, McKenzie, about you running off to do battle, waving around a fucking empty two-two automatic?"

I tried to look up at him, but he appeared to be in a fuzzy, soft focus. I squinted, trying to sharpen the image of an angry man in black suit. "It was empty?"

Marty shook his head in disbelief. "You didn't fucking

check?!"

I don't know how loud he said it, but I'm sure all conversation around us stopped, and it felt like everyone was watching and waiting for one of us to start the world turning again.

Just then my angel returned, pushing a collapsible wheelchair. Without asking Marty's permission, or asking if I needed help myself, he straddled my legs, put his hands up under my arms and lifted me onto my feet.

"Okay, soldier, time to take a ride."

I closed my eyes and tried to help as much as I could. But I was far too tired. With an ease which comes from practice, he walked me backwards a couple of steps, then lowered me into the wheelchair.

As I was being pushed away, I called out to Marty, "That two-two is probably what killed Wesley Greagson." After that I just gave up and went with the flow.

27

Several hazy days later I woke up in a private hospital room, courtesy of Roger Llyle. I'd had my head wound sorted, my left hand put in a cast, and had what felt like a mile of elastic bandage holding my cracked ribcage together. Nurses came and went, their sole duty to ensure I had enough medication, food, warmth, light, and pillows. At least I was allowed to go to the bathroom by myself.

Once the doctor had signed off on my concussion, I would be as free as a bird. Until then I had to stay.

I spent some of my time catching up on sleep, meals, and even surfed some cable TV channels. But, by Tuesday morning, I was well and truly bored out of my skull. Then Marty Beddows appeared in the doorway, wearing a black serge overcoat, and looking for all the world like the Grim Reaper. I greeted him with a friendly wave of my hand.

"Yea, though I walk through the valley of the shadow of Death…."

He came in, closed the door, and flipped me the finger. Without saying a word, he pulled a chair to the side of the bed and sat down.

"Now that the dust has settled, even I've got to admit you left an impressive trail of devastation, Kimosabe. You want to tell me anything you haven't already told DuMont?"

I tried to read his face, but he kept it deadpan. I waited, but when he didn't fish out a notebook or a recorder, I asked, "Shouldn't you be taking this down or something? I mean, you're going to want a proper statement from me, at least."

Marty shook his head. "We can take that later, if we need to. Karrel reckons he can get by with just the Fairfax woman, old man Llyle, and the butler. The D.A. wants to keep you out of it as much as possible, seeing as how all the important questions have been answered." He paused, then added, "I'm still curious as to why a butler carries a SIG P220 in a back sack, but the papers are in order and old man Llyle has him registered to carry a concealed as part of his personal security team."

I slipped into a Dick Van Dyke cockney accent. "A classic case, guv'nor. It was the butler what did it, an' no mistake."

Thankfully there was a knock on the door and a nurse entered. She smiled warmly at me, took my temperature, made a note of it on my chart and asked if I was comfortable.

Marty cocked an eyebrow. "Comfortable? When someone else is footing the bill for all of this? Are you kidding me, or what?"

She glared silently at Marty, smiled nicely at me, then left us in peace again.

Marty glanced down at his interlaced fingers. "In case no one's told you, thanks to you it looks like Harrison Tylor is going to survive after all."

The sharp memory of Tylor in a pool of his own blood filled my mind for several seconds.

I tried to sound casually interested. "As I recall, he looked like the wrong end of a hit and run. Almost no pulse and barely breathing. Lindsey Fairfax had stopped the bleeding with rags and bubble wrap, but I didn't expect him to survive until the medics arrived."

"They pulled him from the warehouse and had a surgical team prepped long before the ambulance had cleared the highway."

"What about Lindsay Fairfax?"

"It looks like the Llyle kid had kept her regularly sedated with a cocktail of prescription drugs. She took a while to drop back into the real world, but the experts reckon she hadn't taken enough of the crap to cause physical damage. The psychological damage will take longer to heal."

I didn't want to ask, but I had to know. "And Harrison Tylor?" I tried to keep concern out of my voice, but Marty looked at me before he continued.

"The Tylor kid was a complete mess. The surgeon said he shouldn't have survived that kind of trauma. They operated twenty, maybe thirty hours, reset shattered bones, removed skull fragments and blood clots. His family are paying for a private room at the Willard Memorial Hospital. They're pretty sure he'll survive the attack, to a degree, but with oxygen starvation, plus the pressure and damage from the blood clots, it looks like he'll be on life support until he shrivels up and dies. It's what they call locked-in syndrome. He can hear, see, think, and feel like the rest of us, but his body's totally paralysed. Well, except for an eyelid. His parents are getting some computer experts flown in to see if they can get him to communicate, and I know the D.A. is keen to have some kind of question and answer session. Harrison Tylor had an impressive gift for a variety of illicit activities. Designer drugs, child prostitution, loan sharking – quite the entrepreneur."

I took a sip of water and put the glass back on the nightstand. "He's not going to admit to anything. Let's face it, Marty, a defence team will have a field day with any statement, no matter how it's obtained."

"No, he's out of the picture now. Like the D.A. says, if we prosecute and win, then he goes to jail and the city picks up his medical bills. Even though his parents have now publicly disowned him, his family are still covering them – probably because it helps to keep their name sweet with the press for the time being. The D.A. is going to have to make a decision sooner or later, but for now it's all wait and see."

He organised his thoughts, then said, "We've been able to connect the Llyle kid to the Greagson murder, but he's no good for Bobby Weams or Evangeline Mallory. You turn up anything?"

Carefully I shook my head. "I'm pretty sure Tylor had a hand in it somehow, but probably not directly. I don't see him getting his hands that dirty. No doubt he had someone inside his organisation do the killings."

I didn't want to dwell on Harrison Tylor longer than I had to, on the grounds it would be more than just tempting fate. Marty wasn't stupid, and no doubt he suspected there was a lot more to it than I was letting on. I didn't know if the computer pen drive I'd given back to Tylor had been picked up during the various police searches, but I was hoping it had. If so, then I was sure Karrel would realise the woman on the edge of the videos was probably Tylor's girlfriend, Valentina Melo.

I changed the subject, without it seeming too obvious, and we chewed the fat about this and that for another half an hour.

Then Marty got up to leave, placing the chair back against the wall. "Next time, Harry, you talk to us, okay? I don't want to end up getting called down to the morgue to identify some dead yutz by the name of Rhimes. For one, I got better things to do. For another, it's damn hard to get the smell of that place out of a quality suit like this."

"You think I want to give Karrel the chance to dance on my grave? Get the hell outta here."

He shook his head, opened the door, and walked out into the corridor. As the door closed behind him, I heard a heartfelt "K-rist" rise above the day-to-day hospital noise. Somehow it made things feel right again.

28

The end of October rolled into November, and while I took time to recuperate, things around the house got fixed, or adjusted, or just left in peace. Whatever I saw fit.

Elizabeth visited now and again, as did Freddy, and after a while they swapped the Chrysler for my beat up old black Ford. Not that I was good to safely drive it until some of the chest wrappings and finger splints had been removed, but it was gratifying to see the old PoS back.

As Elizabeth said when she'd returned it, "You bad mouth it all the time, yet you hang onto this old clunker as if it were some kind of security blanket."

"Not so. I've just not found something to replace it with, is all." Which we both knew was a half-truth at best.

The D.A. was true to Marty's word, and I was never called to supply an official statement, or to testify. The whole thing had been placed in the hands of family lawyers, and would, no doubt, be deliberately tangled, disputed, and hog-tied in red tape for years to come. So much for Wesley Greagson, Harrison Tylor and Preston Llyle.

Bobby Weams and Evangeline Mallory remained another matter. I figured Tylor was somehow good for both murders, but didn't know how to prove it. And I doubted it would be of any consolation to the families, even if I could.

On the positive side, the D.A. had stacked up enough

charges to close Tylor's operations down for good. There had been a rush of news coverage when Bobby Weams' video footage had hit the news networks. It had helped bring to book most of Preston Llyle's clients in the sports drugs rackets. The networks had been tipped off to the anonymous postings on the Internet, which had gone viral within hours. By the time people started looking, the original source had vanished without a trace. When I heard about it, I sent some flowers to Dixie by way of a thank you.

Getting Tylor to stand trial, on the other hand, was going to be a major problem. Some tabloids tried to make an issue of it, but after the initial flood of ink, even the banner headlines quickly dried up and the reporters moved on to fresher scandals and outrages. Today's news was always destined to be tomorrow's fish wrap, regardless.

By the end of November, I was fit enough to start exercising, building up muscle strength to support the healing process.

Marty came by to drink my coffee, eat my food and generally help set the world to rights. We have an unspoken agreement to steer clear of religion and politics wherever we can, but we never keep to it.

He kept me updated in regard to investigations into the Bobby Weams and Evangeline Mallory killings, but with little to go on, it looked like it was destined to be marked inactive. I'd mentioned to him about Valentina Melo – thanks to the news channels she was no longer a woman of mystery – but she had vanished.

"K-rist, even down in Florida the state cops still call her Lady Loco. She's wanted for questioning down there in regard to several murders. The Feds have started getting the hots for her as well, which will probably take it out of our hands sometime soon."

And I'd even started getting myself together enough to move back into the master bedroom. It had been an effort. But the more I walked around the house, putting unwanted things into a couple of large cardboard boxes, the easier I had begun to feel about getting rid of emotional, as well as physical, baggage. Come the finish, the weight of my subconscious depression lifting and dissipating had made me feel almost light headed.

I doubted I would ever truly get rid of the Bad Fairy from the shelf in my scary monster cupboard, but clearing out the stuff which wasn't mine helped to jam the lid down tight for a while. And in my physical condition, rebound sex was thankfully a non-starter.

As I still didn't trust myself to drive, I called Ruth Crawford, to see if she'd collect the cardboard box, plus a garbage bag of other stuff. Her voice was cheerful when she picked up.

"Harry! Good to hear from you. What can I do you for?"

Ruthie's Thrift & Gift Shop helped fund the Concrete Rehabilitation Centre. Her own past was chock full of drug and solvent abuse monsters, so supporting the centre was her way of saying thank you for their help in getting her clean.

"I've got a box full of donations. Plus a bag with some clothes, paperbacks and CDs. I've also tossed in a couple of old suits to make your journey out here worthwhile."

"Aw, you didn't have to do that. I'm going to be out your way in a week or so to pick up a consignment of Simple Sally soap. Alice Bartelletski's donated a whole batch of seasonal stuff to the rehab centre for free. You going to be able to hang onto your stuff 'til then?"

I looked down at my left hand and grimaced. "Doubt I'll be

going anywhere for a good couple of weeks yet. Drop on by whenever you're ready."

Then, at the end of the first week of December, I was out on the kitchen veranda, having brunch with the Richardsons' dog, when a white mini-bus with tinted windows pulled up in the driveway. The side door slid open, Steadman stepped out, then went to the rear of the vehicle. Moments later, he came back into view, pushing Roger Llyle in his wheelchair.

I put down my fork, and looked over the veranda railing. Steadman looked calmly back up at me.

"Good morning, sir. Mr. Llyle was wondering if you are in today, and if you are, whether you are receiving visitors?"

I was bemused and dumbstruck, but Steadman held his ground, waiting for me to say whether I was at home, or not. Resisting the urge to ask if Atlanta was still in flames, I nodded. "Give me a minute to get the door," then headed down.

Opening the front door wide, I ushered them into the living room. Steadman swiftly positioned Llyle's wheelchair so I could sit on the sofa, and hold a conversation with ease. Job done, he stood behind Llyle, his face blank and emotionless, staring at some distant spot way beyond the confines of the lounge.

I hadn't seen Llyle in person since the Saturday evening in October, and his health had declined further. He was dressed in the now-familiar deep blue three-piece suit, starched plain white cotton shirt, and a simple little light blue bow tie. But the body the suit had been designed for looked like it had sprung a leak somewhere, and was now two sizes too small for his clothes.

There was an oxygen tank attached to the back of the wheelchair, and Steadman's hand hovered near the valve most of the time. From the nebulizer unit ran clear a plastic tube which rested under Llyle's nose, each of the two tubelets positioned under a nostril.

But Llyle's eyes were clear and sharp, and he still projected an air of confidence. I had no idea what the visit was about, but the more civilised part of me thought it might ease things if I paid lip service to polite protocol. At the very least, Roger Llyle deserved some respect.

"Before we get down to business, whatever that might be, I'd like to offer my sympathies at the loss of your family."

Llyle took several deep, laboured breaths. "I might be crippled, Mr. Rhimes, but I'm not stupid. Jacqueline wasn't my natural daughter, in the same way Preston wasn't my son."

There was no way I could mask my surprise.

He almost smiled, and there was a touch of smug laughter in his husky voice. "I may no longer be able to play hide the salami, but I've been firing blanks since my teens." He gasped another couple of breaths. "It's certainly had its advantages. In my youth I was able to sleep around, safe in the knowledge I wasn't going to sire any bastard offspring. Another was that it meant my first wife, Angel, couldn't contest the divorce settlement."

I thought back to my first meeting with Llyle, and how much I had been struck by his indifference. Then later, Preston's comments about how Roger had treated both children with equal distain. Yet something still didn't sit right.

"So what about the money? The locked down trust fund? It's what motivated Preston, after all."

I waited as he took another series of breaths before he answered.

"It doesn't exist. Never has." Again, the wry smile. "Oh,

there's possibly an old draft of a will somewhere in the house. Probably loose in a drawer where anyone could find and read it." Another breath, then "But the real one, Mister Rhimes? The real one is held by my lawyers. It's what I pay the leeches for, after all."

I was amazed and inwardly horrified at how this crippled old man had manipulated so many people, for so long, and yet still managed to remain alive.

Llyle's mouth started to open and shut repeatedly like a landed fish, and Steadman's hand turned the oxygen higher. Ten seconds later, Llyle twitched his hand several times and Steadman turned the flow down once more. With his breathing back under control, he said, "Don't be so quick to judge, Mister Rhimes. In the real version, my staff are fully cared for, financially, and the remainder goes towards medical research. I intend to build a neurology centre, specialising in reversing spinal cord injury."

When he tried to breathe again there was an odd, rasping sound, as if his throat had closed. Before Llyle could start to panic, Steadman had turned the valve back up, then with a finger he'd pushed both tubelets firmly into Llyle's nose. As Steadman adjusted several controls on the nebulizer, Llyle started to breath regularly, the red flush of his face fading back to what little colour had been there before.

He licked his lips several times to moisten them. "Most people want their family name to live on, each successive generation crawling further up the annals of history. Finding out I was sterile forced me to look at how I was going to continue the family name in a much different light. Not forgetting, of course, if Preston did manage to inherit the family fortune, it was likely to disappear in a very short time.

The neurology centre will be named after me, and will continue for a damn sight longer than anything I could have created biologically. Just think of all the medical advances such a project could accomplish."

I started at him. "And that's supposed to make everything right?"

He huffed more oxygen and looked thoughtful. "Well, since she was discharged from hospital, I've allocated funds to pay for Ms. Fairfax's counselling and therapy sessions, regardless of how many she needs. Something I feel is only right, considering what Preston put her through. Then there's the matter of your reward."

"My what?"

"Your reward. You found Jacqueline's killer. When the police failed, I put up a reward for information leading to the successful prosecution of the murderer. As you uncovered the real culprit – and given that it's impossible to prosecute a dead person – I think, by default, the money is rightfully yours."

On cue, Steadman reached into the back pocket of the wheelchair and extracted a plain manila envelope.

When I made no move to take it, Llyle said, "Don't worry, there's no strings attached. I'm not trying to buy you, if that's your concern."

When I didn't answer, his face showed his anger at my refusal. Sucking hard on the medicated oxygen, he said, "If it's any consolation, I have a host of employees, all of whom are more than willing to do my buying and selling for me."

There was a long, stony silence between the two of us, then Llyle said with disgust, "Steadman, we're done. Leave the God-damn cheque, and get me away from here."

Steadman hesitated, his hand still extended towards me,

holding the envelope. When I made no effort to reach out and take it, he dutifully laid it on the arm of the sofa, then wheeled Roger Llyle back out to the mini-van. I didn't see them off. I just kept looking out of the patio windows, staring at the far side of the canyon.

Sometime after they had driven away, I picked up the envelope and headed upstairs to the kitchen. Out on the veranda I breathed heavily several times, long and slow. Filling my lungs with clean air and purging myself of my anger as I exhaled. Leaning on the railing, I looked out across the canyon, and thought back to that Monday morning when a young woman had hired me, despite her knowing it would probably take more money than she had in the whole of her world. I ran the brown envelope through my fingers several times. I doubted if the cheque it contained would even make a dent in Roger Llyle's loose change.

*****

Three days later, after Ruth Crawford had collected the boxes and the garbage bag, I got a call from her.

"I've just gone through all that stuff, Harry." She paused, not really sure as to how she should carry the conversation forward. Then, "The cheque. It's – it's very generous. I, er…."

I cut her embarrassment off at the pass. "Just say Merry Christmas, Ruthie."

"Merry Christmas, Harry."

I dropped the handset back in its cradle, then settled back to listening to the record on the stereo.

Epilogue

The Willard Memorial Hospital, January 1ˢᵗ. Less than two hours before the first sunrise of the New Year. This early, the medical staff walked softly, talked in whispers, silently made notes on patient charts. If they were lucky, they'd catch a little sleep. The time of the morning when the hospital slows down, just enough to catch its breath before the dawn chorus of fresh casualties. Some accidental. Some not.

> *Lancette e forbici,*
> *al mio comando.*

The paramedics picked him up on a stretcher, strapped down, neck brace, face uncovered except for the mask. Paramedics fussing and buzzing around him – one holding an IV drip full of something, another prepping one of those large syringes they use with the long needle, probably loaded with a kick-start shot of adrenaline. You don't do that for a dead man. Ambulance had sped away, lights flashing, siren screaming – even a couple of motorcycles clearing the route.

They had pulled the woman out alive, too. People milled around, but they weren't as frantic.

They drove The Man straight here. Into major surgery, with eighty-twenty odds against. But The Man refused to stay down.

Preston should have made sure of the kill, not left it to chance. He never had the stones the way The Man *did, dealing with the gangs.* The Man *knew how to work a deal so everyone was happy, even when the goods were cut to fuck.*

But with The Man down, business has been stone cold. Can't fight against that kind of negative shit. Can't hold a crew together either, not when the fuckwads refuse to sell us the goods. Time to cut and run – go somewhere else, set up business again.

The Man *was a good find, always did what he should, always rode up front, always stood his turf. But now we gotta save ourselves and tidy up the loose ends.*

Okay. Playtime.

Through the hospital entrance. Cross the main area as if we've done this journey a thousand times before. Look over to the nurses' station – smile nicely at the nurse. Don't walk too fast, keep the shoulder bag from swinging too much. The little overnight flight bag is so commonplace, it makes the ideal cover. Press the elevator call button, step inside, press eight. The long-term patients are up on nine, but we're not ready for that stage just yet.

Into the waiting area, lights low this time of the morning. Ask the nurses station where the restroom is.

She looks up briefly from her paperwork, "Down the corridor, third door on your left." *Then back to her clipboard and forms.*

Along the corridor, past the cleaner pushing his cart along the passageway. Into the restroom. Straight to the far stall, inside, lock the door. Put the lid down and put the overnight bag on it. Unzip, take out blue scrubs and latex gloves. This time of a morning things are deserted, but the possibility of discovery still adds an addictive tang of excitement.

The Time starts: now.

Put on gloves, strip down to bra and panties. Blouse and skirt into the bottom the flight bag. Get into the scrubs. Quick check in the hand mirror – wipe away make-up with a disposable wet-wipe. Drop the wipe into the bag, then check the wig is firmly in place.

Peel the lid back from the small plastic lunch box. Check the syringe and contents are still okay. Fine. No need for a needle, just a protective cap over the plastic barrel. Slip syringe into a pocket. Now stuff cotton padding in mouth to change shape of face. Okay, we're ready.

Out into the hall, then to the elevator. Press and wait. Doesn't matter if there are people in the elevator, just one floor up and out to an identical corridor.

Room 923. Sign says Mr. H. Tylor. *In we go.*

Money can buy you comfort, even in times of pain. Strange to see him alone in bed. So peaceful among the ventilator tube, wires, bandages, and plaster casts. They cut him for hours. His people can afford good medical.

The laptop computer. Reporters said something – one blink for yes, two for no – nothing more than a ghost at a séance.

It would be easy to just turn the machines off – but that would sound alarms, and people would arrive long before the job was done. No, this is the right way to do it. This way he gets to chill happy. This close his face looks angelic, innocent. Brush the side of his cheek lightly with a fingertip. The left eye opens immediately.

Move into the line of his vision. The eyelid blinks a rhythm – one-two-three, pause, one, two. One-two-three, pause, one, two. A waltz?

Now, gently lift the blanket, fold it back to expose his chest and stomach. Follow the tubes and there it is – how they feed

The Man, via a percutaneous endoscopic gastrostomy tube. The PEG. They won't fit a button, but the feeder tube has a spur with a valve on it. Pop the protective cap, and connecting to the valve is easy. Don't need a needle to deliver the goods. Hold the syringe steady, then a gentle pressure to push the fluid through the tube and into his stomach. Two grams of uncut crystal meth in a water and glucose solution. One gram is probably enough, but best to make sure, and it's important to get out before he starts failing.

Disconnect the syringe, snap the valve cap back on, pull the covers back up. Syringe into pocket, nice and tidy.

Just watch him for a moment. A lasting memory to share with all the other good times we've had. His eyelid rapidly blinking – one-two-three, one-two-three, one-two-three – now the first signs of a stutter. The crystal kicking in, rushing around his bloodstream. No idea what the buzz feels like when paralysed – what it's like inside his head. The rush – the high – the overload....

> *King of kings,*
> *Forever and ever*
> *Hallelujah, hallelujah....*

Out of sentiment put two fingers to my lips, then down to touch his. A farewell kiss. Both his eyes are crying – the right one still permanently shut, the left blinking so rapidly that it looks like a spasm or a tick. And the monitoring equipment is also starting to get excited.

Time to go, time to go!

Down the passageway to the elevator – don't run, look calm. Drop down one floor, to the washroom. Still all clear. Change into old jeans, baggy sweatshirt, loafers. Toss scrubs in the bag with the wig, cotton out of the mouth, the latex gloves. Trash the whole lot later. Simple, smooth, fast.

The sweatshirt feels cool against skin – keeps the adrenaline in check – don't want to look hot and flustered on the way out, do we? Check hair and face in the rest room mirror, a little dark lip-gloss, then head casually towards the nearest elevators. Tap the down button and wait without any sign of panic. On the floor above, The Man's life support alarm will sound as his heart races beyond the point of no return.

Ride the elevator down and casually walk out. Find a nearby dumpster and get rid of the bag with the clothing in. Then just blend into the night, safe in the knowledge that Alpha males come and go.

But there's only ever one Alpha bitch to a pack.

If you have enjoyed California Twist and would like to read more of Harry Rhimes, then don't miss the next in the series:

So Long Ballentyne

Bette Woodstock sat at the kitchen table, drinking her first cup of coffee and taking some of her daily meds. Her husband, Mike, had been up before 7am and was still working in the back yard, taking advantage of the pleasant early morning coolness. His chore for the day was planting out some bean seedlings in the raised troughs which served as their garden area. Their son, Denny, had built the elevated beds out of recycled scrap timber, and she was still fascinated by the faded paint marks, bruises and large, rusted nail holes. So much so that, after a while, she'd found she'd slipped into the habit of casually running her hands across the thick, damaged planks as she walked by them. Some had clearly been scaffolding boards and rescued railway sleepers, while the various paint spattered ones had been used in a variety of building projects.

"Just like us," she'd confided to Mike evening. "Recycled."

Today, though, Mike was already out working on the garden, and on his own this time. Bette was usually out with him, giving him a hand, but this morning she'd woken up with a stiff hip and, despite her regular medication, it sometimes took a while for her joints to get oiled and working again. All Mike had to do was plant the French beans out into the beds, then pull the canvas sun screen over the top so as to keep the harsh light off the plants while they were still young. Later, with bamboo canes and plastic netting to hang from, they would fight and tangle with each other for the best positions.

She reached across the kitchen table, picked up the stainless steel coffee jug and refilled her breakfast cup to the half-way point. All things in moderation, especially at her age, even though the previous evening had resulted in her waking with a stiff hip. Maybe next time she'd let Mike ride on top? She smiled as she remembered Denny's looks of distaste at his parents' little shows of affection. Each time she and Mike kissed in front of him or – heaven forbid, *in public* – his face would scrunch up in disapproval. God knows what he'd do if he realised they were still having sex. And enjoying it all the more. At 66, Mike was delightfully adventurous, and energetic – no need for any chemical enhancements in that department. Also, when you're 70, it's good for a woman to know she still had the ability to launch the occasional pocket rocket into orbit.

She slipped the small green and white capsule between her lips and washed the last of her morning meds down with a delicate sip of coffee. The more she thought about it, the more she couldn't figure out where their son had gotten his strangely puritanical attitude from. Certainly not from his parents, nor from his wife, Anne. But then, thinking back on it, she could never remember being able to visualise her own parents indulging in a round of satisfying coitus perfectus, even though they obviously had done. Five little Montroys were testament to that.

She took another small sip of coffee, finished off her toasted English muffin, then unfurled the newspapers. *The Reporter* was a local paper from Eureka, about the only place of any real habitation close enough to generate an interest in the local goings on. The other was a copy of the *New York Times*.

She flicked through to the financial section and did several mental calculations. It looked like their retirement funds had taken yet another dip. But as most of the portfolio consisted of blues and gilts, they'd been able to salt enough away to keep them on a comfortable level for a little while longer. Provided they didn't decide to go crazy. One day she would have to show Mike how to track things – make him take an interest in the damn pension fund for once. You could call her paranoid if you like, but she always worried over the likes of heart attacks, dementia, or even a stroke. She and Mike were both long-time ex-smokers, but it was only now that some of the side effects from the assortment pills and potions they'd been readily prescribed in the 1970s and '80s were finally starting to come to light.

She looked back down at the columns of share prices laid out in front of her, and silently wished Mike would take more of an active interest in the way their lives were, period. Just in case. In case of what? She grimaced and flattened the newspaper out with her hand. She didn't want to go there this early in the morning.

She broke the NYT down into various more manageable sections, then started to flick through those pages she thought might contain any news or articles she'd be interested in. Sometimes, if she was feeling low, she'd just go straight to the funnies and cheer herself up. Today, though, she spread the newspaper out in front of her, turned the pages and just scanned. That was how she nearly missed the short piece towards the bottom of the page.

It was a report of a possible jumper on the New York subway. It seemed to have attracted more column inches than such an item usually would, mainly because the video system had been down for emergency repairs and the eye-witness accounts all seemed to conflict with each other as to just exactly what had happened. But that wasn't what had caught her eye. It was the name of the deceased. Anthony Wolfe. She swallowed hard several times, re-reading the piece again and again for five minutes, before slowly getting up, opening a kitchen cabinet drawer, and pulling out a well-worn address book. She paused for a moment. Maybe it was a mistake? There must be more than one Tony Wolfe in New York. Hundreds – thousands, even. She took the wall-phone off its hook, thumbed through the index of addresses until she got to the penultimate page, then dialled the number written in faded green felt tip pen.

It rang four times – as she knew it would – then a flat, emotionless female voice came on the other end. "How can I help you?"

Without hesitation, Bette replied, "I'd like to leave a call-back request for a Mr. Anthony Wolfe, as in the writer, W-o-l-f-e." She carefully spelt his name out just in case the service had another person on their books with a similar name.

There was a click as the line was put on hold for a moment or two, then the female voice came back on the line. "I'm sorry, that service is no longer available through us."

There was an embarrassing silence as Bette desperately tried to think of something more to say. But the finality of the other woman's words left no room for any hope, or further conversation. In a quiet voice, Bette said, "Th-thank you." But the far end had already hung up.

Carefully she returned the phone back onto its hook. Closing the address book she slipped it back into the drawer, pushing it shut as she did so.

She couldn't remember when she'd sat back down at the kitchen table again, but the shrill ringing of the phone finally cut through her confusion and startled her back to the present,

She stared at it as it rang six or seven times, until Mike came in through the kitchen door to see if she was okay. Spurred into action she pushed herself away from the table. Moving too quickly and immediately feeling dizzy from the sudden rush of blood, she snatched the receiver from its cradle.

In an unusually timid voice, she said, "Hello?"

The voice on the other end sounded as if an old bullfrog had learned the art of speech. "Hi Bette." There was the laboured noise of large intake of breath, then, "Have you had a chance to read the papers yet?" Frankie Nixx paused to take another long breath. In the background she could hear Frankie's television set fighting for dominance over the radio. Both were tuned to different sports channels. Over the top of them he said, "I mean the piece about Tony." Pausing again, he then went on, "They say it might be suicide."

She tried to keep her voice calm, but it sounded fragile and a little wavering. "That doesn't make sense, Frankie. He had no reason to do anything like that."

Frankie's cancer-ravaged voice barked unintentionally loud in her ear. "We haven't heard from him," his voice paused for a moment, "in – what? – twelve – eighteen months?" Again the pause as he drew breath, "How do you know he was still okay?"

"Because he trusted us, Frankie!" Her voice tailed off into a little sob of despair. "He trusted us. He would have told us if something was wrong." Without saying goodbye she put the receiver back on the wall.

As she turned round to sit back down again she realised Mike had moved up beside her. She pointed to the newspaper article, sitting back down as Mike picked up the loose pages, folded them in half, and started to read – holding the newsprint at a distance rather than go looking for his reading glasses. After a few moments a look of comprehension appeared on his face. "Oh...."

Sitting down at the kitchen table he put the newspaper to one side, reached across and held both her hands in his. "Well, sweetheart. It looks like we really are on our own now, doesn't it."